INTO THE FIRE

GWEN RIVERS

ELEMENTS UNLEASHED MEDIA

ISBN: 978-1-951215-33-0

✺ Created with Vellum

INTO THE FIRE

It's always darkest before the end of the world....

Bound without power and in the hands of the mortal authorities, Nic Rutherford can do nothing to save her supernatural friends trapped beyond the Veil. She can't even save herself from the psychological interrogations and vivid dreams of destruction that shred her to the pit of her soul. All she has to hold onto is hope of rescue and a new friend with a magical secret of her own. Is her faith in new love enough to keep her sane?

Nothing can keep him from her side.

Aiden has one goal—to get to Nic as soon as possible. But dark forces from his past want his life magic. For he is the key to unchaining the god Loki and bringing about Ragnarök—the end of the world. Will his determination to rescue his mate be enough? Or will old ghosts steal the future he is now desperate to embrace?

Family meets fantasy in this epic conclusion to the Unseelie Court series.

INTO THE FIRE

FIRE AND ICE

Some say the world will end in Fire.
Some say in Ice.
From what I've tasted of desire
I hold with those who favor Fire.
But if I had to perish twice,
I think I know enough of hate
To say that for destruction Ice
Is also great
And would suffice.

Fire and Ice by Robert Frost

DARK DREAMS

The cave looms large in front of the woman, a forbidding mouth that will swallow all that is bright in the world. She doesn't hesitate as she moves closer, her gait purposeful. Flanking her are two cloaked figures, their features obscured by the dark cowls. In front of her are the dead, a solid wall of corpses.

Bodies that stand at attention, hers to command.

She takes in their gruesome visages. Her hands come up and a golden light filters out of her palms. Her rune marks, the two symbols that allow them to walk long past the point when their souls have abandoned the tattered flesh.

But it's their flesh she needs. The physical forms that are as unstoppable as they are repugnant.

Men, women, children all in different parts of decomposition. Faces half missing, wings shredded to gossamer strands of spider silk. They were fey once, forever young. Children of the goddess Freya. They schemed and fought, stole and laughed. Now they are the perfect army, never stopping to sleep or eat, a relentless wave of death.

And they obey only her.

At the smallest wave of her hand, they move apart as though pulled by giant magnets. She and her entourage continue down into the abyss.

The light is blotted out as they twist and turn down into the suffocating darkness.

A ball of light appears in the woman's hand. Its glow illuminating her pale skin and midnight hair. Fey light—pulled from the elemental magic that all the fey possess. She is not one of the immortal fey, though her skin holds an ageless quality. She is tall, almost six feet in height with a voluptuous figure like that of a fertility goddess. But she is not a goddess either.

A shudder rumbles the cave walls. The trio pauses, but they do not speak. When the tremors subside, they continue on down into the darkness as if nothing happened. This place is a prison, one of the oldest in existence. It is fraught with traps to dissuade any from unleashing the soul condemned within its walls.

The company strides onward into the darkness. Their steps sure and purposeful. They don't talk at all. Talk could give them away. No one must interfere with their purpose.

As they wend their way into the bowels of the world, a dim green light appears. It is their destination, built by the gods to cage one of their own.

His release will bring about the end of everything.

There are two people in the cave. The one standing is a petite blond woman. She is wearing a white sleeveless gown several centuries out of fashion. She hovers by the side of the prisoner. A man. He is naked and bound to the slab of rock. A man with hair the color of flame. Above the man's head, a serpent is coiled around a stalactite. From its overlarge fangs, a sickly yellow green venom drips down. The woman holds the bowl out and the poison is caught before it can splash on the bound man's face. Old scars mar his features from where the venom found its target.

His eyes are a piercing green and are filled with madness.

The female traveler moves forward. Her voice is melodic as she speaks. "Greetings Loki, Lord of Chaos and all that burns."

The woman in white starts, turning to face the newcomers. Those leaf green eyes lock on the newcomers. He doesn't speak, instead he begins to laugh. It isn't a pleasant sound.

"What are you doing here, Pharaildis?" The woman in white asks. "You know it is forbidden."

The woman named Pharaildis lowers her hood. "Sigyn. Why, the way I hear it, we are practically family. My daughter, your son."

Loki cackles. "I met her you know. She came here, seeking her immortality. Tricksy Underhill, land of the fey that they all worship and revere. How many deaths have you brought about on your little quest?"

"You, my lord Loki, ought to know better than any that worship and freedom are not the same."

His laughter cuts off abruptly and he stares at her with a burning intensity. "You don't have the means to free me, Underhill."

"Oh, but I do." She gestures to the cloaked figure on the left. One hand reaches out and removes the cowl from the face within. "I and the ruler of the Shadow Throne. Together, we wield all the powers of the Unseelie Court. With Fire and Ice he shall be freed."

"Hello, Father." The voice is feminine, with a soft Southern drawl. The round face belongs to a young woman, the eyes to an immortal beast.

Sigyn blanches and in a horrified whisper mutters a name. "Fenrir?"

Loki laughs even harder.

"Nothing is impossible," Underhill bends down until her face is inches from his. "Not when you have the patience and relentless nature of an immortal. Loki, by the blood and entrails of your youngest son you were bound. By the blood and bone of your eldest you shall be free."

3

Sigyn's gaze goes to the other figure. "Váli?" She breathes as though in disbelief.

Underhill closes in for the kill. "Great Loki. The world is ripe and the gods are weak. Science has replaced magic beyond the Veil and the ancients are gathering for the final battle."

"Ragnarök," Loki breathes the word like a benediction.

Underhill nods. "The dead are walking and the great winter is at hand. We offer this sacrifice to free you."

Without warning, she grabs hold of the third figure. Fenrir moved behind the other and holds his hands captive. From the depth of her pocket, Underhill withdraws a silver knife.

"Any last words you wish me to relay to my daughter, Aiden?" she asks.

The figure shakes his head once, the hood falling back revealing shaggy dark locks and the same piercing green eyes as Loki.

"I think a rib will work," Underhill puts her free hand on his chest as though marking her place. The knife flashes in the torch-light and then is buried in his heart.

I AWAKE WITH A JOLT, Aiden's name on my lips. Had it been only a dream? Or had Underhill really captured my wolf?

My love. I never should have left him.

My body shakes with small tremors, making the chains tethering my wrists and ankles together rattle. A leg iron cuffs each ankle over my grubby and blood-stained jeans and bracelets connect my wrists. My shoulder throbs and so does my leg—both the sites where I'd been shot.

Shot by the FBI.

It's what they do when fugitives run. Even teenage girls.

And I am so much more than your average teenager.

It helps, repeating my mantra. *My name is Nic Rutherford. I live in the mountains of North Carolina. I am the Risen Queen of the Unseelie Court. I have died twice and been resurrected. I hunt murderers and rapists and kill them with my goodnight kiss. Aiden is my mate.*

It helps my confidence to recite my little mantra. At least it distracts me from the unforgiving reality. That I am cold, in pain and utterly terrified.

I've been incarcerated. Captured. *They know what I can do.*

Trying not to panic, I take in my surroundings.

Four concrete walls with an oval doorway, like something on a submarine. No windows though, not even an arrow slit. All the light is manufactured and comes from the humming overhead fluorescents. The people who shot me have stuffed me in this cell, inside some FBI stronghold. Crusted blood cakes my clothing from where I'd taken a bullet to the shoulder, another on my thigh. The clothing has been cut away to expose the injuries, which are covered with thick swathes of gauze.

I have no memory of the treatment or being dumped in this cell.

At least the mask—that horrible thing they'd wrapped around my face is gone. I take a full breath and try to slow my pounding heart. It was just a dream. Aiden is across the Veil, true. He has to stay there until he manages to break the evil spell of madness Pharaildis—aka Underhill—put on him.

But she doesn't have him. I would know it. We are mates, bound by fate and by choice. I can feel when he is in danger or in pain, just as he can feel me. We share a connection that carried over from my last life when I'd been queen of the Shadow Throne.

I'd been meant to rule again. But Pharaildis had tricked me into bringing Gretchen, Fenrir's human host, to her. The Shadow Throne had accepted him and now Aiden's half-brother, the wolf who is destined to swallow the world, rules in my stead.

And I have been banished to Midgard, the mortal realm where the FBI waited to spring their trap.

I picture Pharaildis in my mind and think, *Mother, you are such a bitch.*

Prison. I look down to see my hands are shaking. Terror courses through me at the thought of incarceration and all it might entail. What will the mortals do to me? Tests? Experiments?

I take a deep breath to steady my nerves.

As a serial killer in the hands of the FBI, I am in seriously deep shit. And I don't see a way out. What's more, since my banishment, I don't have access to my magic anymore. My allies, the fey of the Wild Hunt might come for me. Then again, they might not be able to leave. The Hunt is bound to the Unseelie queens, and I am not one any longer.

Besides, it's not in my nature to skulk around and wait for rescue.

Shoving aside my clawing panic at being trapped in a windowless prison, I push to my feet to take stock of myself. They've taken my boots but I still have on the thick gray socks. My pants are shredded, my shirt hanging open. The garments had been along the sites where I'd been bleeding. Though I am filthy and aching, my rapid healing is already kicking in. It's a good thing the FBI wants me in top working order, otherwise they might not have bothered to patch me up.

I've got enough explaining to do as it is.

A wave of nausea rolls through me, but I shove it aside as I take in my holding cell.

A bed with a lumpy mattress that looks like it was stolen off some dorm curb on trash day sits on a metal frame. A miniscule sink stands in the far corner. I trudge that way, ignoring the pain in my leg. The shackles that encircle my wrists and ankles give me enough wiggle room to take care of my personal needs over the single toilet. A camera is mounted in one corner, the red light indicates that it is on.

Perverts.

Otherwise, the place is bare. I'm a minimalist by nature but this is ridiculous.

Another lurch in my stomach and I lunge for the toilet. The smell of the chemicals within is the final straw and I heave, emptying the meager contents of my stomach down into its murky depths.

When is the last time I ate? I can't remember. So much had happened, what with me going from a prison in Underhill to one here.

I'll send her back and she can resume the course she was set upon.

That had been the deal Underhill had cut with Aiden. But not really Aiden. My Aunt Addy had glamoured herself to look like my wolf.

Another ripple of nausea goes through me. What if it was Addy who'd been stabbed in the heart? Can a silver knife kill a Norn—one of the goddesses of fate?

The chains rattle as I turn on the water and splash some on my face and rinse the taste of bile from my mouth.

I take a deep breath, trying to scent the air. It's all canned, recycled through a vent system. So, we're underground somewhere. Even without fairy queen magic, I have always had an affinity for air. The details are foggy, the haze of pain that infected me clouds my memory of the journey to this place. Sooner or later someone will have to come though. To feed me, to interrogate me.

To vivisect me.

I shy away from that thought. The one notion that keeps panic clawing at my innards is the idea that these people knew enough about me to cover my mouth when they'd captured me. How had they found out how I kill?

My goodnight kiss has been my biggest secret for most of my life. Up until last spring, I'd used it only in self-defense or to protect an innocent from a monster. I'd been the butterfly no one suspected, the stalker in the shadows, the being who went bump in the night and took out the biggest predators around.

No one who saw me guessed the petite blonde with corn-flower blue eyes was killing full grown evildoers. And had been since I was six-years-old.

Men. Women. Those who hurt others for no reason other than they were scum. I'd laid the traps, often using myself as bait, and closed it on those who fell into it. They culled the herd like a disease, and like a vaccination, I destroyed them.

Really, it had been a public service.

My aunts, Chloe and Addy, had helped cover for me. They disposed of the bodies whenever possible. A couple had slipped through our grasp though and the FBI had been tracking my victims. But I hadn't killed a mortal in months. So how had they caught on to me?

My hands clench into fists as the answer surfaces. The diary. That damn diary where I'd stashed the licenses of all my prey. I'd done this to myself, kept those trophies and incriminated myself. How many times had Addy warned me that doing so was foolish? That I was helping the feds build their case?

Note to self. When a Fate says something is a bad idea, *listen*.

So okay, they have the diary. It had my fingerprints all over it0 and the IDs inside. They knew who and how I killed. But still, I could get away.

I just needed to find an angle.

"You're awake," a disembodied female voice says from a tinny speaker.

I stare straight at the camera and will my eyes to water in

fear. It isn't difficult to conjure a few tears. "This must be some kind of mistake."

"No mistake," the being within says. "You're Nic Rutherford, adopted child of Chloe and Addison Rutherford. You live on a farm in the North Carolina mountains. And I have been hunting you for a very, very long time."

A chill goes through me at those last words. "Who are you?"

"You'll find out soon enough."

Gas filters down through the vent in the ceiling. I cough and choke, eyes stinging, lungs burning. This is why the room was airtight, so they could gas me whenever they chose.

I fight, trying to hold my breath, even struggle to reach for magic. But it's no use.

Terror courses through me as the world around me tunnels and I slip into oblivion.

BURN IT DOWN

THROUGH THE WOLF'S EYES

He sees his destination ahead. The fortress that holds the Green Throne and his target. The man who shares his skin cautions him to use stealth. There is wisdom to the man, an ancient knowledge that comes from his long years. Perception and many times courage as well.

The wolf hadn't appreciated those traits before.

The place is set in a valley, surrounded by trees and a mystical enchantment of protection. A blockade of air. The magic smells of his mate. The wolf had run for leagues, intent to get what he needs from the place and then cross back through the Veil to Midgard so he can be with her. She needs him, he can feel it in his bones.

He knows she is not within but her spell crafting has held fast. And would until the new queen of the Shadow Throne arrives, waves her hand, and obliterates it.

No time. The man thinks. The people don't know what has happened. Don't know that a new queen sits on the Shadow Throne and that she is really an immortal wolf who hungers for their blood.

How many people still live within the boundary? He has come across no others. Underhill is a wasteland of corpses.

He studies the scene in the valley below his perch. This place should be abandoned as lost. The wolf is a survivor and the unnatural dead things walking are growing in numbers.

A sea of them swarmed in front of the barrier. They are thick on the ground, like leaves after a hurricane. Relentless, unwavering. They hold no doubt, remorse or fear. They have a singular goal—the annihilation of all that lives.

From what he witnessed on his way here, they have mostly succeeded. Every village empty, every home abandoned. The dead don't need a home or a place. They have no feelings and nothing can alter their course once set.

The siege would continue indefinitely.

Unless we do something to stop it, the man's voice whispers in his head.

The wolf hesitates. It's not his nature to muck about in the affairs of men or fey. They are different, complicating things which should be simple.

We can't cross without them. His other self reminds him. *We need their help to reach her.*

The wolf stares at the throng of animated dead and paces in a circle. *You could transform,* he tells the man. *We need not engage the dead.*

But the man refuses. *My magic can't get us through that shield. They have to lower it from within. And without Nic there to put it back in place, their city will fall.*

The wolf growls. This is taking too much time, all these strategies and tactics. He needs to do something, to be somewhere else. With her.

What can kill the dead? he asks the man.

Fire. The man answers promptly.

The wolf's eyes glitter. *Then you do your part and I will do mine.*

11

He begins to run. As a unit, they charge down the hill for the ranks of the dead. From the city beyond, a cry arises. One of the fey spots him. Even with the barrier in place, he can scent them and the earth magic that emanates off of them. As well as the fear. He knows what it must look like, a lone wolf heading to his doom. Many beings crowd the limbs of trees to watch the army of the dead tear him to pieces.

A gust of wind ripples through his fur. The man's spark ignites. Flames lick out from his coat and the breeze carries stray sparks from him down to the dead.

Some of the newer dead wouldn't go up so easily.

These have been out in the elements for a time. They are dry flesh, quickly losing moisture that living beings need to sustain themselves. His embers in the tight space catch like a wildfire, with that breath of wind spreading it throughout their ranks. The dead start to smoke and then flames lick hungrily up, an unending appetite. The scraps of skin and brittle bones catch like well-seasoned wood, one into the next into the next. It doesn't stop them or slow them. They surge forward as they burn. He approaches the first line and then turns right before the flaming dead fey can reach him. He will snake through the entire dead army, spreading the discord, the chaos.

They don't scream, don't make a sound. Can feel no pain. It's part of what makes them so unstoppable. The only sound is the roar of his wildfire the pop of sizzling marrow. Bones char and the smell of roasting meat is thick in the air.

Tongues of flames lick out from his unburnt skin until they caress the dead.

"It's Aiden!" a familiar voice calls. An image floats to his mind. The man carries names but the wolf holds her face close to his heart. The young nymph girl is pack.

"Taj, lower the shield!" A female calls, this one older.

"Are you sure?" An unfamiliar voice asks her.

His wolf ears pick up the deep cadence even over the roar of the burning dead.

"Yes," his young ally says. "Mother, we have to help him."

"Hunt, to me!" The older female voice is accustomed to command. "Prepare for battle."

No, the man thinks. A protracted battle is the last thing they need. Too much confusion and the man worries that some of his allies will fall. He can't pull the flames back or risk the dead escaping the inferno.

The wolf turns again and blazes a path straight through the reaching limbs of the dead. Skeletal hands grab for him but he dodges and weaves their grasping clutches. The fire burns hotter. He is immune to the heat though the fey behind the shield of wind are not. If the fire reaches inside the city, all the fey within might die.

Including the one he needs.

"He's coming this way!" The mature woman calls.

A wall of bodies stand in his way, several of them armed with swords and spears. He dodges most, but some penetrate the fire and slice into his skin. He snaps and yanks, writhing with all his fury to make enough space to surge through. The fire inside him burns hotter still, the need to defeat this deathless foe prompting him to dig deeper, to burn them all to ash. The intensity of his split soul—part man and part beast—fuels the flames, encouraging the blaze to burn hotter and brighter than before. A river of fire, a moat surrounding the last stronghold of living fey.

A sizzling line of demarcation between life and death.

The dead began to crumble. The air is so thick with ash it chokes him. The smoke sends plumes up into the sky, a signal fire for any who may be left to read it.

Swallowing, he turns and surveys the carnage. Every-where the bodies are burning, some still upright, others decaying to the point of no return. His massive pyre is a testament to the destruction of which he is capable.

Inside him, the man's heart is heavy.

Victory, but at what cost?

The land is burnt. Nothing will grow. What was once a thick forest of dense trees and fertile soil, is only a plain of death.

But the wolf has no time for regrets. He turns and faces the city, seeking an ally.

"Lower the air shield," the woman with the commanding voice says.

"But we are defenseless without it." Another voice cries. Male this time with a high-pitch whine.

The woman snarls, "He just saved us from the immediate threat. We can't stay here forever or we'll starve. Lower. The bloody. Shield."

A moment later, a gust of wind blows out from the city. Icy wind carries his mate's scent. He breaths in deep as it sweeps over him like her gentle caress, taking the last of the flames with it.

"Aiden?" A young girl with pointed ears approaches him. Her eyes are bright. "Are you all right?"

Give over. The man whispers to him. *It's Jasmine.*

The wolf is reluctant to cede control. *Can I trust you not to linger here?*

He sense's the man's determination. *Nothing will stop me from getting to her.*

With one last look at the carnage, the wolf recedes. Satisfaction radiates through him.

This is what awaits anyone who would harm my mate.

Through the Man's Eyes

HE NEEDS to cooperate with the beast inside him, to gain its trust. Aiden looks around at the flames licking across what remains of the dead. The beast's instincts had made this possible. It had ignored pain, the stabs of the blades. Wounds he can still feel oozing from his back and legs. and he can't help but agree with the creature's final sentiment. He too would do anything to protect Nic.

"Lady Jazz," Aiden says as soon as the transformation is complete.

"Where have you been? Did you find the queen?" The girl throws her arms around him and squeezes for all she was worth. "I've missed you."

He hugs her back. "It's good to see you, too."

She backs up and frowns at the streak of white in his dark hair. "What happened here?"

The only outer sign from the kiss of madness.

"Nothing you need to worry over." He pulls away to study her. "You've grown since last I saw you. How much time passed on the mortal plane?"

"A little more than a year from the time you left."

A shudder goes through him. Time moves differently across the Veil. Nic might live years to his minutes, or vice versa.

"Where is she?" Freda is much less welcoming than her daughter. "Where is our queen?"

Aiden shakes his head. Though the giantess Angrboda told him Nic had retreated to her family's farm in western North Carolina, he doesn't want to share that with Nic's first. Her loyalties might be to Nic but she commands the Wild Hunt. Which is now controlled by the Shadow Throne's new queen.

The Wild Hunt is a powerful ally and an even more deadly enemy.

"Gretchen was taken over," he says. "By Fenrir. She—or rather the wolf—sides with Underhill. Together they rule the Unseelie Court."

Freda curses.

He scans the throng of fey, who wear woebegone expressions. They are slack faced and appear as though they've witnessed one too many horrors.

Lowering his voice, he urges Freda, "You need to get these people out of here. Underhill is no longer safe for the fey."

Freda is frowning at his bloody shoulder. "You're hurt."

Aiden waves it off. "I'll heal."

She blows out an impatient sigh. "First thing's first. Put on some clothes and for the love of the gods, put out this fire."

He waves a hand and the flames die down to coals and smoking embers. "I can only help with one, I'm afraid. No garments."

"Well we can't bring you bare-assed before the king." Freda turns to her offspring. "Daughter, go find something for the wolf to wear. And a healer. Nic will flay me alive if he dies."

"Yes, *jord*." Jasmine runs off to obey her mother's command.

"You were in the other Seelie kingdom?" Freda removes her black cloak and hands it to him. "Does the Gray Throne still stand?"

"The throne stands but not much else." He shakes his head as he recalls the rubble of the sea glass palace. "Underhill brought it down as a message to Wardon and any who would oppose her. And when she figures out the shield is down…."

"She'll do the same thing here." Freda finishes his thought

Jasmine returns with a pair of pants that are a good deal

too short and a battered linen shirt which has one sleeve ripped off. "This was the best they could do."

Unsurprising, since the fey have no textiles or industry. All their clothing has been stolen from the mortal realm.

"A healer?" Freda asks.

Jasmine's smile dims. "None are available."

Meaning none would come help him after what they saw him do. He forces himself to show no reaction. "All I really need is a hot meal and I'll be as good as new."

"I'll show you where the kitchen is." Jasmine snags his hand.

Her sweetness and light are a balm to his shunned soul. If none of the other fey are worth saving, little Lady Jazz certainly is.

"I need to oversee the dispatch of any that aren't finished." Freda dons her winged helmet. "I'll meet you in the throne room in one hour."

She moves away from the field of battle where the Wild Hunt is dealing with any of the straggling Draugar.

"Come, Lady Jazz. I believe a hero's feast awaits us."

She grins and then leads him over the barrier to the inner sanctum of the last standing fey kingdom. The trees are taller than most skyscrapers and come in every color of the rainbow. Silver with purple leaves, gold with blue. Their branches intertwine and stretch on to create roads and bridges through the air. Beneath the boughs, small huts and houses have been constructed, more like nests with roofs than any real house. The fey gawk as they pass by, their expressions ranging from amazement to distrust.

He doesn't meet their stares, uncomfortable with their scrutiny.

"Did Nic find you?" Jasmine asks him. "She was desperate to reach you."

Desperate to reach him. The thought causes a small smile to tug his lips up. "I saw her."

"That's good." Jasmine leads him down some stairs that seem to be carved from nothing but roots and dirt. "The food is all down here."

He follows her down more cautiously. The wolf is uneasy with the confined space but the smell of roasting meat goads him onward.

"Rask?" Jasmine asks a potbellied fey with long white eyebrows and a scowl who is stirring a large cauldron of bubbling brown liquid. "The First told me to ask you for a meal for my friend here."

"Hmmph," the fey called Rask grumps. "Next meal's not for another three hours."

Aiden opens his mouth to tell the fey that he's going to keep the king and his court waiting but Jasmine is faster off the mark. "Please, Rask? I know you don't like to feed anyone between meals, but he only just arrived."

The chef drops his spoon into the pot with a clang then gives the nymph a reluctant smile. "Oh all right. But only because it's you asking."

Jasmine beams and hurries into the larder where she retrieves cold ham, cheese, apples and a huge loaf of bread. "Thank you, Rask. You're the best."

The grumpy fey gawks at her haul but says nothing.

"Come on," Jasmine gestures for him to follow her up another set of stairs. "I'll take you to the garden."

Aiden follows, relieved when they are aboveground once more.

This is taking too long, His wolf snarls.

Aiden lets out a breath. *Food, then we'll get what we came for.*

Namely, a kiss from a king.

❄

I WAKE UP ON A GURNEY. Naked, with only a thin, white sheet covering me from breasts to midthigh. My shackles have been replaced by a series of metal bands. One on each ankle, then above the knee. One on either wrist and then a large one over my midsection and finally around my neck.

There is something wedged in my mouth, forcing it open like a bit for a horse. I try to scream around it but it is muffled. Struggling, I attempt to wrench myself free of the cold metal bands. No use.

I look around the space where the gurney's been parked. It looks like some sort of futuristic medical lab. All white walls and white countertops, silver instruments and computer screens. My knowledge of medicine is limited to my Aunt Addy's veterinary clinic, but something about this room feels more like a laboratory than a doctor's office.

My gaze goes to the corner where, sure enough, the eye in the sky is pointed directly at me.

I clench my hands into fists, wishing I had access to my magic.

But it isn't my magic, at least not anymore. It's the magic of the Unseelie queen. My magic is limited to my deadly kiss. And my enemies have effectively neutralized that threat.

A woman wearing a blindingly white cleanroom suit appears over me, holding a needle. I shriek and the sound is muffled by the gag.

"It'll go easier if you hold still." She studies me a moment.

Terror makes my stomach twist. What exactly are these people going to do with me? The needle looms massive as it comes closer and closer. I whimper in fear, I can't help it.

Contact. Then the overwhelming sting as the needle sinks deeply into my upper lip.

Tears spill over. The woman's focus is on her work, her

eyes completely unsympathetic. I can feel the sickening tug as blood is forcibly removed from my body.

She extracts a vial from the syringe and then adds another. Two vials later, the needle is withdrawn.

A sob escapes. I want to beg, to ask who she is and why she is doing this. But why ask questions I already know the answers to? The people who caught me know what I can do. They know how to contain me and they want to find out how I can kill with a kiss.

They don't appear to care if I'm hurt on their quest for answers.

The medic returns with a fresh needle and repeats the process again. And again.

Return to the path you were on.

My mother set me up for this. Put me back on the course I've been destined for, the road that leads to this hell. A prisoner, a medical curiosity in FBI custody. Would they try to weaponize the toxin in my goodnight kiss? What will their tests reveal? I shudder to think of the outcome. Contained to me, my deadly kiss has only ever been used to take out murderers, rapists, people who prey on the weak. But if the feds find a way to weaponize the poison....

I shudder at the thought. It would be used for power, political gain. Magic unleashed on the wrong side of the Veil.

Finally done using me as a living pin cushion, the medic collects her bags and vials and departs. There is a hiss as the door closes behind her. I am left on the table like a rotting carcass at Thanksgiving.

No wonder I'm a vegetarian.

Please, I implore the empty space. *Anyone.*

A mist gathers. It's a strange sight in the closed room, but I see the little red light on the camera wink off. A moment later the mist takes shape.

A hideous shape. Part bird, part woman, all evil. She is a

Valkyrie spirit. A wraith I'd secured to serve the Wild Hunt. To serve me.

And she hates me for it.

"Little queen," Nightweaver appears in the room. "What has been done?"

I glower at her. With the gag in my mouth there isn't anything I can say. Talk about asking a stupid question.

She drifts down and studies my mouth closely. A trickle of blood has curved over the bow of my lips and down past my gag. The coppery tang of my own blood makes my stomach roil. Would serve them right if I choke to death on my own vomit.

"That looks painful." Nightweaver's soulless eyes gleam.

I shudder at her nearness. The Valkyrie still smells slightly of carrion, even in death. My nausea grows worse.

"Nahini sends me with a message. Underhill has discovered the ruse."

I close my eyes. Addy. She'd found out Addy is pretending to be Aiden.

"I'd ask if there is anything you would like me to tell her, but it's obvious you aren't up to conversation."

I glare at the cantankerous spirit, who drifts off, silent laughter echoing behind her.

Trapped. I am trapped by the mortals. My magic is all but gone and I have nothing, nothing nothing….

Including a plan.

You win, mother, I think tiredly. *Kill them all, there isn't a damn thing I can do about it.*

I can't protect the fey. I can't even keep mortals from tying me down and taking my blood. Most of the people I care for are on the other side of the Veil, but even if they were here, could they find this underground place and me within it?

Aiden could.

My heart cracks as I think of my poor wolf. Trapped beyond the Veil, held there by the threat of looming madness. I have no doubt Aiden will find me, eventually.

I stare at the medical equipment lying well out of reach. Scalpels, scissors, bone saws, scanners. The ominous blinking red light from the camera in the corner.

Will there be any of me left for him to find?

Eventually, two guards also wearing clean room suits enter the medical torture room and wheel me—gurney and all—to my cell. The guard steps to the door and presses a button on a remote. With a hiss of hydraulics, the metal bands part. The door is sealed behind them before I sit up.

First thing I do is reach behind my head and unfasten the straps of the gag. I hurl the thing with all my strength against the far wall. It bounces then rolls to the middle of the floor.

My hands shake as I raise them to my sore lips. Blood crusts one side of my mouth, but at least the wounds have clotted. My wardrobe—or lack thereof—is a bigger problem. I am freezing with nothing more than a scratchy sheet to warm myself. What, do they expect me to make a toga out of the thing?

"So this is how it's going to be," I snarl at the camera. "No clothes, strapped down like a lab rat. I have rights, you know. I want a lawyer."

There is no reply, not that I really expected one.

Wrapping the sheet around my nude form, I move to the bed and sit with my back to the cold concrete wall. Can an immortal die of exposure? I doubt it. Most of the fey have spent their lives going without clothing. It's still not a comfortable proposition.

Footsteps sound in the corridor. A slot opens beneath the oval door, a bar of light shining down on the dim gray floor tiles. Through the slot a tray is shoved then the mini hatch clangs closed. The footsteps recede.

I move forward and study the tray. Meatloaf, mashed potatoes smothered in gravy and anemic-looking green beans. Plastic wrapped disposable flatware, a paper napkin and an empty metal cup. One would think the FBI would feed their prisoners better than my high school cafeteria.

"Hey," I say up to the camera on the wall. "Something to add to your file, I'm a freaking vegetarian."

I can't hear a reply, but, in my mind's eye, I imagine them scowling at their notes. Some prune-faced man jotting down a note, *the serial killing vegetarian*.

The Fates are not without a sense of irony.

Ignoring the food, I pick up the cup and head to the sink. The water out of the tap smells like chlorine but I drink it down anyway. At least it's coming from their communal plumbing so I know the water isn't tainted. After another cupful, I set it on the sink and then slink back to the lumpy mattress and wait.

My best chance of escape is as soon as possible. If I linger, time will be my worst enemy. My muscles will atrophy and my mind will grow sluggish. Especially if the diet around this place doesn't improve. They know about my goodnight kiss and though Freda trained me to use various weapons, I don't have any within reach.

Surprise is my only advantage.

In spite of my resolve, my body is exhausted and soon my eyes drift shut.

"You," Underhill hisses as she looks down at the flickering image as the glamour melts away. The woman on the ground is all too familiar. One of her jailers.

She didn't have Váli at all.

On the slab, Loki laughs, the sound hysterical. Beside him, his wife shivers.

The fate, Atropos, looks up at her. "Power hungry as always, Pharaildis."

Underhill's nostrils flair in outrage. "You are interfering with the natural order."

"I am," the Norn wipes the blood off her chest, showing the flawless skin beneath. No mortal weapon could kill her. "Nic and Aiden have born the weight of everyone else's misdeeds. Someone needed to interfere on their behalf."

"There's got to be more to it." Underhill narrows her eyes on the Norn. Why would this ancient creature risk her position for Nicneven and Váli?

Unless...

Loki laughs. "The One True Queen is coming."

"No," Underhill whirls and storms from the cavern.

"My lady? What of the prisoner?" Fenrir asks.

"We can't hold her." Underhill turns back and smirks. "It matters not. By her actions, she has sealed her fate."

"Stand up, face the wall, hands behind your back." I jerk awake as the disembodied voice echoes into my chilly prison.

Addy. My heart pounds.

"Move." The command comes again.

I hesitate and then do as I've been told. My cover has always been normal teenager. Playing a scared, confused girl instead of an immortal fey should help me gain....

Well, not their trust, but maybe security will grow a bit lax.

When I am in place, more footsteps come. There is a hiss, like an airlock being unsealed and then two figures swathed in clean room suits appear. The fabric is so white they glow under the harsh fluorescent lighting. The duo step in unison over the threshold and enter my room.

The larger of the pair holds some sort or weapon on me. Not a gun, but something that looks sort of like a Taser. Message received. I do anything squirrely, I get zapped.

The other moves forward and snaps a pair of handcuffs

on me. Then produces that damned hood and slips it over my face.

Okay then, time to meet the wizard.

With the hood and cuffs in place they wrap some sort of sarong style outfit around my body. The fabric fastens with Velcro and feels like terrycloth. Not that I'm in a position to complain. I am escorted out into the hall, barefoot. It's just as bright out here and I wonder why whoever it is I'm going to speak with doesn't just come to my cell.

Unless this little outing isn't for a pleasant conversation. The US government wouldn't have me executed sans trial and sentencing. At least I don't *think* they would. I may have failed my tenth-grade civics class due to absence, but I know enough about the judicial system to understand that criminals get a trial. I'm in custody, I should get a trial.

Still, my insides twist.

We move past room after room with the same oval doors. If there are other prisoners in this facility, I don't see or hear them. The corridor joins with another identical one. We turn left, then right. I barely stifle my frustration as we make yet another turn. I have a shit sense of direction, even on my best day.

Which this isn't.

Aiden, I think. *Now would be a stellar time for a helping hand.*

But there is no reply. Our bond has gone silent. More than anything else, this has panic rising in my chest.

Underhill hadn't caught the real Aiden. Nightweaver would have said.

Worry about yourself, I think. My welfare used to be all I worried about. But I have changed. Aiden has changed me.

Finally, we stop in front of a nondescript door that looks no different than any of the others. The guard to my right knocks three times and then stands back.

The door opens and I come face to face with a gorgeous

woman. She doesn't smile but satisfaction shines from her dark eyes. Her short stature does nothing to revoke her sense of authority. A gun rests at her hip. Is she one of the agents who'd shot me?

At least she's not wearing a lab coat.

"Sit her there." The woman gestures to a ladder-back chair. It has ankle cuffs and a bolt in the back to run a chain through.

I am frog-marched to the chair and bound to it. My bare feet freeze on the cement floor and when my ankles are bound, I can't do anything except wiggle my toes.

"Leave us," the female agent says once I am secure.

There is another of those hissing sounds as the door seals shut behind them.

She moves forward and unzips my hood. I suck in air in a greedy gulp.

"Nic Rutherford." She circles the table to sit opposite me. Her eyes are so brown there is no distinction between iris and pupil. The intriguing color emphasized by a light dusting of eye shadow.

"And you are?" I put a little quaver in my voice and let my gaze dart around as though in panic. It isn't hard to fake being terrified.

"Agent Yasmine Hanson." She reaches for the single manila file folder on the table and flips it open. "I've been following you for quite some time. Since almost the beginning of my career."

Her tone is conversational but I'm not fooled. The folder contains the picture of a dead man slumped over the backseat of a bus. A man I'd killed a few years ago in Nashville when he'd tried to rape me.

Schooling my features, I do my best featherhead routine. "I don't know what you're talking about. This has to be some sort of mistake."

"Did you know, Ms. Rutherford, that this man, one Harrison Downey, was a convicted sex offender when you killed him?"

"Killed?" I manage a squeak. "I've never killed anyone."

She narrows her gaze on me. Then sits back and folds her arms over her ample chest. "Is that right?"

I nod, trying to sell the big-eyed innocent caught up in something out of her control, shtick. Lie and deny, bob and weave.

"What about Paul Anderson? Or Minnesota St. John?"

I shake my head even though my gut is churning. Those names are all on the IDs in my diary.

Agent Hanson raises one dark eyebrow. "I see. This is all a big mistake is it?"

I don't like her tone. This woman has studied me, knows how I will play, but there's no way out but through. "Yes, that is…I slipped out of the house to meet up with my boyfriend and then the next thing I know I'm being shot."

"Your boyfriend. That would be Aiden Jager?"

Cold dread seeps into me. How does she know Aiden's name? As the son of a god, he has the ability to blend in with the mortal world seamlessly. There would have been no paper trail, no way for her to find out about him.

The diary was one thing, but in order for Agent Hanson to know Aiden's name, she had to have an immortal informant. Who? Someone who also knew to warn them about my goodnight kiss. Not Chloe or Addy. My aunts would never betray me.

"That's right." Aiden's across the Veil. Safe from their reach. There's no reason to deny our relationship.

"And is Mr. Jager also the father of your baby?"

"Baby?" I blink. "I have no idea what you're talking about."

She pulls a paper from the file and spins it around so I

can see it. "We did a blood test on you when we patched up your wounds. See here?"

She points down at the block red print. Six weeks pregnant.

The world tunnels. No. *No.* I can't be pregnant. Cannot. We hadn't even had sex. It had been close but…

Is it possible?

Those midnight eyes survey my every twitch. "Congratulations, Ms. Rutherford. You're going to be a mother."

MIND GAMES

"**T**here must be some kind of mistake," I shake my head, unable to believe what the paper is telling me. "I'm only sixteen."

Agent Hanson frowns. "It says here you were born in 2001. That means you're eighteen."

"Right." Swift, Nic. I've forgotten that I'd missed eighteen months in the mortal world while I'd been screwing around beyond the Veil. I still feel sixteen.

Hanson's dark eyes narrow. "This…changes things."

"What do you mean?" No vivisection?

"I was under the impression that you were a serial killer. And yet you're sitting there looking like nothing more than a teenage girl."

"I am a teenage girl." And so much more.

But the other woman shakes her head. "You're not. I have the photos taken by one Gretchen Hamill and the diary with your fingerprints all over the licenses belonging to the victims. Look me in the eye and tell me you didn't kill those people."

I meet her gaze. "I didn't kill those people."

She blinks as though I've surprised her. As though she hadn't expected me to be able to lie. I hold my breath for a beat and wait.

"So, who killed them?"

It's difficult to shrug with my hands secured behind my back, but somehow I manage. "How would I know?"

"And how did your fingerprints come to be all over this?" She reaches into her bag and withdraws my fuzzy heart shaped diary.

"Brought it to school and I lost it."

She shakes her head. "Your prints are on the licenses, not just the book."

I inhale and then do the one thing I swore I'd never do. I throw someone else under the bus. "It belongs to Gretchen Hamill."

Agent Hanson leans back in her chair. "You're telling me that Gretchen Hamill is responsible for killing all these people? She's the one who sent us this package."

"Look, all I know is that I saw Gretchen with the diary after I lost it. It was in her bag. So, I snatched it out and flipped through it. I thought she was making fake ID's or something and thought I could get her to set me up with one. I didn't know she was killing people!" My shriek by the end has a hysterical ring.

Sorry, Gretchen. You're not going to be able to come back here.

Agent Hanson studies me for a moment. "I don't believe you. There's too much oddness about you."

"I want to talk to my aunt." Though Addy is MIA, Chloe is still around.

"We can't find her. Besides, you're legally an adult."

"A lawyer then." I square my shoulders, as though I'm the girl who is going to assert her rights, instead of the tricksy fey who is only buying time.

"Ms. Rutherford, I don't believe you fully comprehend your situation." Agent Hanson waves a hand around the room. "This is a secure facility meant to hold creatures like you."

At her words my blood starts to frost over. "What do you mean, like me?"

Her smile doesn't reach her eyes. "Come on now, Nic. You don't think all the fey activity has gone unnoticed, do you? We know about the Veil and the big tear in it. We know there are creatures that abduct innocent people from their homes, their lives, and use them for their own nefarious purposes."

I swallow hard. They know about it, about all of it. The Veil, the fey, possibly even Underhill.

"What will that baby you're carrying be able to do?" Agent Hanson eyes my still flat midsection. "Wield fire? Water? Fly? Will it have horns?"

I shake my head. It's not difficult to fake my overwhelm. Knowing I was being held by mortals who know of the fey is bad enough. But the baby….

I need to get out of here.

"I'm going to be sick," I breathe.

Hanson is on her feet and thrusting a garbage can in front of my face before the last word escapes. I hurl my guts up, though it is all bile this time. Morning sickness. I have freaking morning sickness.

No. It's a trick. Aiden and I hadn't gone all the way. I am not pregnant. Just freaked out.

She curses and then moves to pound to the air-locked door. "Take her back to her cell. Send a medic to run some more tests."

"What sort of tests?" I gasp.

"We won't hurt you or whatever it is you are carrying." Hanson assures me. "We're too interested to see the result."

I shiver at her matter of fact tone. It's a lie. No baby, she's fucking with my head.

I sit still while the agents unchain me and then shuffle back to my cell. On the third turn, or maybe it's the fourth, we pass another team perp walking someone else in the opposite direction. It's a girl, small, with honey brown hair, and blue gray eyes. Our gazes lock. She looks to be the same age as Jasmine, maybe even younger. Is she fey, too?

We are past them before I can get a word out. Then I passively stand back while I am deposited in my small, dank room.

"The medic will be with you shortly," the guard on the left says.

"Can't wait." I lie back on the cot, pulling my knees up into the fetal position.

I'm not really pregnant. I can't be. Agent Hanson is playing some sort of game with me.

I trundle through my mental archives, trying to remember the first day of my last period. It's no use. The time shifts between Underhill and the world around me are too vast. It could have been a few weeks or a few months.

I'm going to hang on to hoax as long as possible.

No matter what year it is, I still feel like a sixteen-year-old girl, not an immortal fey. I've lived more than most girls my chronological age could ever imagine, seen more, traveled through the fairy realm. I was within a few heartbeats of killing my own mother and claiming a throne.

Damn it, why didn't I kill her?

I wonder again where Aiden is. Before my meeting with Agent Hanson I'd thought our reunion would be peaceful and sweet. Now, panic fills me as I imagine his reaction.

Especially if I am knocked up.

In my past life, I had also carried Aiden's child. A child he hadn't really wanted. A child I'd planned to use to take my place on the Shadow Throne so I would be free to ride with the Wild Hunt.

"How the mighty have fallen," a sibilant voice hisses from the dark.

I glance up to see the hideous shade lurking in the corner. "Nightweaver." I should have known the ghost would still be skulking around. I try to keep my lips from moving too much and displaying my conversation for Agent Hanson and company.

The dead Valkyrie drifts over to the camera. She tilts her birdlike head to one side and then I see the red light go off.

"Nahini? Did she get free?" Last I'd seen of my second in command, she had been caged in the great room of the underground palace.

"No." Nightweaver shakes her head. "She wants you to know the Fate is still alive."

I sag a bit in relief. I don't believe Underhill had the power to kill Addy. It was the fates who trapped my mother after all. Hearing the confirmation takes a weight off my shoulders.

"Do you wish to relay any messages back to her?" The Valkyrie asks.

I think it through a moment. "Tell her to do whatever Underhill asks."

Nightweaver studies me in that odd way of hers, head tilted, beady eyes fixed. "You want Nahini to help your enemies?"

I hold her stare unflinchingly. "If it means she might have the chance to escape, yes."

The ghost nods. "So, she can free you?"

"No. I don't want anyone else crossing the Veil. The FBI know about us and they won't hesitate to kill any of us on sight if they can. Midgard is no longer safe." As an afterthought I add, "Get that message to Freda, too, if you can."

Nightweaver nods and then fades into the translucent mist that the dead of the Hunt dwell in.

I exhale a moment before footsteps sound from down the hall. The medic. I coil my muscles, ready to pounce. It's time for me to decline the invitation to stay at Club Fed any longer. Time for me to get back across the Veil. To save my real home and kill my mother.

For good.

When the door opens, I groan theatrically, hoping a show of pain will throw the medic off stride.

"Is it your wounds?" The voice is matter of fact.

I nod, rattling the chains as I grip my stomach. "I think whatever you gave me for the pain is making me sick."

She moves forward and I prepare to headbutt her when I spy two armed guards at the door. Damn it. This is supposed to be my escape. But even if I knock the medic out, the guards in this place won't hesitate to shoot me.

Letting out a breath, I settle in to wait for my next opportunity.

WITH A FULL BELLY, Jasmine escorts Aiden into the empty throne room. It smells of fresh cut wood and green and growing things. A live oak table sits in the center, with the infamous Green Throne situated at the head. Freda is already seated, her winged helmet on the table within easy reach.

"Jazz, go back to our quarters." Freda says to her daughter.

The nymph looks from her mother to Aiden and then back. "But, jord—"

"Now." Freda's tone brooks no nonsense.

Jasmine squeezes his hand once and then retreats.

"There you are, lad!" A thunderous voice booms and a beefy palm claps him on the shoulder.

"Thor." Aiden grins at the god. "I'm surprised to find you still here."

"I promised your little dumpling I would look after the place. Besides, the food here is some of the best I've consumed in recent memory." The thunderer pulls out a seat and drops into it with enough force to make the hearty wood groan.

No wonder the fey are worried about the food stores. Thor's appetite is the stuff of legend.

"What happened to you?" Freda turns to face Aiden. "The last we'd heard you were going to help Wardon secure his heir."

Aiden nods. "Jedda. And the boy was successful. The Gray Throne has a new ruler." He looks in the direction Jasmine had darted off. "One younger than your daughter."

Freda's tone is coated in permafrost as she accuses, "And you left him alone?"

"I sent him across the Veil. I thought he would be safer there." What he didn't say is that he'd turned one of the four fey monarchs over to a giantess he'd hated his entire life. Certain details are unimportant and would only cause Freda's infamous temper to get the best of her.

"I need to see Soladin."

Freda scowls at him. "Didn't you know? Soladin rode out with Nic."

Dread coils in his gut and the wolf lunges for control. If Angrboda had been right Nic had crossed the Veil. Was Soladin with her, taking with him any chance of staving off Aiden's madness?

"Then who lowered the air shield?" Only one of the four monarchs could command such magic.

"Taj. He's Soladin's longtime consort and the new Seelie king." Freda sucks in a breath. "He won't be happy to hear that Soladin's been captured as well. He'll want to mount a rescue."

Aiden couldn't blame the other man. All of his thoughts focused on getting across the Veil to retrieve Nic. "Where's *Seelenverkäufer*?" he asks.

"Nic had it with her."

Aiden shakes his head. Could nothing go right?

They fall silent, each lost in their own thoughts. Off to the side, a fire roars in the massive stone hearth—the antlers of a large animal mounted above it. Aiden recognizes it as the great stag the god Pan slaughtered while he reigned supreme in this court.

A man with dark skin and cat eyes strides into the room. His expression is grim as he approaches the Green Throne. "This is the wolf who burned the dead?"

Freda nods once. "He's Nic's....well, he's Nic's." She shrugs as though she doesn't know how to qualify their relationship.

Instead of sitting, Taj steps forward and offers his hand. "Your mate has told me much of you, Aiden. I am honored to have you here."

Aiden gets to his feet but before he can take the fey's hand, there is a stirring within him.

Bloodprice, the wolf whispers. Taj's male had abducted Nic. Soladin isn't here but the wolf swore vengeance.

We need him, Aiden tells the beast.

The wolf is poised to tear the Seelie king's throat out, but at least he doesn't try to wrestle control away.

Aiden refocuses on the king. "You know Nic?" And she'd

told this man she was Aiden's mate? His heart pounds. He will never tire of having her claim him as her own.

The large male's eyes gleam. "Not as well as I would have liked. Do you bring news from the other courts?"

"I do, but there's something I need from you first." Aiden takes a step forward.

"And that is?" Taj raises one hairless eyebrow.

"The Kiss of Clarity." Briefly he describes how Underhill had infected him with madness. "It is the only way I can rejoin my mate."

Freda tilts her head to the side and he can feel her scrutiny. "You don't look mad."

"It's dormant. One of Underhill's games. I can't cross the Veil until it is removed or risk unleashing my wolf to run rabid across Midgard."

Taj studies his face. "I've never bestowed it before. I'm not sure if I even can."

"You sat on the throne." Aiden gestures to the branch and leaf seat that thrums with life magic. "You must be able to give the gift of the court."

"For Nic's sake, and for the sake of true love everywhere, I will try." Taj moves forward and takes a deep breath. "Hold very still."

Aiden does. He doesn't close his eyes but lifts his chin to receive the kiss. Taj's lips are soft and gentle on his. A steady pressure. The intimacy of the moment stretches out but there is no pulse of magic. Aiden closes his eyes in frustration. Worry courses through him. What if it doesn't work? What if he can't cross the Veil? Nic's been banished.

I might never see her again.

A single tear tracks down his face and lands on their joined lips.

Suddenly there is a brilliant flash. Power radiates from

Taj's body and floods into his own. A sharp pain stabs into his mind but as quickly as it came, it dissolves.

"Did it work?" Taj asks.

Aiden hesitates and searches his thoughts. Smooth, clear, focused. The wolf too seems on point.

"Well, that was an interesting spectacle." Says a familiar voice, peppered with Latin spice. "Too bad our queen missed it."

Aiden pulls away and turns to the seer, Harmony Gold-feather. The purple-skinned fey tosses him a wink. "Two royal consorts necking in the throne room. The end of the worlds must be at hand."

"Watch your tone, slag," Freda barks. Aiden is surprised that the First would bother. Of course, the leader of the Wild Hunt is eternally loyal to his mate.

As loyal as he himself.

It's done. The wolf rises again. *Bloodprice.*

No. Aiden thinks. *We must get to her.*

Again the beast crouches. It wants Nic more than it wants vengeance. It helps that Soladin isn't here and that Taj isn't a threat. Aiden needs to get out of here and away from the new Lord of the Land.

"Where is the nearest in-between." Aiden turns to Freda. "Or how far is the tear in the Veil? I need to get over there immediately."

"Slow down, lad." Thor holds out a hand. "What's wrong?"

"Everything." Having his mind cleansed lifts one weight from his shoulders but there are so many others. Against his wishes, he sinks back into the chair.

"Our queen is in mortal custody." Harmony takes the chair on the opposite side of the table from Freda.

"You saw this?" Freda inquires.

As a seer, Harmony has visions of events before they

occur. Their abilities are so rare that seers often rise to the highest ranks of the courts.

Harmony bobs her head. "I did. She was betrayed and in turn captured by a special unit of federal agents." Her lips curl up as she turns to face Aiden. "And she just received some very interesting news."

Aiden doesn't give a damn about news. "Is she hurt?"

"She's been shot twice but is healing."

Pain pierces his heart. The mortals shot her.

We'll shred them to ribbons, the wolf vows.

"Mostly, she's worried about what is happening here. With you." The seer holds his gaze. "If her mother has captured you yet."

Aiden shakes his head. "That doesn't make any sense. I'm nothing to the Unseelie or Underhill for that matter. Why would she want me?"

"The prophesy." Harmony whispers.

He frowns. "What prophesy?"

Her eerie gaze is transfixed on him but he gets the feeling she is looking through him to something he cannot see. "Ragnarök. Once Loki has been freed, the end is unavoidable."

Even Thor appears uncomfortable with that.

The prophesy of Ragnarök—the end of the worlds. Aiden knows it well. "What does that have to do with me?"

Harmony's dark gaze meets his. "Underhill intends to free your father and hasten the end."

His lips part. "How?"

Her expression is somber. "The gods used your brother's intestines to create the trickster's bindings so he is held by his own blood. They need your bones to break them."

A shudder travels through him. "And once he's free he can unleash Fenrir." The wolf who will swallow the world. His half-brother.

39

"Fenrir rules from the Shadow Throne," A sibilant voice says.

Aiden turns and spies a ghost hovering in the doorway. Taj's guards draw their fey blades but the king holds out one hand to stay them.

"What do you want, Valkyrie?" Taj asks.

At the same time, Freda narrows her eyes. "Nightweaver."

"I come on behalf of she who was queen." Her gaze rests on Aiden. "I was just with her across the Veil."

His heart pounds. *Nic.* "How does she fare?"

"She is intact," the ghost says, making all the hackles rise along his spine. "Her message is for the First. She bids that no one cross in an attempt to save her."

Freda frowns. "What? Why?"

The ghost drifts farther into the room until she is situated above the table, her transparent form like an untethered balloon. "She has been captured by mortals."

"Tell me where she is." He'd find a way across even if he needed to tear the Veil himself.

The first shakes her head. "Did you not here the part about how she doesn't want rescue, wolf?"

He meets Freda's stare. "I am her lover, not her soldier. I go where I will." Nic saw to that.

Freda smiles. It's gone in an instant but he saw it. "Fine, but if we can't cross to Midgard, where shall we go? Without you and the dead of the Hunt to protect it, this stronghold will fall."

Harmony steps forward. "We need to evacuate these people. Without Nic's barrier we're all sitting ducks here."

"Where can we go?" Taj asks. "Where is safe?"

"The lands of the Vanir." Aiden breathes. "There is a portal, two days walk from here. It will take you to their world."

"It's forbidden." Thor's face is stern. "The gods exiled the fey."

Aiden turns to face the Asgardian. "Better to court the wrath of the gods than stand against the dead. Help us, Uncle. Plead a case for the fey."

Thor shifts and then nods. "For you, Váli, I will try." There is a clap of thunder and then light explodes through the room. When it dissipates, the thunderer's chair sits empty.

"Organize the evacuation," Aiden tells Freda. For once, the First doesn't argue.

"And you won't come with us?" The Seelie king asks.

Aiden shakes his head. "I need to get to Nic. I will retrieve her and we will meet up with you as soon as we free the others."

"It's too dangerous," Freda says. "You don't know what you will face over there."

"Worried for me, First? I didn't know you cared."

"I don't." As a turned mortal, Freda can't lie, as she proves by adding, "But my daughter does. And you stand the best chance of freeing Nic and getting her back on the throne where she belongs."

"Nic wouldn't want me to risk anyone else. She would want you to see these people safe."

"What will you need for your journey?" Taj asks.

"Perhaps some more food." It would save him time if he didn't have to stop and hunt.

"I'll take him to the kitchens," Harmony offers.

"Good luck, wolf." Freda holds his gaze a moment and then turns to make plans with the Seelie king.

Harmony is already on her feet. Aiden follows the seer through the wooden hallways, past a giant tree and down stone steps into a bustling kitchen.

The grumpy old cook is nowhere in sight. At least Aiden

won't have to argue with the fey over what he is taking. He hunts for some sort of satchel to carry his haul and settles on a nearly empty potato sack.

"Why didn't you tell them about Angrboda's suggestion?" Harmony asks as he lays out the food. Cooked chicken and ham, three varieties of cheese, fresh fruit and vegetables. It's enough to feed a fey army.

Or one hungry wolf.

"I don't know what you're talking about." Something about Harmony unnerves him. She can't lie anymore than Freda, but the seer has a nasty habit of not sharing vital information until it suits her.

She tilts her head to the side, her expression inscrutable. "I think you do. The giantess intimated that Nic could still rule in the Unseelie Court."

"You mean by claiming the Fire Throne?" He shakes his head. "Her magic is based in air. She can't wield flames. The magic of the throne would destroy her."

"So that's it then?" The seer studies his face. "You're just going to walk away and let the worlds burn?"

"Ragnarök is unavoidable."

"But it doesn't have to be now. Loki isn't free yet." Her lip curls up in a snarl of contempt. "You just don't want to risk your precious mate."

A warning growl echoes in his chest. "You're right, I don't. If Nic really wants the Fire Throne, I will help her obtain it. But I'm not going to force her to face off against her mother and Fenrir, never mind an army of the dead, just to see her burned to ash by that bloody fey chair."

"So that's it then." Her face falls. Is the seer disappointed in him?

"What would you have me do?"

"Remind her of her promise. She told Freya she would kill Underhill."

Aiden steps closer to her. "I won't pressure her. Nic makes her own choices."

"And what of you?" Harmony's chin juts up. "When will you start making your own decisions?"

"I owe Nic my allegiance, not the Unseelie Court." He shakes his head. "Trust me, Harmony. You're better off without my assistance. Nothing good comes from my bloodline. Nothing."

Harmony's lips part as though she is about to say something, then she shakes her head. "I'll leave you to pack. There's a room down the hall that's empty. I'll have the servants draw you a bath."

"There isn't time—," he protests but she holds up one hand, cutting him off.

"Freshen up for your journey, while I find you some real clothing. Better than drawing mortal notice."

It's easier to acquiesce than to argue. Besides who knows when his next bath might be? "Thank you."

After securing as much as he can carry that won't spoil, he cinches his bag and totes the bundle to the room Harmony had indicated. The door is ajar and he steps through.

The smooth wooden tub sits along the far wall. Steam curls enticingly from the water. There must be some sort of herb mixture within. He can smell rosemary and lavender and something else he doesn't recognize. It is familiar though. Some servant must have just filled it. Setting his food down on a low table, he strips off the tattered clothing Jasmine pinched for him and sinks down into the warm water.

He lays his head back and sighs in pleasure. His lids are heavy. How long since he last slept?

No time. The wolf argues. But the animal's voice is distant. His lids slide closed as he breathes in the perfumed water.

When his eyes open, he's in another place entirely. White marble, ornate gilt. Even the tub itself is different.

And he isn't alone.

"Hello, Váli," Freya's hands wrap around him from behind. "You've come back to me at last."

FRIENDS AND FOES

Days pass and I'm beginning to give up hope that I will have an opportunity to escape. It's not just because I'm incarcerated—a fact that sets my teeth on edge. Part of the problem is that I have nowhere to run. Undoubtedly the feds made sure all of my finances are frozen. With no magic and no safe haven, escape will only delay the inevitable.

Of course, there is the possibility of going back across the Veil—death sentence or no. Underhill can't kill me if she can't catch me.

Nightweaver returns in intermittent intervals, passing messages back and forth across the Veil. If not for her to talk to, I would go insane.

The Valkyrie's reports are grim. The dead are everywhere and the few fey remaining are evacuating to the Vanir lands. Worst of all is when she tells me Aiden has vanished.

"What do you mean he disappeared? Did he cross the Veil?" My heart thunders against my ribs. Maybe my wolf is on his way to come save me even now.

I'm not a girl who likes to depend on rescue, but any port in a shitstorm….

But the Valkyrie spirit dashes my hopes. "That was his intent."

I roll onto my back, trying to ignore the pain in my arm from the new batch of blood tests. "He'll be coming for me."

"Of course." The shade disperses and a moment later the red light on the camera winks back to life.

"He'll come," I say and face the wall. "And I will have to be ready to rabbit when he does show."

The days marking my incarceration start to take shape. Medical checks three times a day. Heartrate, blood pressure, blood draw. At least they let me keep my sarong thingy. Followed by shower time down the hall from the medical center. I never see another prisoner, except for the girl the first day.

A few staring sessions with Agent Hanson. The day before she laid out photos from the tornado that ripped through my high school and the apartment complex that had been taken over by Valkyries.

"How many of these people did you kill?"

"None." I'd given up on my innocent act and instead employed a new tactic—the truth.

"Then who killed them?" Her finger slams down on the pile of rotting meat that had once been people. "Because they sure didn't die of natural causes. Not with their bones ripped out."

I stared at the image, haunted by the memories. The smell of carrion, shit and rotting meat that were telltale signs of a Valkyrie nest. The battle. The Wild Hunt had cleaned it up but not before Gretchen had gotten her pictures.

"Did you ever think it was staged?" I hold Hanson's gaze. "That someone is playing a prank on you?"

In response she shuffled through her briefcase and

extracted a stack of papers. "You see this? Missing persons. All of them lived in that apartment complex. We have the wood chipper from your farm. All it will take is one hair, one fiber, and you'll be locked up for the rest of your natural life."

Again, I try to imagine running. There are way too many people in the building for my comfort, all of them armed except for me. I can't get close enough to kill them all and escape.

I miss the rest of my magic. Not that I could have wielded it in front of Hanson. I sit and stare at the ceiling, trying to plan. What are my resources? Nothing much on tap. They know about my kiss and take extra precautions anytime they move me. Allies? One phantom Valkyrie can't do much except deliver messages and haunt people. I shiver as helpless vulnerability wafts through me.

Even though I am 99.9 percent sure there is no baby, I can't help thinking about it. What would the progeny of a shape-shifting wolf and a teenage serial killer with a deadly kiss be like?

A predator, a hunter of men. Maybe he's been right to worry that his offspring would join his father in Ragnarök. I had almost sided with my mother. Before I knew what an evil bitch she is.

My thoughts turn to Aiden. He will freak out. Like some biblical old-testament catastrophic meltdown. He never wanted kids, not with so many monsters in his family tree. Our relationship is so odd, so new. I know him and yet in so many ways we've barely had any time together. Our union is older than time. I love him, I know this. And I am certain he loves me. But that doesn't mean we're ready to be parents.

Gas leaks through the vents for the first time since my first exam. Memories of that day make the sight even less welcome.

This isn't going to be pretty.

I come to, not strapped down on a gurney, but face down on a blue exercise mat. And I'm not alone.

The young girl I saw is huddled in a corner, knees bent, her hair hiding her face from view. Her shoulders shake but she doesn't make a sound. Her entire body trembles as though she has too many emotions and nowhere to put them.

Neither of us are chained.

"Hey now," I say. My voice cracks from disuse.

She looks up and I see the silver sheen of tears in her eyes. "Are you going to kill me?" Her voice is small and terrified.

I hold my hands up in front of myself. "I won't hurt you."

"They told me you killed people."

How to answer that one honestly without scaring the crap out of her? Deciding I can't, I change the subject. "What's your name?"

"Astrid," she sniffles.

"Hi Astrid. I'm Nic." I hold out one hand.

She stares at it but doesn't move.

Did the FBI put us in here because they want us to fight? I study the large room. There are cameras, but no other occupants. My hands aren't tethered there is no facemask covering my deadly lips. "Is this some sort of test?"

Astrid shakes her head, her brown curls bouncing out of the way. "I don't know."

There's something about her, something familiar that I can't place.

Slowly, I get to my feet. Even though I'm still barefoot in my sarong, I'm not about to squander the opportunity to move. "Do you want to walk with me?"

She scowls at me as though I've suggested something obscene.

I head off, deliberately turning my back on her. It's a risk, but trust has to be given in order to be received.

After a moment, she falls into step beside me. "Tell me about the baby's father. What's he like?"

I stumble. "How…?"

"I overheard the guards talking about you."

My eyes narrow. Okay, I've seen this movie before. Put seemingly innocent person in with the target to gain her trust and then so called-innocent rats out all her secrets to the bad guys. Could Astrid be a plant?

"He's complicated," I say after a pause. No acknowledgment of the pregnancy thing. *Denial ain't just a river in Egypt.*

"Do you love him?"

"More than I thought I could love anyone." It's a painful truth, one that leaves me vulnerable to hurt.

If your enemy knows where your heart lies, they'll know just where to strike.

She flashes me a smile then and I see that underneath her tattered sarong and stringy hair, there is a very pretty person with the promise of rare beauty in a few years.

She likes this topic, likes the thought of happily ever after. "So, have you ever been in love?"

She shakes her head. "I can't wait to fall in love."

Maybe Astrid is a better actress than I am, but I actually believe her. I want to ask what she's doing here, why the FBI put her in this place with me.

"What's it like?" She tucks some hair behind her ear.

"What's what like?" As we walk, I scan the room looking for doors or windows, or something I could climb to get to the air ducts that are a good fifteen feet overhead.

"Falling in love." She casts me a shy smile.

"It's not for the faint of heart." Only the one door, no windows, more of the same industrial cinderblock architecture.

"Was it love at first sight?" she probes.

"Not even a little bit. No, he sort of snuck into my heart when I wasn't looking." Damn tricksy wolf.

Astrid's gaze meets mine. Her blue-gray irises flicker. Swirl.

My breath catches. Oh gods. Is it possible?

I shift my own gaze, the way Nahini taught me, so I can view the soul plane. It's not a skill I've practiced with much, but when viewing the aura of a living being, it's invaluable.

Most souls are blue, bright blue, like an electric storm flash. But a scant few glow golden like the summer sun on a field of wheat. They are not of this world, the beings the gods fear above all others.

Addy's. Chloe's. And now Astrid's.

The girl the FBI have in their custody isn't a fae. She's a fate.

I let out a shaky breath. Does she know the truth? Should I tell her?

"Nic?" Astrid tips her head to the side to study me. "Are you all right?"

"Fine." The word comes out in a dishonest sounding cough. "Just really ready to get out of here."

Her smile is faint and she shakes her head. "There are worse places to be."

The words send a chill rocketing through me. "Like where?"

"On the streets," she licks her lips. "I won't ever go back there."

"Someone hurt you." My heart clenches and my murderous impulses surge to the fore.

She just looks at me with her eerie gaze.

"You won't go back to living on the streets, Astrid. You'll come with me." I don't know where the declaration comes from, but I can't leave her behind for the FBI to experiment on. Not when she might be related to my adopted family.

She stops and turns to face me, putting her reed thin body directly in my path. "Why? You don't even know me."

"Maybe not, but we're jailbird buddies now. Who else can I talk to about my time in the trenches?"

She smiles a little at that and then continues to walk around the indoor track silently.

I, Nic Rutherford, teenage serial killer and daughter of Underhill have a new soul to protect.

Maybe two. My hand rests on my still flat belly.

Gods help them both.

AIDEN SURGES up out of the water and away from the goddess of love and beauty. The wooden tub has morphed into white marble, the water in it swirling in rainbow hues.

Bifrost. That was the familiar scent. Someone tethered the magic from the bridge to Asgard in his bath.

He's been transported to Freya's temple in Asgard. He hasn't been here in centuries. Nothing has changed. The goddess favors white and it is reflected in the milky flooring and arches, rugs, chaises and pillows.

Even the flames burn white hot in the white stone firepit in the center of the space, as though the element dare not disobey the goddess's preference.

"Why have you brought me here?" he rounds on her with a snarl.

Ignoring his ire, she stands, letting water sluice down her perfect body. "Welcome home, Váli. I have spoken to the All-father on your behalf. He has agreed to release you from your banishment."

Her arms reach out as though to embrace him.

He steps away, not wanting to be any closer to the goddess. "Why would you do that?"

She trails one finger down his sternum. "Because, you belong here."

He shakes his head and retreats further. "I don't. You like playing games, Freya, but I'm not the same boy I was when you used me long ago."

She actually laughs at that. "*I* used *you*? I don't remember you complaining when you were naked in my bed."

Maybe once he would have believed her honeyed lies. But having accepted Nic as his mate, he understands just how one-sided his relationship with the vain goddess had been. How empty of real feeling. "You found me the day I first saw my father with Angrboda. Pretended to offer me comfort. I was drowning and had no one to confide in. You manipulated me when I was vulnerable."

She drops her arms to the side, her gaze narrowing. "And you enjoyed every minute of it."

"Yes, because I was young and alone and didn't have anyone else watching out for me. I was just a toy to you. But no longer."

She moves around him, surveying his body like a side of beef. Though he'd spent most of his life sky clad, her scrutiny unnerves him and he covers himself with his hands.

"Shy?" Her tone is mocking.

He lifts his chin. "Send me back."

She sighs and snaps her fingers. Within moments, they are both dressed, him in loose white trousers and a matching vest, her in a diaphanous red dress with a long sweeping train. It pools on the floor behind her, like a puddle of blood.

His jaw clenches. He's dressed in the style of one of her servants. "Vindictive bitch."

She crosses to a chaise and lowers her body onto it. "And

you really think that your mate is any better? Look at what she's done to you."

"Nic's done nothing." Aiden shakes his head. "She's innocent."

"Innocent?" The goddess scoffs. "Of the crimes against the fey? Most of them are dead, thanks to her. I gave her a task. To kill Underhill and she hesitated."

"And so would I if you asked me to kill my own mother."

She waves that away like it's of no importance. "Underhill will kill us all if it means her imprisonment ends. That Fate took your place and stalled her for the time being. Until she is terminated, the fey will suffer. The only being capable of taking her out is Nicneven. And if Underhill gets her hands on you…." she trails off.

Understanding dawns. "That's why you brought me here. You're worried that Underhill will carve me up and use my bones to free Loki."

She snaps her fingers and a glass of red wine appears in one perfectly manicured hand. No offer of refreshment for him. "The All-father told me. You're the key to releasing the trickster. He in turn can release Fenrir's corporeal body and Ragnarök will begin."

"You know better than anyone that fate can't be altered." Aiden studies the room he hadn't seen in a millennium. Everything is white and bright. Outside the open windows, birds twitter in the trees. The scent of Idunn's orchard waft on the breeze. The apples that keep the gods in their physical prime. "Where is the rest of the welcoming committee?"

"There's a little hiccup." Freya reclines so her lush curves are on full display. In his youth he would have taken that seductive pose as an invitation. Now he could barely hold her gaze. Everything about the goddess is just…wrong.

Because she isn't Nic. Isn't my mate.

The wolf is oddly silent. He frowns, wondering why it hasn't lept out and shredded Freya already.

"What sort of hiccup?"

"Your beast has been lulled into a temporary sleep."

His lips part. "You can do that?"

She rolls her eyes as though the question irritates her and sips from her glass.

"The key word there is *temporary*."

"The gods fear the beast within me more than most." He studies her face. "They already tried to kill me. Tried and failed."

"The wolf is a living being and as such, it can die." She waves her hand and a pink bubbly liquid appears on the table. "Drink that and your curse will be lifted. You will be welcomed back with open arms."

He stares at the vial in disbelief. "I've grappled with the beast for centuries. And all this time you've had the ability to kill it?"

When she doesn't answer, he swallows. He could be free. Free of the monster that had murdered his brother. Vengeance at last.

"What will happen to its magic?" Magic could neither be created nor destroyed. The wolf had its own set of abilities that had melded with his fire magic over the centuries.

"Oh, but that's the best part." The goddess says. "You know that giant tear your mate created in the Veil? The wolf's magic will seal it tight. No more in-betweens, no more crossings. Underhill will be contained. Midgard will be safe. Your mate will stay with the mortals. You get to live, so does Nic."

"And the fey still in Underhill?"

"Sacrifices must be made." She holds her arms out as if in welcome. "Drink it, Váli. Drink and be welcomed back to Valhalla."

EMPTY PROMISES

Three meals have come and gone in my new cell. At least now I have someone to talk to other than a spirit.

"Where are your parents?" I ask Astrid over our breakfast of crappy instant oatmeal and orange juice from concentrate.

Surly mortal parents wouldn't be okay with a young child being held imprisoned this way.

She lifts her spoon and lets gravity take hold of the gluey mixture until it lands back in the bowl with an unappealing plop. "I don't have any. I ran away from the foster home I was in after…the incident."

My ears perk up. "Incident?"

Her gaze meets mine and she looks down. "I don't want to talk about it."

Having a wealth of my own secrets means that I'm not about to push her for a confidence she doesn't feel.

She eyes me curiously. "You're the first person I've seen, other than *them*."

"Same. Are there other prisoners here?"

She shakes her head, dark curls bouncing. "No."

I fish, still trying to decipher if Astrid knows what she is. "Do you know why they took you? Why they have held you here for so long?"

There is a pause. "I see things...things other people don't see."

"What kind of things?"

She shoots me a repentant look. "I lied to you before. About hearing the guards talk about your baby? They never talk around me."

She's clearly worried that I'm going to chastise her for fibbing. I shovel the oatmeal in without comment, waiting for her to say her piece.

"I know because of my...ability. The baby you're carrying? It's a girl."

My lips part. "You're sure?"

She nods. "I can feel her soul. It's like a big bright glowing string of red energy. You have one too. But yours is darker, like a deep purple."

Chills shoot down my spine and my hand reaches instinctively for my stomach. It'll take months for the proof to manifest, at least if I remembered my biology lessons correctly. Still. Eerie.

She looks away. "You think I'm a freak, don't you?"

"No, not at all." I offer her my palm and, after a moment's hesitation, she takes it. "You have a gift, Astrid. A special one."

I don't say any more than that, sure that Agent Hanson is monitoring our every word. If she doesn't know about the Norns, then I'm not going to be the one to enlighten her.

"What is it the FBI do to you?" I ask.

Her shoulders bob up and then down. "Nothing. They don't keep me shackled anymore."

"Do you ever get to go outside?" I fish, wondering if we'll ever get a chance to escape.

"No," she shakes her head.

"Then we'll have to get our exercise in here." I stack my tray on top of hers and carry them to the corner by the door. "You ever learn to fight?"

She shakes her head. "I'm only twelve."

I snort. "I knew a twelve-year-old who could kick my butt. Come on, I'll show you some moves."

I crouch down into a fighting stance, knees bent, hands facing toward her. We are an army of two, with me as the default commander. I don't know how long Astrid and I will have together, but I plan to at least teach her how to defend herself. It might pay off in the long run.

After a moment, she copies me. "This won't hurt the baby?"

Fake baby. "As long as you don't kick me in the stomach." I wink. It's not a gesture I would have made before. Winking and laughing, two habits I'd picked up from Aiden.

Her eyes round and she shakes her head with vehemence. "I won't, I promise."

"Good. Now, try and grab my wrists, to hold me still."

She does and I break her hold almost at once.

She squeaks and leaps back.

"That's good, you have fast reflexes."

"I'm not very strong." Her tone is apologetic.

"The best fighter I know is the fastest." In my mind's eye I can picture Nahini, moving like a blur. "Strength only matters if you can lay hands on your opponent. Now this time, I'm going to grab you."

I lunge and she darts back. I'm fast too though and I manage to get a hold of her wrists.

She struggles and then steps away.

"Not back. Don't retreat," I tell her. "Step into me."

She does.

"Now, circle your arms in and around, the way I did, to break the hold."

Astrid does, though not fast enough to get free.

"Try again, but move faster so that I don't have time to adjust my grip."

The speed of her movement increases and I fumble my hold enough that she can spring back.

"I did it." Her eyes are alight with excitement.

"You did. Let's try again."

We work for hours. I show her how to break different holds and use whatever is on hand to break free and put distance between herself and her attacker. I don't bother trying to teach her to attack. Astrid is too worried about hurting me. Our goal is escape, not takedowns.

She may never become one of Nicneven's Nymphs but as I watch her move, I feel good that I've taught her a valuable skill that might one day save her life.

We're taking a breather when a hiss stems from the air vents. I leap to my feet, but there is nowhere to run.

"Nic," Astrid grabs for my arm, panic wild in her eyes.

"It'll be all right," I say, even though it isn't.

But when our eyes meet, I see hers are swirling silver gray. A tear slides down her cheek. Dread fills me.

"If you get the chance to run, Astrid. Don't wait for me."

Her lips part but then her eyes roll back in her head. I catch her before she hits the ground. Lowering myself so that I don't fall, I cradle her in my lap.

"Bastards," I exhale, swearing that I will one day kill Agent Hanson and all her cronies if it's the last thing I do.

I AWAKE with the damned hood over my face. Agent Hanson is looming over me, dark gaze laser focused. My terry sarong is gone. My flesh is covered in goosebumps against the cold metal gurney. My arms are pinned at my sides by the metal bits again.

"You're an interesting young woman, Ms. Rutherford. A stone-cold killer who spent the last several hours teaching a girl she just met to defend herself. I half expected you would kill the girl, especially when she knew about your offspring." Her gaze travels down to my stomach.

Fake baby. Mindfuckery. I want to ask her where Astrid is, but speech is impossible with the hood covering my mouth. It dawns on me then that this is going to be a different sort of interrogation. Agent Hanson still wants her answers, but if my mouth is covered, we've moved beyond talking.

A medical tech moves around her, putting a sensor down by abdomen.

My eyes go wide as I hear the rabid little *thrum thrum thrum* from the microphone.

"Your baby's heartbeat." Hanson says. "In case you didn't believe our report."

Tears sting my eyes. Oh gods, it's true. It crashes down on me with the weight of an avalanche. I really am pregnant. Up until this moment, I had ignored it, pushed it aside. But I really am going to have a baby.

Aiden's baby.

The tech places more sensors, at my throat above my breasts. My adrenaline spikes, the sound of my own rabid heart drowning out the little flutter of the infant. She said she didn't want to hurt the child. What is she going to do to me?

Hanson dons latex gloves then reaches for my hood's fastenings. She uncovers my face.

I suck in a lungful of air. "You know not only does the food suck in this place, but the hospitality leaves a lot to be desired. My Yelp review is going to be scathing."

She ignores my tone. "Tell me where Aiden Jager is."

"Oh good, an easy one." I pretend to think about it then hold her gaze. "I have no idea."

She gets close, not close enough for the kiss I'm longing to give her, but still in my face. "I will break you, Nic."

I hold her gaze in silent challenge.

"Last chance. Tell me where to find the wolf."

I force myself not to react. She knows what Aiden is, or at least that he can transform into a wolf.

"I already told you, it wasn't my turn to watch him. So, what are you going to do to the pregnant teenager?"

In answer, she waves a hand. All the lights in the room dim. Above my head, the ceiling is transformed into the face of a dead man. His cheeks are ruddy and he is smiling.

Goosebumps rise up on my arms. Familiar faces.

"You were found by hikers in the Black Forest." Agent Hanson circles around the table. "Just six-years-old. The one who stayed behind to wait for you was found dead. No apparent cause of death for a healthy thirty-two-year-old man. Left behind a wife and two young sons."

At her words, the image shifts to the man and his family. The woman is dark haired but the boys have the same sandy blond hair and ruddy cheeks as their father.

Hanson leans over me. "Care to tell me what happened to him?"

I force myself to stare at him. He looks like a model on a photo booth wall, not the man who'd tried to exchange a chocolate bar for sexual favors with a child.

"You said it yourself, he died."

She leans in closer. "It's the how I'm curious about. Do you regret this man's death?"

Do I regret offing a pervert? No. "What do you think? I'm psychologically scarred by that encounter."

Her full lips turn up. "I think you lack remorse. I think

you are devoid of compassion. I think you're glad he's dead. I think you're some sort of vigilante and you and your boyfriend have been at this for a very long time."

The image flicks over to a blonde woman in a white dress with red flowers. She's standing barefoot on a beach. "Do you know who that is?"

When I shake my head the image enlarges. "Look closely. Something about her must seem familiar."

My lips part. "Is that...?"

"Your mother. The woman who gave birth to you."

I have had two mothers. One is Underhill, the deathless realm whose life force is tethered to the land beyond the Veil. She was the mother to Nicneven, the Queen of the Unseelie Court. When I died, Aiden merged her soul with that of an infant girl so I could be reborn as Nic Rutherford, current prisoner of the FBI.

"Her name was Sophie. Sophie Ann Nesbit. Do you know how she died?"

I stare up at her, barely breathing.

"She was killed by a creature like you. One who could kill by no means we can detect. She left behind an infant son and a husband."

Aiden had told me my birth mother had passed away. I'd never once thought to ask about the how. And she'd been killed by magical means?

Underhill. It had to be.

But Underhill couldn't reach through the Veil. So, who could have done it?

"Does it bother you to know that an innocent woman died because she brought you into this world? You might as well have killed her yourself."

The image shifts again, this time to a little boy. So thin I can count every rib through his grubby t-shirt. "Do you know who this is? His name is Garret Stevenson. You should know him. You killed his mother. And after she died, he went to live with an uncle. The man had a gambling addiction and he left Garret alone, and locked in his room. He died trying to climb out of a fifth story window."

My lips part. The mother with Munchhausen's-by-proxy. I had patted myself on the back for having helped that boy, kept him from a slow, painful death at the hands of the woman who was supposed to care for him.

What was it Addy always said? *When your time is up, it's up.*

The images turn into video. Flashes of the crime scenes. No blood, I didn't draw blood. But the bodies, the sightless eyes that transitioned to their loved ones.

A web of death and misery. And I was the spider who'd woven it.

"Ma'am? Her heartrate is erratic." A tech says to Hanson.

The woman's hawk like gaze is on me. "The child's?"

A pause. "Stable."

Hanson stares down at me, her gaze pitiless. "Then we proceed."

AIDEN STARES down at the small glass in his hand. Freedom from the wolf. Safety for Nic.

Death for the fey.

He holds Freya's gaze, then slowly turns the cup upside down, pouring the liquid across the fluffy carpet.

Her nostrils flare in outrage. "You fool. Do you have any idea what I had to go through to procure that for you?"

"Put. Me. Back." Midgard, Underhill, he doesn't much care where she deposits him as long as it's away from these soulless creatures that call themselves gods.

She rises and moves to stand before him. Unlike Nic, she's the same height as he is and holds his gaze with her own steady one. "It's not so simple. There is no way back, not for you."

"You got me here." He frowns in thought. Heimdall, the watcher, isn't a fan of Aiden or anyone in his family. And his is the only hand that can operate Bifrost.

"Who put the Bifrost in my bathwater?"

Freya's lips curve up seductively. "You wouldn't believe me if I told you. So, I'll show you, instead."

A figure moves forward, a familiar purple-skinned figure.

"Harmony?" he blinks, stunned.

Freya moves to the seer's side. "She has been my faithful servant for centuries."

The fey woman stares at him in the most unnerving way, as though she wishes to apologize. And is that longing he sees in her gaze?

He shakes his head, unable to believe the seer had turned on them. "You swore your loyalty to Nic."

Harmony's dark hair and purple skin stands out like a splash of paint against Freya's colorless decor. "Actually, that doesn't sound like something I would do, since I can't lie."

"You swore not to betray her."

She shakes her head, her tone insistent. "And I haven't. I said I would be part of her court, but that was all."

He stares between the two women, wondering at their connection. Harmony Goldfeather is a rare beauty and normally, Freya's vanity would cause her to subjugate someone who might outshine her own attractiveness. There is more to this relationship than meets the eye.

"So why trap me?"

"Haven't you been listening, Váli? You are the key to unbinding the trickster. Underhill will stop at nothing to possess you." Harmony holds his gaze, demonstrating no remorse for her actions. "I have seen it come to pass, the destruction, the chaos. You must stay here."

"The hell I will." Aiden leaps across one of the pillow strewn chaises and bolts for the door.

He doesn't make it. Freya sighs and uses her magic to toss him to the floor. He slides into a wall face first. There's a crunch in the region of his nose and blood streaks the pristine marble.

"What a mess," The goddess puts her hands on her hips. "See what you made me do? Obstinate fool."

Another flick and he sails into the other wall. Another crunch, this time in his shoulder. Dislocated for sure.

"Stop," Harmony falls to her knees beside him. "You said you wouldn't hurt him."

Freya moves forward, blue eyes narrowed. "I'm not hurting him. He's hurting himself."

Aiden lunges up and snags Harmony into his grip, wrapping his useless arm under her chin and preparing his good arm to twist. "Release me or I'll snap her neck."

Freya actually smirks. "Go ahead. She's served her purpose."

Aiden doesn't relent. She might be bluffing.

Another wave of her perfect hand and then the breeze is suddenly cut off as the doors shut with a bang. "The temple is warded, no one can come or go unless I say so. And if your wolf wakes cranky and thinks to kill me, let him know he will be trapped in here until the end of time."

With that, she vanishes.

"Damn you, you heartless bitch." The goddess was more selfish than he recalled.

Harmony makes a soft noise. "Go ahead, Váli. Kill me."

"I should," he snarls. "If not for you, I'd be in Midgard right now with my mate."

She doesn't plead or beg or offer any explanation. She waits for his decision in total silence.

He huffs out a breath and releases her. Stumbling to the

nearest arch, he slams his shoulder back into the socket. A wave of dizziness washes through him and he sinks to the floor.

A tearing sound causes him to look up. The seer rips another strip off her dress and then offers it to him.

"Are you all right?"

"I'll live." He holds the fabric to his broken nose. "Why are you helping her?"

"I told you—"

He cuts her off. "Freya is only interested in the welfare of one person—Freya. You're too intelligent to have missed that fact when she told me to kill you just now."

Her jaw clenches.

"Help me escape here. Help me reach Nic."

She swallows, looks away. "I can't."

Can't, not won't. Centuries of dealing with the fey have made Aiden aware of the importance of word choice. "Did you have a vision? Something specific about me? You know as well as I do that visions of the future can change."

She holds his gaze and her tone is sincere as she murmurs. "They can. But in all of mine, you die."

WHAT'S LOVE GOT TO DO WITH IT

S omeone is singing. A sweet, light voice. It pulls me
out of the darkness.

Long ago and far away
In a field kissed with golden sun
A sprite flitted from branch to flower
and there she met the one
Her love as fresh as a summer breeze,
her heart as big and warm
His eyes guileless and serene
gave no hint to the coming storm

Together they danced and laughed and played
until the light faded from view
For then he turned into a monster there
and she his victim anew.

A HAND IS on my shoulder, shaking me awake. "Nic? Are you all right?"

Sensing a presence, I surge up from my hidden place inside, ready to kill whoever is near. So much loss, so much pain. Do intentions really matter when you spread misery around like pollen?

It's unforgivable.

I attack. It's all I know how to do.

"Nic." A feminine voice. Not Agent Hanson.

Astrid. The Norn girl. I'm choking the life out of her.

"Sorry," I gasp and roll away from her. Those bastards. They fucked with my head and then dumped me back in with her. Are they hoping I will kill her?

Can I even kill her? Norns are not of this world.

Her eyes are huge. "What did they do to you?"

"Nothing I didn't deserve." I close my eyes and imagine my mother's face. Not Underhill. Sophie Ann Nesbit. Killed because she gave me life.

Astrid is quiet, sitting in a corner, arms wrapped around her legs.

"Are you okay?"

She nods but doesn't speak.

Normal. I have to bring the tension down for both our sakes. I cast around for an idle topic of conversation. The girl has no family, and doesn't want to talk about her gifts. Understandable, even if I am still suspicious. "Tell me... what's your favorite food?"

"Chocolate," she whispers.

A smile creeps out. "I have an aunt who is a total choco-holic. She once ate five pounds in one sitting. Special dark, with almonds. I thought she was going to be sick." I vividly remember Chloe had bitched about an excruciating stomachache for days after. *"Just kiss me, Nic and put me out of my misery."*

"Why did she eat so much?" Astrid sounds intrigued.

"She'd made a bet with my other aunt, Addy, that she couldn't go without eating chocolate for a solid month. Well, she made it and then gorged when the month was up."

"Your aunts sound so awesome." Her sigh is wistful.

"They are." My throat closes up as I think about Addy. Is she still alive?

I know it is possible to kill a Norn. Addy and Chloe had annihilated the third sister, Lachesis. They'd done it because she'd broken the cardinal rule of the Fates and tampered with mortal destiny.

Just as Addy had done for me.

"What's wrong?" Astrid asks.

I shake my head. "It's nothing."

She frowns. "Nic, you don't need to protect me."

Except I do. But she's right, I shouldn't handle her with kid gloves. "Okay, well, I'm trying to figure out how to spring us from this place. Got any ideas?"

She shakes her head.

"Yeah, me either." Some freaking magic would come in handy right about now. *Screw you and the horse you rode in on, Mom.*

"Where would you go?" Astrid asks.

"Back to my family's farm." And from there across the Veil and into Underhill where I would kill the treacherous Underhill once and for all.

"What's it like there?" It takes me a minute to realize she's talking about the farm, not the land beyond the Veil.

"This time of year, it's very quiet." I close my eyes as I picture the icicles hanging from the roof of the house, the snow layered over the ground like a thick blanket. The icy north wind whipping a blast of chilly air between the barn and the other out buildings, making the powdery snow dance.

Astrid studies me. "Are there any animals?"

"Not that we own. But Addy has a veterinary clinic where she takes care of dogs and cats. I help out there sometimes after school." Or I had until my destiny had blindsided me.

"It sounds nice."

"It is my favorite place in all the worlds. My home." It's true. My memories from my life as Nicneven had shown me wonders beyond human imagining. I'd seen the in-between —the space behind the Veil that separates Midgard from Underhill. I'd grown wings and flown, bathed in a biolumi-nescent pool and dressed from a magical wardrobe in a sea glass and sand castle by the sea.

But Dorothy had it right—there's no place like home.

I wonder if I'll ever see it again.

"Someone's coming," Astrid says a moment before I hear the footsteps.

"Stay behind me." I put myself between her and this new threat.

A hiss as the airlock door opens. Two guards stride through the door, both armed, both wearing the required clean room suits. "Get up."

I am slow to comply. I don't threaten them but neither do I try to pull off poor, pregnant teenager. These people have no mercy, so playing the sympathy card is a waste of time.

"Step forward."

I do but when Astrid moves to follow the other levels his sidearm at her. "Not you."

"It'll be all right." I tell her.

She doesn't answer.

The guards lead me out into a hallway. As we walk, I make an effort to mentally map the twists and turns. Note the cameras perched in the corners of every intersection. Is there anything here that can aid me in an escape?

Astrid might know.

And then we come to the room that has become a familiar part of my day, interrogation 101 with professor Hanson. Time to sit and stare blankly at the wall behind her. Pretend I hadn't cried, hadn't begged for her to stop relating the tragic lives of my victim's families. I hate her for that more than all the rest.

But Hanson isn't inside the room. The guards don't bother to tether my shackles to the chair. I scowl and look down but before I can decide if it's an oversight or an order, they exit the room, the hermetically sealed door hissing behind them.

I sit and wait. Is this some sort of test? Best not to respond at all. There is no camera in here, no two-way mirror, only a thin vent in the ceiling. In the quiet I can hear the fan thrumming as air circulates through the ductwork.

I count to thirty. Then one hundred. Nothing happens. I'm used to waiting, it's in my nature, but I'd be lying if I said that, under these circumstances, it isn't unnerving.

The door opens and a woman steps through. She is tall and statuesque with blood-red hair wound up in an elegant chignon.

The Hag of the Ironwood. My heart leaps when I recognize her. But is she here as a friend or a foe?

"Don't say anything," Angrboda sets her briefcase down on the table. "We don't have much time."

"How did you get in here?"

"I had to wait until Hanson was off the premises to ensorcelle the other mortals so they'd let me in."

I stare at her, the woman my mother forcibly evicted from Underhill. The mother of monsters and the giantess who Aiden held responsible for ruining his life.

"I'm your lawyer, hired by your aunt, as far as they're concerned."

Chloe. "Is she all right?"

The giantess nods once. "Worried about you though. We have a plan to get you out of here. Soon."

"What is it?"

"I don't want to reveal too much. Just know that I'm going to slip an order into their heads on the way out to move you from this facility to a more secure location. When they transport you, we will be at the ready."

I pick at a hangnail. "There's a girl here, her name is Astrid. Do you know anything about her?"

The giantess shakes her head. "No. Is she fey?"

Unwilling to say the words out loud I murmur, "I want to help her, too."

She studies me. "I'll see what I can do."

"Do you know where Aiden is?" It's the sort of question any normal girl would ask.

She shakes her head. "No one has seen or heard from him for days."

The hangnail rips free. That's why my eyes sting.

"One thing at a time. We have to set you free then we can worry about the wolf."

"I'm pregnant," I'm not sure why I tell her this, other than that it feels good to tell someone since everyone else has been busy telling me. It should be my news, fucked up as that is. "I've heard it's a girl."

The giantess's eyes go wide. "The One True Queen."

"What?" Where had I heard that before?

"Nothing." Her green eyes fix on my face. "Does Aiden know about the babe?"

I shake my head. "I'm worried about his reaction though."

"Worry about yourself, Nic." Her gaze goes to my midsection. "For you carry the key to saving all of us within you."

AIDEN WAKES to the feel of warm hands sliding across his naked back.

"Nic," he breathes, but the second the scent hits him, he knows it is wrong.

Leaping out of bed, he turns his back on the goddess. "Keep your talons to yourself, goddess."

"Is that what you really desire?" She is wearing a sheer white gown that reveals more of her flesh than it conceals. She skims her hand along her side. "Do you not find me...irresistible?"

He glowers at her. "Somehow, I'll manage."

She falls back, her touches growing bolder. "Why must you make this so hard on yourself?"

He catches her hands. "Don't try me, Freya."

She lets out a breath. "So, this is to be our fate? You denying us any sort of pleasure? Do you not remember how good it was between us?"

His gaze narrows. "What I remember is that you abandoned me to Midgard, you let my brother die and didn't bother to say a word against the gods. And you've all but abandoned your children to Underhill."

She sucks in a breath. "Oh, here we go. Váli, you are *centuries* old. Don't you think it's time you learn to let things go? These grudges aren't becoming."

"Tell me what I need to do, Freya." Aiden paces the room. "Tell me what it is you really want. You know you can't keep me here forever."

"Fine, you insist on leaving and dooming us all...." She rises from the bed, hips swaying as she prowls closer to him. "I want to carry your child."

He stares at her, uncomprehending.

"It's the only way your father will spare me. He's always

had a soft spot for his progeny. If I am the mother of his grandchild, he will let me live in peace instead of destroying me with all the rest."

"I will *never* have a child." He closes in on her, wrapping his hands around her arms. Barely refraining himself from shaking her. "Do you understand me? My entire line is tainted, filthy. I will not spawn, especially not with the likes of you."

Her face grows mottled in her fury as he speaks and she vanishes out of his grip.

He sinks down onto the bed. What a mess Loki made. Why couldn't his father have been content with his mother? Why couldn't they have spent eternity together as a family? It had been idyllic to be a child of the Trickster.

Right up until the moment that it wasn't.

Angrboda had been right. He must accept his past and all it had taught him. He'd been trying. Now that madness no longer threatens, he can think clearly for the first time in centuries.

Fact one. He loves Nic. His wolf accepts her as his mate.

Fact two, she, for whatever reason, loves him as well. The last night they'd been together was all mixed up with the pain from the past and the thin thread of hope for the future. And then they'd been separated again. The cycle repeating as it had since he had first met her.

Why can't they be together? In Midgard or Underhill, the Vanir lands or the deepest corner of Hel. He doesn't care where as long as it is her and him.

Fact three, it might be all his fault.

Freya is an idiot if she believes having a child with him will protect her. His father had been jaded and tortured for thousands of years. And now, with the end of the world at hand, he will be even more vicious. And there is the ever-present worry that any child of his would side with Loki,

Fenrir and all the rest come the last battle. The odds are already stacked against the world. Aiden refuses to do anything else to aid its downfall.

His gaze takes in the room around him. Freya's white motif abounds but on a shelf in the corner sits a ruby red dragon's egg in a small glass case. It had been there the first time she'd brought him here. He recalls the first time he'd been in this room, after he'd seen his father and Angrboda together. Freya had found him in her garden. He hadn't been paying attention to where he was, his mind trying to reconcile what he'd seen.

"Why was he with her?" Aiden shook his head.

"They were making love." The goddess handed him a drink.

"That wasn't love." It couldn't be, not with a woman who wasn't his mother. "She must have bespelled him."

"Sweet boy, love comes as it comes." Freya's cat eyes had glittered. "Let me show you."

Aiden squeezes his eyes shut.

Deep in his chest, his wolf stirs. He's oddly relieved to know the beast is with him.

He rubs his thighs as though they itch. The creature within him detests being caged almost as much as he detests being separated from his mate. So how to escape?

Harmony. The seer is his way out. So what if she foresaw his death? The future isn't set. He must convince her that the world will best be served if he gets out of this place as soon as possible.

With that thought in mind, he follows his nose, tracking the seer's wisteria scent. Her room is down a long open-air gravel path. Moonlight illuminates the white cobbled walkway. A fountain burbles merrily. Everything perfectly austere. Not a pebble out of place. Perfect and cold, like the bitch who lives here.

He knocks softly, not wanting to wake the seer if she is resting.

Harmony opens the door. She is wearing a blue silk bathrobe and her jet hair is pulled up in a high pony tail.

She smiles softly when she sees him. "How's your head?"

Though he had told himself he needed to make nice with her, her question enrages him. "Why the concern, Harmony? You delivered me into the hands of my enemy."

"We're friends, Aiden. And she's not your enemy. In case you missed it, we are trying to save your life. And Freya isn't all bad. She petitioned the other gods to allow the fey to evacuate to the Vanir lands."

"And?"

"They're discussing it." She stands aside and gestures for him to enter her space.

He does and then frowns at the room. Fluffy white bed covered in purple and pink pillows and a white lace canopy. Stuffed animals cover a chaise lounge by a picture window that overlooks a glittering silver stream.

It's a child's room.

He studies the seer anew. "How long have you known Freya?"

"All my life." Her chin goes up and she crosses to the bed, seating herself on the edge of it. "She rescued me from certain death."

"How so?"

"You're not ready to hear the story." She tilts her head to study him. "I assume you're here to try and convince me to help you escape?"

He doesn't bother to fight a smile. "Am I so obvious?"

She shrugs. "It's what I'd do in your place."

He studies her a moment. "Please try to understand. I have a mate out there. You know how rare that is?"

When she nods, he pushes, "I have no idea what's happening to her, no idea if she's too hot, too cold. If she's hungry and doing without. It's my job to protect and provide for her."

The seer shakes her head. "It really isn't, Aiden. Nic has been taking care of herself since she was six-years-old. She's a survivor."

"And that means what, that I shouldn't worry?" His laugh is hollow. "Tell me, have you ever gone without protection from a goddess?"

Her expression grows shuttered. "You know I have. Wardon kept me locked in his castle."

"Where you were dressed in finery and given plenty of food and a place away from the elements?"

Her stare is unflinching. "A gilded cage is still a cage, Aiden."

She sounds like Nic. "There are worse things than being chained, seer. Part of me still longs for Ragnarök if it means I can forget all that I have done, all that has been done to me."

She shakes her head in clear denial. "You don't mean that."

He didn't, not anymore. Not if total eradication meant his mate would die. For her, he will endure, even with the cruelty and suffering that plagues him. "There's a reason the dead of the Wild Hunt are so formidable. Nic can't turn a corner without coming across another evil soul. They are sprouting up everywhere like weeds among both human and fey populations. The worlds are only getting worse."

She rises up and moves to the door. "Hungry?"

He frowns. Why the abrupt change? Or is she just sick of hearing him moan and groan over things that neither of them can change?

He can't blame her. Sometimes he is sick of himself.

At the notion of food, the wolf surges up. "Is there actual food here?"

Harmony nods. "It's been Freya's practice to keep it around ever since I came to live here."

He follows her down the path once more. Instead of turning back toward his room, she takes another turn and heads in the opposite direction.

They entered a humongous gourmet kitchen. Aiden gapes at the marble countertops, the island that is really more of a continent, the two side by side refrigerators. Though Freya could adorn her home by any magical means, she had never bothered following human custom before. Just what did Harmony mean to her that the goddess would put herself out this way?

"You said Freya rescued you?" He follows her into the gleaming white space. "That doesn't sound like her. She only does things to suit herself, in case you haven't noticed."

"Says the selfish wolf who'll see the worlds burn so he can get to his mate. Who is perfectly fine where she is. Omelet?" She holds up a container of eggs.

Aiden sighs. "You're not going to try and mick me with that wolf-be-gone potion, are you?"

She holds his gaze. "I'll tell you flat-out with no word-twisting so you know I can't lie. No, I will not try to slip you any drugs or altering substances."

He's tempted to bring up that she'd dumped herbs in his bath so he wouldn't detect the scent of Bifrost, but restrains himself. "Then an omelet sounds excellent." Harmony isn't a natural cook. More eggs land on the counter or the floor than in the bowl but finally she has enough to make an omelet.

Aiden releases a sigh. "As for Nic, I never claimed to be farseeing, or to care about those who don't bother with me or mine. I'm selfish and single-minded. It's not a crime."

Harmony extracts mushrooms, onions, peppers, butter, bacon, cheese and bread and lays them all out on the counter.

"Did you ever stop and think that maybe the world you are so eager to let burn would be a better place if all those people could see beyond the ends of their noses?"

He had, actually, but even with the powers of a god, Aiden possesses no ability to interfere with mortal or even fey choice. Serving in an advisory role for Nic is as close as he's ever come to political power. Harmony, maneuvering in Wardon's court has far more experience.

"Why do you dislike her so?"

She plops a pat of butter in a pan and then lays cold bacon over it. "Whatever you think, I have never hated Nic. Not in her last life and not in this one. But she's no longer a queen, Aiden. She didn't sit on the Shadow Throne."

No, she didn't. And the throne which had sat vacant for so long had accepted another. "There must be a way."

Harmony whacks away at the vegetables, like they are fighting back. "Have you ever asked her if she wants to rule, Aiden?"

He opens his mouth, then shuts it again.

Harmony whips the eggs with preternatural speed and mixture slops over the side of the bowl. "Fenrir sits on the Shadow Throne because your mate didn't claim it. She never made it a priority. Why do you think that is?"

"It's her destiny." But even as he says the words, he recalls all the times Nic's eyes had glazed over at talk of ruling. "She protects the people, the court. She rides with the Hunt."

"She did all that in her last life." The bacon pops, releasing a delectable fragrance in spite of its mistreatment. "And she wasn't a great queen or even a good one."

"And you think Fenrir will rule well?"

Harmony shakes her head. "I want you to stop and think, Aiden. About something other than yourself. Nicneven was born of Underhill. She has fey in her blood. But the monarchs are tainted. The entire court system is biased.

You've seen firsthand how those without magic struggle. Do you really think a former mortal with all the life experience of a sixteen-year-old can make things better?"

The truth in her statement unsettles him. He remains quiet until she slides a massive omelet in front of him.

"She's been doing her best. The best that she knows how. The Fates didn't tell her who she was because they wanted her to have as normal a life as possible for as long as she could."

She whips more eggs and adds them to the pan, before shooting him a pitying look. "Aiden, she started killing when she was six-years-old. Do you really think Nic ever had anything resembling a normal life?"

PLANS

More days drag by as I stare at the four walls of my cell. I do what prisoners have done since the beginning of incarceration. I work out. Though the medics who tend me warn not to overdo it—I had been shot recently and am *expecting*—I do sit ups, planks, squats and lunges, mountain climbers and burpees. Freda will kick my flabby ass if I let jail soften me.

At night—or what passes for night as the Feds control even the lighting—I talk to Astrid. She has a funny quirky sense of humor. I tell her about my friends, about Freda and Nahini and Jasmine or Lady Jazz as Aiden calls her. My hair has grown out again, the white blond now down past my chin, with the dyed black bits hanging past my shoulders. If I had something to cut it, I would.

"He sounds perfect," Astrid interjects as I finish a story about the house Aiden had planned to build in the North Carolina Mountains.

"No one is perfect." It has taken me a long time to come to terms with that.

"So were the two of you just going to live there, in the woods, all alone?"

I open my mouth to respond, then close it again without speaking. "I guess it was supposed to be more of a retreat. You know a vacation spot?"

"So where were you going to live?" she asks.

The Unseelie underground palace. Where the queen of the Shadow Throne always resides from Samhain to Beltane. "Wherever we had work."

Would I have to kill Gretchen to get Fenrir off the throne? The thought sickens me. Even with the wolf at the helm, I still had liked Gretchen. She was an innocent, much like Astrid. And like Astrid, she is paying the price for getting roped into our supernatural world.

"Tell me about you, Astrid."

She is cautious, maybe even more paranoid than I am. While I think she believes me when I say I want to help her, she doesn't seem to believe that I can. Or maybe that I will.

"What do you want to know?" she asks.

"You said you ran away. Were your parents...bad?" *Did you kill them?*

"Foster parents. I've never had the real kind."

"An orphan then?" My heart lurches as I think of the blonde woman on the beach.

"Something like that. Being placed in a house doesn't make it a home, you know." Her tone is hard and unyielding.

"Wasn't there anyone there you liked?"

She gnaws on her thumbnail. "There was one boy, Declan. He was only there for a few months though. His mom got out of rehab and he went back to live with her."

"What did Declan look like?" I ask.

"I thought he was a giant."

I blink and then, realize she isn't talking about the kinds of giants I knew. She just means large for a mortal.

"He told me how it happened. A neighbor had called to report shouts from their apartment. I guess one of his mother's boyfriends had knocked her around. Declan came home from school and beat the hell out of the guy."

"How old was he?"

Astrid shifts, I can hear the creak of her bedsprings. "Probably around fifteen. He was big for his age though. The cops came and took him into custody. They were going to send him to Juvie for assault, but his lawyer got him off. He had only been protecting his mother. She had to get clean though before he could go home. It took her about six months, then she came and got him."

"And he was your friend?" It seemed odd to me that a large boy with serious anger issues would look after a delicate flower like Astrid.

"He was the best friend I ever had. He would take me down to the river, teach me how to fish. Sometimes we would just sit together." Her expression is soft.

Astrid, who loves to hear about love had already given her young heart away.

"And so he went home with his mom and they lived happily ever after?"

Her gaze darted away. "I never heard from him again. That was a few weeks before Agent Hanson picked me up."

Which didn't mean her gift hadn't told her exactly what had happened to her friend. I don't pry though. If Astrid wanted to tell me, she would. I glean some insights from her tale. Declan had been important to her. The oversized boy who would fight off a full-grown man to protect his mother, the drug addict. And that the longest connection Astrid has ever had with anyone is a few measly weeks.

"Astrid, tell me what it is you can do. Why are you here?"

"I'm a freak." She whispers the words that jab a cold shard right into my heart.

"I can kill with a kiss." It's a leap, trusting this stranger. Gods know I have never benefited from demonstrating trust before. *You have to give a little to get a little.* It's what Addy always said about the injured animals that were brought to her veterinary clinic. *They won't bite or scratch me if I don't hurt them first.*

Addy had plenty of practice gentling wild beasts.

"You can?" Astrid's eyes go wide. "You've actually killed people?"

"I call it the goodnight kiss." Briefly, I tell her about being found in the Black Forest, how I'd accidently killed that hiker. I leave the Norns and the fey out of my tale. If she's anything like I'd been, her brain won't process all that exists beyond the Veil without seeing it.

Hell, I'm still trying to understand it.

She lets out a breath. "So that's why you're here. You killed a bunch of people who attacked you?"

"And a few who hurt young children. I guess I'm a vigilante. Like your Declan." At least I thought I was before seeing the ripple of destruction my actions had caused.

Astrid is back to working on her nail.

"Do you believe me?"

Blue gray eyes take me in. "I do. I'm not sure why, but you don't sound like a liar."

"So, tell me what it is you can do." She's given hints, that she knows my baby is a girl, that she can see things, but I need more detail if I am to figure out how much I should tell her about the Norns.

"Someone's coming." Astrid scrambles to her feet.

Footsteps stop outside our door and then it is pushed inward. I turn to face the hazmat suited guards.

One steps forward, a bag in hand. He isn't moving toward me though, but reaches for Astrid.

"What is this?" I snap, pushing up off the floor until I am standing between the two of them.

"Back off, now." The guard blocking the doorway levels that weird gizmo that is sort of like a Taser at me. "Hands up, or we'll gas both of you."

I swallow and then raise my hands. Goon two steps forward again, reaching for Astrid. Her gaze darts to me as if she's looking for reassurance. "Nic," her voice cracks.

"It's okay," I tell her, praying that I'm not lying. "It'll be fine."

Then my hands are bound behind my back, the hated hood coming down over my face. I am frog-marched out into the hall beside Astrid. I want to say something to her, but don't know what.

"Where are you taking us?" My words come out muffled. Are we on the verge of the rescue Angrboda promised me?

"Walk." The terse reply is accompanied by a sharp jab in the lower back.

Prick.

Side by side with my new friend, we are led around twists and turns until we reach an elevator. More guards join us, eight in total. All armed to the teeth. I can't tell if any of them are Hanson, but she's never bothered with the hazmat gear.

The elevator is too small to fit our entire entourage, so Astrid and her four guards go first. When the empty car returns, I step inside without a fight.

The concrete slab where we disembark leads to a ware-house of sorts. Cracked and fogged glass let in a little natural light, but it's so much better than the recycled air I've been ingesting. Hanson's lair is underground. Ahead of me I see Astrid, still unbound, still surrounded by a wall of guards.

Not FBI, I realize with a start. Maybe it's the fresh air working on my brain for the first time in a while but I realize that while Hanson may be FBI, the rest of her team is made up of hired thugs.

We push outside into a hardscrabble dirt parking area. I wince at the brightness of real sunlight reflecting off snow. I inhale all the way down to my toes, picking up the crisp scent of winter. It's almost too bright after the artificial darkness of the past few days.

One of the thugs jabs me again in my lower back. That's going to bruise.

We walk as a unit toward a large blue panel van, like the one they had transported me in. From my angle I can't see the plates, no idea what state we're in. Still no FBI logo. Whatever this is, it's not an obvious operation.

The tall trees are a mix of evergreen and deciduous. I want to scan the area for any sign of Chloe and Angrboda. They knew this would happen, that I'd be moved. Where are they?

Astrid is shoved roughly into the van, where she is secured. I'm up next, but have trouble balancing with my hands bound behind me. I fall and go down to one knee. One of the guards jerks me up roughly by the hair. Tears spring into my eyes, but I don't let them fall. Not yet. I need help, can't take out eight of them on my own.

The guard hauls me to the seat next to Astrid and shackles me in place.

I suck in as much fresh air as I can through my hood before the guards shut the door. Three left, one in back with us and his wicked looking weapon that may or may not be a Taser. Two up front on the other side of the mesh webbing. A driver and another, both heavily armed.

Soon. I'll be free soon. And I will free Astrid as well. Because regardless of what else she is, she's become my friend.

And I don't leave friends behind.

The van travels down a dirt road. Having grown up in a rural area, I know the jounce from trucking over potholes at a good clip. The ride to the facility is foggy, filled with pain and shock. No landmarks, just trees, snow and more trees. I tap my toe against the floor. I see the guard frown down at my bare feet.

"What?" I mumble through my mask.

He looks away, as though unsettled.

Yeah, well your bosses took my shoes and gave me nothing else. So here I am, barefoot and pregnant. I shift on the seat, trying to ease my discomfort.

"Settle down," he snaps as though the reality of my situation makes him uncomfortable.

Freedom is at hand—I can feel it in my bones. Eagerness courses through me. I am ready to move on to the next phase, to find Aiden and my friends. I haven't figured out what I will do with Astrid but one thing at a time. She will be safe we all will be….

The thunderous boom accompanies an explosion of earth. Flying dirt pelts the side of the van. Another massive reverberation knocks us all to the right. Then the van is rolling, rolling, down an incline of some sort.

My head hits the side and blackness consumes me.

"Nic," Aiden shoots up in bed, sweat soaking the twisted sheets. His heartrate thunders and her winter apple scent is stuck in his nose as though her head had been on the pillow beside him.

So real. It had been a dream. He knows it had. Her bound and gagged in the back of a mortal vehicle. But it had felt real. Felt as though she were hurt, bleeding.

Their bond, their connection, couldn't cross the Veil. He knew this and yet...

"Help," he calls out, not sure who he's summoning. No one living in Asgard would help him, not the cursed son of the trickster, and yet he feels as though someone is nearby.

"I need to get to her. Please," he implores.

"Then do as Freya wishes," a sibilant voice hisses.

Aiden jerks his head to the side. "Who are you?"

The creature, for it is no god, smiles. "A serpent in the garden."

"Wrong pantheon." Aiden tosses the covers off and climbs out of bed. "How did you get in here?"

"The same way you did, I imagine. Your friends are looking for you, wondering what happened."

"You crossed from Underhill?"

His companion bobs its head in what Aiden assumes is a nod.

"A dwarf." He sits back and studies the being anew. Dwarves are typically considered separate from the fey. Their bodies twisted from the dark magic they practice to create their great weapons and impressive gifts. This being has some snakelike features but it also had hands, with fingers like thick sausages. It wears garments that are mostly rags.

"My name is Grendel," the creature shuffles to the right. "I am her magnanimous supreme delightfulness's appointed jeweler. And it would serve your interests if you would sire a child on the goddess of love and beauty."

"And create another monster?" Aiden shakes his head. "Think I'll pass."

"What's one more?" Grendel's long face contorts. "The world is full of monsters, Váli Sigynjarson."

He goes still at that. "You know my true name?"

"I know many things about you." Its thin-lipped smile causes all the wolf's hackles to rise.

"You won't help me escape? Even though you know of my mate's need?"

It tilts its serpentine head to the side. "I might be persuaded...for a price."

And this is what the fey and the dwarves have in common. Their penchant for bargains and love of getting one over on a being in need.

He'd be a fool to trust this dwarf.

But Harmony refuses to help. Freya's price is too high. What other option does he have?

"Can you get me across the Veil? Not to Underhill but to Midgard directly?"

"I can, but it will cost even more."

"Cost what?" Aiden asks. "And don't say my firstborn."

"What use would I have with a wolf pup?" The dwarf scoffs. It twists, showing its gnarled back beneath its baggy clothing. "No wolf. If you won't give the goddess what she wants, then allow me to do it."

Aiden's lips part. "Excuse me?"

"Give me three drops of your blood. One for transformation, one for the sight and one for the fire of your heart. I will go to her supreme excellence in your stead and impregnate her. It's the only way."

Aiden hesitates. "How long will this transformation last?"

Again with the thin-lipped smile. "Long enough for my purposes."

There's an idea. Allow the great goddess to bed down with a lowly dwarf. When the scandal of her heir's parentage is known, the gods would make her the laughingstock of Asgard. The shame would never diminish.

"Only if you promise me one thing." He hesitates. "Any

product of your union will not be harmed. Not by the dwarves or the goddess."

Animals learned to eat their young from the dwarves. And much like the American Indians, the small subset of mythical beings frugally uses every bit of their prey. Bones, skin, hair… Aiden doubts he'd be able to live with himself if he imposed that sort of hell on an innocent being.

"I cannot attest to what the goddess will do when she learns she's been deceived, but I vow to all the golden riches in Midgard that no dwarf will ever harm my son."

"Agreed." Aiden holds out his hand.

The creature immediately sinks one of its dirty nails into Aiden's palm. He hisses but the pain is rapidly replaced by a burning sensation. The forked tongue slips from the creature's mouth. Aiden balls his hand into a fist and squeezes. One two and on the third drop, the dwarf begins to shimmer.

Just then the door swings in. "Aiden? I saw the light."

Fast as he can manage, Aiden sprints to cover Harmony's mouth. To stifle her scream. She thrashes in his grip but he doesn't relent.

When he looks over, the dwarf has turned into an exact replica of him. It isn't the first time Aiden has beheld his double, but the experience is as uncanny as ever.

The dwarf waves his hand and the air shimmers. Once more the tang of magic burns his nose.

"Will you leave her here?" The dwarf tips his head to study Harmony.

Aiden doesn't like the way the creature eyes the seer. It's one thing to trick Freya, who demands the impossible. But he can't leave Harmony unconscious at the creature's mercy.

"She comes with me."

Grendel dips his head. "Looking out for family at last."

"Family?" Aiden starts.

The creature blinks at him. "Why your sister, of course."

Aiden shakes his head. "I don't have a sister."

The dwarf tilts his head. "Are you sure of that, Váli Sigyn-jarson? You're sure your mother was not expecting another child at the time of the trickster's capture?"

Aiden's chest seizes up. "A baby?" His mother had been pregnant? "That can't be. She's fey."

"Her most exalted beauty hid the girl under the hill to keep her safe from the gods who were still wrathful against the line of Loki. She looks like one of them, but is a goddess of Asgard."

All the breath rushes from Aiden's lungs. He looks down to the seer's purple face. Can it be true?

"Váli?" The clip clopping of heels approaches.

"We must go," Grendel beckons him forward. "Before she discovers the duplicity."

Aiden tosses Harmony over one shoulder in a fireman's carry. His gaze goes to the mantle where the ruby dragon egg sits. Without thought he snatches it and puts it in his pocket. There is a popping sound and then the dwarf snags his hand. The three vanish into the night.

ESCAPE

Astrid screams as she stares through the front window. A sense of weightlessness comes over us as the van is lifted up into the air.

And a giant eye peers into the front windshield at us. An eye the size of a beachball.

"It's okay," I say to Astrid. "Really. She's a friend."

Well, sort of.

Shots ring out as the armed passenger guard aims to take the giantess, out. The rifle shakes in his hands. He is pants-pissing terrified, and I don't blame him. I've seen a giant at full size before but the sight is still unnerving. She can crush us like bugs. Might do so by accident if she isn't careful.

Angrboda roars and then cracks the van open like an egg, I reach for Astrid as we are falling, falling.

Then land safely in the giantess's palm. She lowers us carefully down to the ground.

"What is that?" Astrid breathes, eyes wide.

"We're like you," I say, hands out. "Astrid, it's okay. None of us are going to hurt you."

"Nic?"

I know that voice. "Chloe?"

Then she is there, a hunting knife in hand. "Are you all right?"

I want to cry. My aunt has come back for me.

"We need to get out of here." She scowls at the shackles. "Angrboda, can you...?"

The giantess appears, her mouth covered in blood. Had she been *eating* the guards? "No, I'm tapped out. Get her loose and Jedda can undo the rest."

"Jedda?" I ask.

"Her ward. We'll explain everything. Later." Chloe lifts the chains. "Come on now, this whole thing is going to go up like a Roman candle."

My steps are small, my gait bound by the chains, but I manage to let her guide me from the back of the turned over van and out into the snow. "What did you do?"

"Trust me when I say you don't want to know. Just keep it in mind that you should never ever piss off a giant."

"Noted," I breathe. There is blood in my hair, though I don't think it's mine. "Astrid?"

Chloe turns and sucks in a sharp breath as she sees Astrid. But before she can say anything a shot rings out. A dot of red appears on Astrid's forehead. The girl crumples to the ground.

"No!" I am on my feet and running. I barely realize that he is pointing his gun at me, don't acknowledge Chloe's scream.

Click. The chamber is empty.

I grab his lapels and press my lips to his, giving him my poison. My goodnight kiss. I don't care about his family, the people who will miss him. He shot an innocent twelve-year-old in the forehead. I can not allow him to draw breath any longer.

He slumps and I drop him like the useless sack of meat he

is. I start for Astrid, ignoring my chains, the stiffness and sore muscles.

She's gone. I recognize death's claim anywhere, the fog over the gray blue eyes.

"Nic, I'm sorry," my aunt says.

"We need to get out of here." Angrboda is shrinking down to human size.

"I can't just leave her here, like this."

"You stay and you're putting us all at risk." The giantess snaps.

Chloe studies my face. "There's nothing more you can do for her."

"I can bury her." I look up and hold her gaze. "Please, I can't leave her out alone like this."

Angrboda holds out a hand. The ground beneath our feet shudders, and then parts. When it stops, there is a deep cavern, deep enough for a girl's body.

"She was obsessed with being in love," I say as Angrboda places her limp form down inside the hole. "There was a boy, Declan. She'd already given him her heart."

"Then he was lucky." Chloe puts an arm around me.

Angrboda climbs out and holds out her hand again. The earth swallows up my small friend.

"Get her to the car," I hear the giantess say. "We don't know how much of a head start we'll have."

I move to the car, let Chloe settle me in the backseat. My feet are numb. My heart is numb.

I'm sorry, Astrid.

"You know, I used to remember humans tasting better than this." The giantess burps delicately.

"It's the diet." Chloe says. "Too much processed shit makes the meat rancid."

"Oh, look who's talking, Miss, I've never met a candy bar I didn't like."

"Not true. They have the ones that don't have chocolate in them. What the fuck is the point of that?"

I laugh, and it is a half hysterical sound. Here I am, in the middle of the woods with my aunt the fate and chocoholic and a giantess who has just gorged herself on an entire special unit. A young girl is dead. And these two sound like the odd couple.

I am free.

But at what cost?

"We need to get out of here. That agent, Hanson, will be rabid in her hunt to reclaim you." This from the giantess.

Chloe looks up at her and winces. "Um, Angie you've got a little special agent on your face."

Angrboda grins, showing off bloody teeth and I feel like retching.

"Don't look, sweets." Chloe hands me a coat. "Giants are known as maneaters for a reason."

"Yeah." I study the back of Angrboda's bloodred hair as she settles herself behind the wheel. "Where are we going? Back to the farm?"

Chloe shakes her head. "It isn't safe. That's the first place they'll look for you."

"Across the Veil?"

"Foolish child," the giantess snaps. "Without a plan? That is Underhill's realm and she will know the second you or I cross back over there."

The sound of gunshots rings out and Chloe throws herself over me while the giantess screeches, "Get down!"

"They can't have found us this fast," I say as the sedan fishtails as Angrboda takes it off road to avoid the hostiles. "There's no way."

"Unless they were tipped off," Chloe's tone is grim, her scent shifting to licorice.

"Tipped off? Gretchen, er…that is Fenrir didn't know about our escape plan, did he?"

"Not now," the giantess agrees. "Chloe, can you take over here? I might be able to work a little magic now."

Chloe scrambles over the seat, but not before pressing a revolver into my clenched hands. "I promise I won't let them take you, not again."

I swallow. A handgun. I've never fired one, never needed to. But with no magic and the people trying to kill me too far away for my goodnight kiss, it's the only option left.

Angrboda shifts so that Chloe can take over driving duties, even as the car careens down an embankment. Luckily the slope is treeless, though we jounce over the uneven terrain.

Ping. Something hits the metal by the left rear door. "They're gaining on us," I call when I dare to look back.

"Keep your head down," Angrboda barks.

My eyes go wide when I see what looks like a ball of blue and purple cobwebs in her hands. That is if cobwebs pulsed with magic.

Giants wield magic better than any other species, including the gods. They are born from magic and can channel it more deeply, unless a god has a tool, like Thor's great hammer or Aiden's flaming sword. The raw talent is why the giants are so feared by the gods. From what Aiden had said, Angrboda's more powerful than most. It was why Loki had sired children on her, so that his monstrous spawn would be the sort to make the Asgardians tremble.

The hand not holding the revolver slips over my abdomen, where my baby is growing. It's too soon to feel movement, yet for the first time I sense something different. An otherness, wholly apart from myself. Part me, part Aiden, all magic. Am I also destined to be the mother of a monster?

"Hang on," Angrboda says and then tosses her magic out

the passenger's side window. Snow erupts like a giant volcano, freezing immediately into a glacier. The wall grows out, curving around the car.

"Ha," Chloe says as she fights yet another skid. "That ought to hold them."

"I can't have them following us back to Jedda." Angrboda says. She turns to look at me. "He is Wardon's heir. Váli freed him before Underhill destroyed the ocean city."

My breath hitches. "She killed them all?"

Chloe's tone is grim. "More meat for her army."

My mother commanded the dead. Every soldier that had ever been cut down beyond the Veil was another in her swelling ranks.

"And Aiden?" I ask.

The giantess shakes her head. "No word."

"Where is he?"

Chloe catches my eye in the rearview mirror. "I don't know, Nic. I really don't."

THE DWARF DROPS Aiden and Harmony off with a thump in the middle of a busy highway. Headlights blind him and horns blare out in protest of their sudden appearance. Aiden leaps, still hanging on to the unconscious seer and vaults up over the hood of a car. Brakes squeal but there is a copse of trees not too far off. He shifts into sparks, praying none of the motorists have their cell phones out to capture his transition and post it online.

Curse social media and smartphones for their very existence.

He lands at the base of a tree and puts Harmony down beneath the shelter of some pine boughs. She looks pale, her vivid purple hue faded to lavender. He regrets having hurt her.

Had the dwarf been telling the truth? Could the seer really be his full-blood sister? He scrutinizes her every feature looking for something familiar. They both have dark hair, but that hardly proves anything. Maybe right around the eyes is the same. But her nose is more delicate than his own, her lips fuller.

Like his mother's had been.

Like Nari's had been.

Blood pounds in his ears. He knows it's true. Deep in his bones he can feel the connection.

"Why did you never say anything?" he asks her.

She doesn't respond. Still out for the count.

Aiden scents the air, searching for any hint of Nic's scent. He can track her across the globe if necessary. The people cursing at him from the vehicles had been doing so in German.

There. He catches the faintest hint of her unique perfume on the wind. Hers is tangled up with several humans. Only it's...different somehow. More complicated than he remembers. Sex could alter a female's scent for a short time.

Had she been with another? Gods, what if she had been raped...?

He'd kill them all. Slowly.

A growl rips from his wolf. The beast is finally shaking off the effects of Asgard.

"Calm yourself, wolf," Harmony's voice grounds him back in the here and now. "She hasn't been violated."

"How do you know what I'm thinking?" He stands and uses his height advantage to tower over her.

"Because you're sniffing the air and clenching your fists as though you're about to do murder."

He makes a conscience effort to relax. "You know for certain no one has used her?"

She nods and then puts a hand to her head and glares at him. "I can't believe you kidnapped me."

"It only seems fair since you helped the goddess abduct me first," he shoots back. "What I can't believe is you didn't tell me that you're my sister."

Her chin juts up and she doesn't look away from him. "You couldn't handle it."

"And what makes you so certain I can now? You do know what my wolf did to my last full-blooded sibling?"

She struggles to her feet. "So now you know. If you think you're such a danger to me, then why drag me along?"

"I couldn't leave you there to tell Freya about the dwarf."

She shakes her head. "Aiden, you never think of anything beyond your mate but do you even know her?"

"What do you mean?"

"She's more than capable of taking care of herself." Harmony rubs her temples. "She has friends and family and she knows this side of the Veil better than any of us."

Her words are laced with bitterness. "Are you jealous of Nic?"

"No."

He taps his nose. "I can smell the falsehood. You must believe it otherwise you wouldn't have been able to say it. But your resentment is clear." He drags a hand through his hair.

"I don't like how she's treated you in the past. Believe it or not though, I actually do like her. Though I know she doesn't like me at all, through no fault of my own. You'd better release me before you jaunt off to her side. You might not kill me, but Nic is another matter."

"So you can run back to Freya and tell her I tricked her? We don't already have enough to deal with, what with defeating Underhill and halting Ragnarök." Sister or no, she'd helped Freya abduct him.

"You can't stop the end." The seer glares at him as though he's being intentionally oblivious. "The fact that we are standing here, together, should tell you that much. Freya wanted to keep you safe. Now that you are no longer in Asgard, Underhill will be after you."

"Underhill has no power in the mortal realm."

She casts him a pitying look. "If you believe that then you really are mad, just like the gods told me you were."

Harmony moves to stride away but before she can, he grips her arm. Her gaze goes from it to him and back.

"Stay with me," he all but begs. If she really wishes to leave, he'll have no choice but to let her go.

Her dark gaze is guarded. "Why should I?"

"So we can get to know one another." After releasing his hold, he lowers himself onto a fallen tree. "Tell me about how you came to be disguised as a fey?"

She glances away. "It was Freya who rescued me from the cave. She helped deliver me. If she hadn't shown up, I probably would have died."

Aiden closes his eyes and imagines the cave where his life had been forever altered. His father chained to the slab, the serpent with the dripping venom and his mother holding a bowl. Never able to sleep or eat…and pregnant. "Why would mother stay there?"

A muscle jumps in her jaw. "She refused to leave him, not even long enough to give birth. The ground shook constantly while she was in labor, until Freya arrived and ordered one of her minions to hold the bowl until I was born. She couldn't hold the bowl and me at the same time so she told Freya to take me with her."

Aiden reaches out a hand and covers hers with his own. Squeezes once. He knows what it's like to have his mother turn her back on him. To deem him unimportant. But he had killed his little brother, was possessed by the wild spirit of the wolf.

Harmony had been an innocent newborn babe.

Her purple hand turns over until she is clasping at his with a desperate strength.

"So Freya took you in?"

She nods once. "At first, but there was always the worry that the other gods would find out who I was and where I'd come from."

No wonder she was so loyal to the goddess. The curse of their line, to forever demonstrate loyalty to those who didn't deserve it. Sigyn to Loki, Aiden to Nicneven, Harmony to Freya.

"How did you come to be in Wardon's court?"

She sinks down onto the log beside him. "Freya hid me in the Seelie Court. She changed my appearance so I would look like the fey family who'd taken me in. Until my drowning accident, when I started to see the future. It wasn't just from the accident. My goddess powers had started to manifest, making my ability to see clearer. Word of my gift spread. Then Wardon brought me into his household." She looks away.

Wardon, the former Master of the Waves. He'd been power hungry and arrogant, but also a visionary. "Did he hurt you?"

She doesn't meet his gaze. "I don't want to talk about that."

He closes his eyes. All this time, he's had a sister out in the world, unprotected and vulnerable.

Pack, his wolf whispers.

"You knew who I was? What I was to you? Why did you never come and find me?"

Her dark gaze holds his. "All I knew of you were the

stories. The mad wolf who'd shredded his little brother. Freya told me it was safer to keep my true identity from you."

He swallows. "Do you still fear me?"

She studies him intently. "I've never feared you, Aiden. But I can't say I trust you, either."

He stands and offers her a hand up. This time, she takes it. "I'll gain your trust. And you can regain mine. If you stay with me."

She searches his face, her expression yearning. "I can't see your future anymore."

He tilts his head. "Why?"

"Sometimes, when someone's destiny is too close to my own, I can't see them anymore. I'm sorry, I'm not going to be much help."

"You're going to be my family." He squeezes her shoulder. "You and Nic. That's more than I've had in a lifetime. For the first time in forever, I am looking forward to the future. I don't need to know what it holds."

She smiles then, and it's a real smile, genuine. "Come on then. Let's go find your spoiled, selfish mate."

ROAD TRIP

"**A**re you ready to tell me where we're going?" I kvetch from the backseat. We've been on the road for hours. I'm hungry, cold, tired. Heartbreak over Astrid burns like acid in my gut.

Plus, I'm awfully sick of looking at the back of their heads.

"Somewhere safe," Chloe says.

"The farm was safe," I grumble.

"Right up until the FBI found out about it," Angrboda quips.

I let out a breath. "And couldn't you just ensorcelle all the humans into letting me go instead of chowing down on them?"

"Agent Hanson is too strong willed. That's why I had to wait until she was gone to approach you and plant the orders in the guards. I've never encountered such a focused human. Any spell I tried to put her under would shatter. Better she finds their remains and fear us." She meets my gaze in the rearview mirror. "Besides, I was hungry."

I shudder in revulsion.

The view out the window changes steadily. Instead of frost-covered trees and fields or icy patches of water, scrubby bushes and sea grass abound as we make our way to the coast.

Angrboda swings through a drive-thru. The speaker thingy has an out of order sign on it so she drives up to the window. The bored looking girl with bad acne at the register slides the glass back and pokes her shaggy brown head out. "What'll it be?"

"Fries and a chocolate shake for me," Chloe wrinkles her nose. "Nic?"

Something coming from inside that place smells heavenly. "What is that amazing smell?"

"Um....bacon?" The girl guesses. "It just finished frying up."

"Nic, no." Chloe turns in her seat, her horror mimicking my own.

"Oh, gods." I breathe even as my mouth waters. Damn it, my baby is a freaking half wolf carnivore.

"Ma'am?" The girl is staring at me through the car window, eyeballing my weird terrycloth dress and blanket ensemble. "You okay?"

"She's on the way to rehab," the giantess says and then makes the decision for me. "Two double bacon cheeseburgers, three fries, and three chocolate shakes."

She forks over a wad of cash, ignoring my cry of protest.

"I can't," I spit when the girl slides the window shut.

"You might not have a choice," the giantess says. "Cravings mean the baby needs something. I tucked entire Nordic villages away when I was knocked up with Fenrir."

The food is passed through the window in a brown sack and a cupholder for the shakes. Chloe passes the bag back to me like grease-stained contraband.

"I've never eaten meat." It's almost a whimper.

"And I never eat sailors named Sven, but somehow I managed while expecting Jormangonder. It's not for you, it's for your child who is destined to save the world. What badass baby wants, badass baby gets." Angrboda holds out a hand. "Quit being such a flipping princess and pass me a burger."

I reach into the bag and remove a paper wrapped sandwich and pass it up to her.

Chloe stares at me as I ignore the burger and start in on the fries. Though they are salty and greasy, the meat smell is stronger and is distracting the hell out of me. I pull the burger out and unwrap it. Hold it up to my mouth.

Chloe's scent has changed to burnt toast, a sure sign of the Norn's displeasure.

"Stop staring," I snap at her. "You're making me even more uncomfortable."

"Sorry." She turns around in her seat, not sounding the least bit contrite.

Again, I bring the thing up into biting position. I think about the fragile little *lub dub* of my baby's heartbeat. She needs this, like medicine.

I sink my teeth in and rip off a monstrous bite.

"Good?" The giantess asks me.

I can't answer. I'm too busy tearing into the thing with all my might. *Best. Medicine. Ever.*

"Oh, Nic," Chloe grimaces.

"Don't judge me!" I shriek around a mouthful.

Angrboda's shoulders shake with silent mirth.

I lick the last drips of grease off my fingers and let out an indelicate burp. No shame. It's Aiden's baby who will be at least part werewolf. I'm almost sorry I didn't try the FBI's meatloaf.

The lighthearted bubble bursts. Almost.

The landscape continues to grow wilder with signs of

civilization fewer and farther in between. There are warning signs about large distances between gas stops. Angrboda, the evil witch, stops at one and when she goes in to pay she brings back a sack full of beef jerky.

"I hate your face." I say around a mouthful of the stuff.

"Wait until you get a steak. You'll want to have my babies."

We drive on, crossing through salt marshes and then the inland waterway.

"What's in the Outer Banks?" I ask when I see a sign.

Instead of answering, Chloe turns to look at Angrboda. "Are we through?"

"Through what?" I ask. We're crossing another massive bridge. "Is there a tunnel or something?"

"Just another minute," the giantess clenches her hands on the steering wheel.

A ripple of *something* washes over the car. It feels like transitioning from our world to go beyond the Veil when crossing into Underhill. "Did we just pass beyond the Veil?"

"Not exactly." Chloe turns around in her seat. "It's a pocket realm. Not a full world like Underhill. It's tucked within a fold of the Veil and can't be breached except with the help of a giant."

"In the Outer Banks?" I raise a brow. "Pretty sure people know about this place."

"Think of it like a parallel dimension," Chloe says. "The laws of physics apply here just as they do in our world. But even if Agent Hanson picks up our trail, she won't be able to cross. It's a mirror to our own world. Same landmasses, same rules of nature, no annoying mortals."

"Pocket realm." I nod slowly. "So what, we're just going to camp out on the beach until the heat dies down? Little cold for that, Chloe."

She turns back around. "We have somewhere to go. Someone we're staying with."

My lips part to ask another question, but then I think better of it. She'll tell me when she wants me to know.

Full of meat and exhausted, I lean back against the headrest. "Wake me when we get...wherever it is we're going."

Though I shut my eyes I can't sleep. Images of Astrid's lifeless face haunt me. Had Hanson found her body? I hope not. Astrid deserved a little peace. I wondered if she realized that I'd killed the man who'd shot her. If she'd take him back to her lab and cut him open to study how my poison worked.

I slip into a light doze and see...her. My mother.

UNDERHILL STRIDES through the underground palace, her smart heels clicking on the polished moonstone floor. She surveys the empty halls with a small smile.

It was as it had been, before the gods and the fey. Back when this land of magic had been pure and lush, ripe with possibilities.

Before the Fates, those retched hags, had interfered.

"My lady." Rodrick, the ingratiating worm, strides to intercept her. He looks nervous, unsure of how he should address she who rules them all. She isn't a queen, the way he is accustomed.

No, she is something more.

"Walk with me," she commands the idiot. "Don't waste any more of my time standing around. There's work to be done."

"It's about the dead, my lady." He begins after taking up a pace to match hers.

"What of them?" The Draugar are her army, the bodies of the fey, the ultimate weapon against the living vermin she is working tirelessly to extinguish.

"They seem.... restless."

"They are fine." The easiest army in the world to maintain. They can't die of starvation or exposure and the more they decompose, the more frightening her army is for the living.

Fear is a powerful motivator.

"Tell me about the city." She commands the fey lord.

He clears his throat in that annoyingly self-important way he has. "Queen Gretchen says there is no shield of air. We're closing in."

The city in question was the last stronghold of the fey, protected by the newly crowned Lord of the Land and the living members of The Wild Hunt.

Rodrick shifts, clearly uncomfortable.

Underhill shoots him a sidelong look. "That city must fall. No fey will escape this land."

"Understood, my lady." *He hesitates.*

She makes an impatient sound. "Is there something else?"

"I was just wondering...what are your plans for the prisoners?"

The beings who had worked to overthrow her new regime. "The prisoners are my concern. Felling the fey city is yours."

"Yes, my lady." *He flinches as he sees the Fire Throne ignite at the snap of her fingers.*

"Leave me." *Underhill paces the room, waiting for Rodrick to disappear. He isn't a stupid man and he has a vested interest in keeping her happy.*

She moves to stand beside the fire throne. Fire is one of the elements she can wield. In her possession is the heart of the last queen of the Fire Throne. She holds her hand out and touches the burning chair.

So close, she'd been so close to having them all.

"Lady?"

She turns and spies a ghost hovering just out of reach. A demonic looking thing that is part bird, part human. A Valkyrie, at least it had been when it was alive.

"What is it?"

The shade drifts closer. "I was wondering if you would be releasing us."

"By us, I assume you mean the souls of the Wild Hunt?"

The creature nods. "Queen Nicneven trapped me into service and I've done her bidding, but we wish to rest."

Underhill considers for a time. "Your rest will be earned."

"How, lady?"

"You can cross the Veil. I need someone to monitor my daughter. Tell me what she's doing, what she's planning. And most importantly, if she is in contact with any fey. Or that wolf. I need them all."

Unlike Rodrick, this creature doesn't ask pointless questions. "As you say, Lady."

I JOLT UPRIGHT. Nightweaver, that treacherous slag. She'd been spying on me the entire time.

If the Valkyrie wasn't already dead at my hand, I'd kill her.

If the dream was real. Could it be? Harmony Goldfeather, the seer, said I might not be able to see the future the way she could, that my talents might manifest in different ways.

Like spying on my mother. The shrew.

The car bumps along a dirt road and I realize it wasn't just the dream that woke me.

"Where are we?" I ask as we drive up to a rickety costal-style home. It has three decks facing the sound side of the sandbar. The giantess parks in the open space next to a rusted out pick up.

"The pocket realm," Angrboda dips her head to the side until her neck cracks.

"There are houses here?"

Chloe turns to face me. "Think of it like a mirror for the real world. Anything there is here."

"Except for the pesky mortals."

"Now you're getting it."

"What is this place?" I glance around.

The two exchange glances as Angrboda pops the driver's side door and chucks her thumb toward the house. "I'll just go check on Jedda."

"Whose Jedda?" I face my aunt. For some reason her scent has shifted to nervous lemon lime soda.

"Jedda is Wardon's progeny and the new Master of the Waves, thanks to Aiden."

My heart pounds. "Is Aiden here?"

"No, sweets." Chloe puts her hand on my arm.

"Oh." Disappointment fills me but I squish it down. I still haven't figured out how I am going to break the news to my wolf about being knocked up. Gods, what if he thinks it isn't his.

No, he wouldn't.

But then we didn't exactly...

Ugh, I can't think about this.

"Whose house is this? I don't suppose they have many rentals in the pocket realms."

Chloe turns to face me. "Nic, I'm not sure how to tell you this…."

I huff out a sigh. "Can it wait? I really need to pee."

She shakes her head, red gold curls slipping free from her bun. "No, you need to know it now. This place was constructed specifically to protect her."

"To protect who?" She must be a big deal if the giants and the Fates had banded together to shelter her. Hell, I was the Risen Queen and they hadn't even gone to such lengths for me.

Chloe takes a deep breath and the words come out in a rush. "Your biological mother."

SURPRISE

I stare at her for what feels like an eternity. All the meat I'd consumed forms a giant ball of icy ick in the center of my stomach. "My mother is dead. Aiden told me."

"Aiden doesn't know," Chloe says. "We faked her death using a changeling."

"*Who* faked her death?" Had Aiden been lying to me?

"Me, Addy, a giant who owed us a favor."

I huff out a breath. "When was this?"

"Years ago. After the first time the fey appeared to her." She holds my gaze. "The fey Underhill sent to capture her."

"I don't understand. Why would Underhill want her?"

"Blood ties are strong," Chloe says. "The stronger the tie, the stronger the magic one can do on their intended target. She probably wanted to summon you to her and Sophie was the closest genetic match."

I shake my head. My first mother had tried to have my second mother abducted. I am a pregnant, virgin serial killer.

Do they have shrinks for people with problems like mine?

"You said her name was Sophie," I say slowly. "Does she know who I am?"

Chloe nods. "I've kept in touch with her. Even sent her photos."

"But she doesn't know what I do." A vigilante, a reincarnated fey queen who hijacked her actual biological daughter.

I'd ruined her life.

And now I am going to meet her. Have to look her in the eye and answer her questions. Talk about awkward.

"What if she hates me?" I whisper.

"She doesn't." Chloe fidgets. "In fact, the opposite of hate."

I study her jerky movements. "What else aren't you telling me?"

She blows out a sigh. "Okay, well, she and your dad, your biological father that is. They're together. And they have another child."

My lips part. "Are you screwing with me?"

She shakes her head. "I just thought I'd get it all out there now. I would have told you sooner but it isn't safe outside the pocket realm."

My biological parents are together and they had another kid. A better kid, one who isn't a freaking serial killer.

I shake my head. "I thought my birth parents were German."

"I know. Addy and I let you think that because it was better that you didn't go looking for them."

I stare at my aunt. "They'll know who I am?"

She nods. "I've been sending them your school picture every year. Well, every year except for last year."

Last year which had passed while I'd been screwing around beyond the Veil. "And where did you tell them that I've been?"

"I said you ran away." She doesn't try to hide a wince.

"And now you bring me here to meet them and I'm a freaking teenage runaway who also happens to be pregnant?

Jeez, Chloe. Way to have me live the troubled teen stereotype."

Her scent shifts to bitter cranberry. "Look, I didn't have many options, what with the FBI monitoring all of our properties."

That much is true. My aunts have multiple investments around the globe but we had to get out of the states and away from the FBI's reach to use them.

She pushes on. "Normally, we would have crossed the Veil. However, that would negate Addy's... sacrifice."

Sadness coats her words. Addy broke the cardinal rule, the only rule for Norns. They can't interfere with fate. By crossing the Veil, pretending to be Aiden and securing my freedom, Addy essentially signed her own death warrant.

"It doesn't have to be death, does it?" I ask.

Chloe rests her head back against the window. "She knows what she's about, kid. There's no coming back from interfering with Fate."

"You don't mean that." Even though my nerves are completely shot, I know Chloe loves her big sister. "There's time, we can find a way to get her back. Her and Nahini and all the rest of them."

Her smile doesn't reach her eyes. She doesn't believe.

I swallow hard. "Okay, pregnant teen runaway, take one. Let's go meet the folks."

Garrett Yates is a burly man in his early forties with a thick head of curly brown hair graying at the temples and a well-trimmed brown goatee. I see nothing of myself in his mammoth form that blocks the entrance to their home more effectively than the door.

"Is it her?" a female voice calls from behind the beast. "Nic?"

"Yeah, it's...uh me." I say stupidly.

She moves out from behind the giant and I get my first

look at my mother. She looks like a Sophie, with her big blue eyes and bright smile. Looking at her is like looking in a funhouse reflection of myself. She's older than me by about eighteen years and her hair is pale blond, though she wears it cut short.

"Nic?" she asks again as though making sure.

"Hi." I wave.

"It's so good to finally see you in person." Tears overflow her eyes.

I don't speak. Chloe nudges me in the ribs.

"Ow. Oh, yeah. Thanks. Uh, that is you too. Thank you for having us." Miss Manners I am not.

A small boy, about six years old, comes running out of the back of the house, heading straight for Chloe. My brother.

"Oh, my goodness, you're getting bigger with every breath." The Norn swings him up into her arms. "How are you, Tate?"

He pops a finger into his mouth and gawks at me.

"Tate, this is Nic." Sophie puts an arm around my shoulders, shocking the shit out of me.

Tate looks like a mini Garret with large dark eyes and unruly brown curls.

She smiles. "He's shy."

"And he was born... here?" Chloe didn't specify how much Sophie and Garret know about the pocket realm.

Sophie nods. "He'll warm up. We hardly ever get visitors so this is new for him."

He knew Chloe well enough. She must have come here often.

I shiver as a cold burst of sea air blows up the back of my dress.

"Oh, you poor thing." Sophie has a soft Southern accent. It's like honey for the ears. "Where are my manners? Come on in out of the cold. I think we're going to get snow, if you

113

can believe that. Garret, quit blocking the doorway. Stand aside and let the poor girl in before she freezes to death."

She smacks him on the chest lightly and he grunts and takes a step back without uttering a word.

Chloe looks at the three of us and then sets the boy down. "Come on, tough guy. Snag your outerwear. How about you and I go out and build a sand monster."

Tate stares from his father to Chloe to me then back as though unsure.

"It's okay, pal." Garret crouches down and lays one beefy hand on the boy's shoulder. "They're staying for a little while."

At this Tate flashes a grin and reaches for his jacket.

Chloe winks and tightens her scarf. "You guys have a nice chat."

"Oh, okay." I feel oddly abandoned and somewhat shell-shocked. She's just leaving me here at the mercy of the strangers who gave me life.

Classic Chloe, out frolicking when times turn tough.

"Would you like something to eat or drink, maybe?" Sophie heads into her small, pokey kitchen that's done up in —what else—nautical décor. "We have coffee, tea and hot cocoa."

My biological mother wants to make me cocoa. My throat closes up a bit. "Don't go to any trouble."

"No trouble. Cocoa?" At my hesitant nod, she smiles. "Garret?"

"Coffee," Garret grunts.

"You take Nic into the living room. I'll be out in a jiff." Her step is light and easy as she moves about the tight space.

I study the man who contributed to my DNA. He doesn't look all that different from many of the high-country types I grew up around. Large, ill-dressed, but washed and relatively groomed. Again, I search for any of my own traits on his dark face and again, come up empty.

"So, Nic. What grade are you in?" The skin around his eyes is tight.

"I'm done with school." It was a truth I hadn't yet admitted to myself, never mind out loud.

"You got your diploma already?"

Slowly, I shake my head. "Nope, no diploma here."

He scratches his beard stubble. "GED then?"

"Nope." What the hell is taking Sophie so long with the beverages?

"Got any plans for the future?"

Hmm, let's see. Free Gretchen from Fenrir, kill my mother—not the kind woman making me cocoa in the kitchen—but the one who bore me during my first life. Find my baby daddy and break the news that his cursed and monstrous line would continue in the next year. Oh, and save the fey who remain beyond the Veil from the dead. Then if I somehow swing all that, I have to convince the nice lady out there building sand monsters with your son that she really doesn't have to kill her big sister.

"Nothing definite, yet."

Sophie returns with a tray, one cocoa for me, two steaming mugs of java as well as a tray of homemade snicker doodles.

"What is it you do?" One of the early social skills I'd mastered was to deflect attention away from myself by asking people to talk about themselves. Most people would rather talk than listen.

"We run a campground in the high season," Sophie says. "This is a big tourist area in the summer. I clean and Garret does maintenance."

"Sounds nice." I wonder if my aunts had sent giants in

disguise here on vacation, funneling money to the people who gave me life.

More uncomfortable silence. I sip my cocoa. It's the best thing I've ever tasted, next to the double bacon cheeseburger.

"You look all done in." Sophie hops up and extends a hand. "I made up the guest room for you if you'd like to take a nap."

I don't want to nap after the nightmares I've been having but any excuse that would get me out of this highly uncomfortable living room is welcome. "Sounds great."

"Nice meeting you," I say to Garret, who is still sizing me up and looking unimpressed. His response is a grunt.

"This is where Angie and Jedda are staying," she points to one wing which is really more of a suite. "How exactly are they related to you again?"

"Cousins." The lie falls easily from my lips. In a way, all the creatures of Underhill are distant cousins. Angie, really?

She nods. "Oh, well we're happy to have all of you."

I study her profile. It's so much softer than mine. Though she has crows' feet, her cheeks are flushed and she also carries laugh lines around her mouth. Salt of the earth, quality people.

It's hard to believe I came from her egg.

My hand goes to my own belly. What will my baby be like?

She sees the gesture and her eyes widen. She doesn't comment though.

"Thanks again for taking all of us in on such short notice." I say to cover the awkward gap.

"It's no trouble," She turns away and leads me to a door. It's a sliding barn door style at the back of the house that leads to a narrow staircase. "This room is a little inconvenient to get to but you have your own bath and the view is amazing."

I follow her up the wooden steps and into the third-floor space. A sliding glass door leads out onto a deck that over-looks the inland waterway. The décor is just as rustic as the rest of the house, with weathered boards and a strong smell of cedar.

It reminds me of Aiden's unique scent.

Everything looks so normal. I want to fall to my knees on the hand braided rug, to bury my face in the candlewick bedspread. I want to climb in between the clean, white sheets and sleep for a week.

Sophie stands there, watching me take the space in and I decide to address the elephant in the room.

"Why did you give me up?" I stand by the sliding glass door where I can see Chloe and my brother making sand angels.

Behind me Sophie sucks in a breath.

"It wasn't by choice. We were still in high school. I grew up 'round here and Garret, well. It was a summer fling. By the time I found out you were on the way, he had gone back to his life in New York."

Again, her gaze drops to my middle. Yeah, cat's out of the bag, there.

Her big blue eyes fill up. "I was young, younger than you are now. And scared. My daddy was a drinker. My mama had passed on and I only had a waitressing job part time. If I had known Garret would come back into my life, I would have kept you. I swear it."

"I believe you," I breathe.

Her arms go around me in a tight hug. My lips tremble and I close my eyes, breathing in her powdery soft scent. She smells of vanilla body lotion and home. My mother.

She pulls away and wipes her cheeks. "I'll leave you to rest."

"Sophie," I catch her hand impulsively. "You did the right thing."

She smiles and then shuts the door behind her.

I wash up in the adjoining bathroom, taking a warm shower and wrapping myself in a white satin robe and then head to bed. Outside, the snow begins to fall. What would my life have been like if Garret had come back to Sophie sooner? If I hadn't been adopted by the Fates?

I fret over the child growing inside me. What will her life be like? And how will mine change? Sophie knew she couldn't have handled the responsibilities of motherhood, even with a nurturing soul. What chance do I stand?

And how will Aiden react when he finds out? He had been vehement about not wanting a child for centuries. Paranoid that his line is cursed. Worried that he will add soldiers to his father's army and bring about Ragnarök—the end of the worlds.

Yet in spite of all that I know Aiden will make a phenomenal father. He's good and true. And I'm...me.

"Aiden," I breathe his name, wishing the wind will carry it to him. "Hurry."

AIDEN STOPS ABRUPTLY, causing Harmony to slam into his back. He turns and steadies her.

"What's wrong?" she asks.

"Her scent is gone." He inhales again. The faint whiff he had of Nic has vanished.

"Do you think she crossed the Veil to find you?" Harmony lowers herself onto a boulder and rubs at her bare feet.

"I don't know." Damn it, if she had crossed back into the fey realm, he'd have no choice but to go after her. "Can you see anything about where she is?"

The seer pauses in her foot massage and shuts her eyes. Her brow furrows as she frowns. "I'm not sure. It doesn't look like Underhill. Too much manmade stuff. She hasn't made any decisions. But the room she's in looks different than where I saw her earlier."

"That's it? She's in a room somewhere?" He can't keep the annoyance out of his tone.

Her purple lids lift and she glares at him. "It's not like I have a supernatural lojack. My abilities are based on individual decisions. If she doesn't make any, I can't see anything."

He huffs out a breath. "Thanks for trying."

One of her jet eyebrows goes up. "So, you trust that I'm telling you the truth? Even though I betrayed you?"

He taps the side of his nose. "I can smell lies. You're not a fey like I thought, but I'd know if you were telling me a falsehood. And I'm fairly certain you aren't trying to keep me and Nic apart. You just don't want me crossing the Veil. And I won't."

Not unless he had to in order to retrieve his mate.

She huffs out a breath. "All right. Can we stop for a rest? My feet are killing me."

Her feet are bare and he can see a fresh crop of blisters. "Can you travel by sparks the way I can?"

She shakes her head. "No. I can barely manage a single flame. If not for my seer gift, I'd be as talented as a fey peasant."

He scrubs a hand over his face. He can transform them both to sparks for a short distance, but without a direction, he'd drain his magic before they found Nic. Not like he was going to get back to her until he picked up her scent again.

He makes the decision. "We'll camp here for the night."

Harmony looks around. "There's no shelter. And those clouds look like they mean business."

"Then we'll build a lean-to." Aiden bends to the ground and starts picking up dead boughs and placing them diagonally from the boulder where she sits. "Gather up some branches. The fire will be our fourth wall."

They gather wood for a camp in silence.

Aiden shifts to the wolf to find food.

"I'll get a fire going," Harmony says.

He's a mile off when he hears her scream.

Wolves, his beast recognizes the scent. *A pack is on her trail.*

Aiden runs as fast as four paws can carry him across the damp ground, kicking up clumps of dirt with each step. How could he have been so stupid? His heart pounds. Harmony is a seer, she's old and clever. She can take care of herself.

But he refused to let anything happen to his sister.

He breaks through the trees and looks down at the scene below. A pack of wolves, larger than any he'd ever beheld, surrounds Harmony. Both hands are out in front of her, a large branch in each one. She clacks them together and the ends ignite until she is holding flaming torches. Aiden leaps, changing from wolf to sparks and back to wolf at her side.

The pack stands down.

It's odd, one moment they are snapping at her heels, surrounding her, but the moment he arrives, they freeze. He can scent confusion coming off of them.

The largest, a gray wolf with a white blaze across his chest, begins to shift. It isn't a seamless transition, not like his own. No, this looks painful, as though the animal is being stretched and misshapen by great, invisible hands.

And then a young man stands before him, naked. He has shaggy dark hair and a long scraggly beard. His eyes are intense as they focus on him, one green and the other blue.

"Who are you?" he asks. It takes Aiden a moment to recognize that the wolf is speaking German. "Who are you that you are not one of our pack?"

Harmony looks to him but she is not his mate and he has no silent communication with her the way he does with Nic. So he shifts, turning back into a man.

"My name is Aiden."

"Váli," Harmony corrects.

Aiden scowls at her but then nods in agreement. "Yes."

The other male steps forward. "Váli? Váli Sigynjarson?"

Did everyone in the nine worlds know his true name? "That's right? Who are you?"

"My name is Liam." The wolf dips his head. "Liam Cooper. And I'm your nephew."

GENERATIONS OF PACK

"So you're telling me," Aiden says as they sit around the fire at the wolf den, "that you are all children of Fenrir?"

"That's right." Liam passes around a jug of ale, offering it first to Harmony, who declines it and then to Aiden. "Although none of us knew that before we died."

"You're Draugar?" Harmony asks with wide eyes.

The term is met with blank looks.

"You died and then were reanimated?" the seer clarifies.

"Not exactly." Liam rubs the back of his neck. "What do you know of your brother?"

"Other than that he is currently sitting on the Shadow Throne?" Aiden asks. "Only that he is imprisoned in a mortal body."

Liam nods. "Fenrir is contained within different mortal bodies. He procreates with others during each lifetime. We are all his children. Gray there is the oldest, at least the oldest of this pack."

Gray, who has the same multihued eyes, though different

shades of blue and green from Liam's, speaks with a British upper crust accent. "I was a mortal over one thousand years ago. Fenrir was my mother then."

Aiden's jaw drops. "You're telling me Fenrir gave birth to you while he was a woman?"

Gray nods. "Yes. His name was Kitty. She died of Cholera. It wasn't until my own death, fifty years later, that I changed for the first time. I was alone, and tried to return to my wife. But she had seen me pass as an old man and didn't understand how I had reverted to this." He waves down to indicate his youthful form.

"The point of death is when the change overtakes us," Liam says. "I was Fenrir's last child, born seventeen years ago. He was male in that incarnation. Hubert O'Leary. We died together in an automobile accident."

Aiden scents the air but detects no lie from Liam or Gray. "How did you find out, what you are?"

Gray takes his turn with the ale. "After my own death and subsequent rebirth as a wolf, I struggled to adapt. And when my Owen died," he gestures to a short stocky wolf with a black saddle and a white tail, before continuing, "I was there to help him transition, to see him through his first change. From that point on, we tried to find as many as we could. But as Fenrir is reborn differently every human life cycle, we never know who he is or who the new progeny will be until the moment of death and resurrection."

Aiden stares around. There had to be at least a hundred different wolves in the territory.

"You are immortal then?"

Liam shakes his head. "No, we just age slowly. Most go mad before age can show in more than a few silver hairs."

"And they found you in time?" Aiden asks Liam.

The wolf shakes his head. "No. But the internet has made

finding the newly changed wolves easier. Always someone nearby with a camera phone."

Aiden lets out a laugh. "I guess that's one good thing about it."

"Why would you stay here though?" Harmony asks. "Why not cross the Veil? Surely, you would have more room to run in Underhill."

Liam and Gray exchange a look. "The Veil?"

"They don't know," Aiden mumbles.

"Know what?" Liam frowns.

Aiden scrubs a hand over his face. Freaking Fenrir sowing his seed since the dawn of time. Or hatching eggs, apparently. And Aiden had been worried about having one child with Nicneven? If he ever got his hands on the wolf, he'd see the bastard fixed.

Although looking at Liam, Gray, Owen and the others, most of them appeared stable.

Harmony speaks, interrupting his thoughts. "Of course, with no one to introduce you to the hidden realms, you don't know anything about magic."

"Magic?" Liam scowls.

Babes in the woods. These beasts knew even less than Nic did when he'd found her.

"How far down the line does the transformation go?" Aiden looks between Gray and his son, Owen. "How many generations?"

"Only two," Gray says as he skins a rabbit and skewers it over a fire. "My grandchildren all died naturally. No wolfing out."

Aiden studies them. He's gone from being the last in his line to surrounded by family. And they are family, even if they are different than the family he'd ever imagined.

"So why do you stay here?" Aiden glances around the cave. "Surely you have the means to have something better."

"We stay here because it is one of the last places we can hide from mortals. And because of our missing one."

"Missing one?"

Liam's gaze is distant. "She who lived among us for a time. It is about twelve years ago now. We smelled you near her house before. It's how we picked up your scent. You smell slightly of her winter apple fragrance."

All the small hairs rise on his arms. "Nic? You know Nic?"

Gray nods. "She came to us as a child. We spend most of our time as the wolves, this is the first time I've regained my human appearance since she left."

"She was never afraid of us," Liam adds. "We took her in, adopted her into the pack. The fragile little one, all alone. She smelled of wolf and magic. She didn't belong and neither do we."

Even then, at the tender age of six, his Nic had carried a shred of his scent.

"You know where she is?" Liam asks.

"Not at the moment. I've been trying to find her scent but it's been hidden from me." Aiden lets out a sigh. "She's my mate."

The wolves exchange another glance. "What is a mate?"

"You really do keep to yourselves, don't you?" Harmony adds, looking out over the pack.

"Life is both easier and more complicated as the wolf. Simpler to hunt, to sleep in warmth and relative comfort. The needs of the wolf are few. It's our human hearts that have suffered. Most of us would prefer not to remember."

Aiden's wolf agrees with their assessment. Life is easier on four paws. Perhaps not safer, but straightforward and without any kind of game playing. Animals hunt and sleep and live their lives.

"A mate is a forever partner. One who is accepted by me

and my wolf and accepts us in return. We recognize a piece of ourselves in the other."

Gray clears his throat. "That's why you smell of her then?"

"Yes." Aiden nods. "It's a rare bond, one I'm willing to do anything to protect."

The threat is layered in his words. Liam growls lightly at the perceived challenge.

"Do you possess any magic other than the shift?" Harmony asks to diffuse the tension.

Liam and Gray exchange a look. "No? Should we?"

Harmony extends her palm and lights her flame. After a moment, Aiden does likewise. The werewolves frown.

Aiden lets his flame go out. "We're descended from Loki, a fire deity. As part of Fenrir's line, you are as well."

"I sense the spark in them," the seer says. "But no one has showed them how to access it."

Aiden studies the massive pack that seethes with untapped potential.

Her eyes glow brighter. "Do you know what this could mean?"

Aiden does. Draugar had to be burned or they would reanimate. And there aren't enough fire fey to make a proper army. But if the wolves could be taught to wield their inborn flames as magic, they could fight the dead the same way he can.

"We might have enough firepower to stop Underhill."

DINNER IS EVEN MORE uncomfortable than I could have imagined. Sophie loans me some of her clothes. I arrive at the table sporting a daisy yellow peasant blouse and a denim skirt. Still barefoot. Still pregnant.

All that's missing is a gods damned minivan.

"Don't you look nice," Sophie chirps when I poke my head into the kitchen.

"Nice," Chloe repeats. "Pastels suit you."

I give her the hairy eyeball and she covers her face with her fist.

Chloe, Angrboda and Jedda are squeezed around a round wooden table with Tate. The boys, one fey the other mortal, are playing with *Avengers* action figures. Iron Man and Thor, if I'm not mistaken.

I wonder if the actual Thor has seen the movies. Dude looks nothing like Chris Hemsworth.

"Need any help?" I ask Sophie who is stirring a big pot of tomato sauce on the stovetop.

"Aren't you sweet?" She flashes me yet another sunny smile from her seemingly endless supply of them. "You can set the table. Dishes are in the cabinet to the left of the fridge. The silverware is in the drawer under the coffee pot."

Chloe lifts Tate off her lap and sets him on the floor. "Better go clean-up, Champ."

"Do you know him?" I murmur to my aunt as I set a plate down in front of her.

She shrugs. "Remember that veterinarian conference Addy and I attend every year?"

When I nod she adds, "Funny thing about that, there is no conference."

I roll my eyes and turn to face the giantess. "Any news from Aiden?"

Angrboda shakes her head.

Sophie lays a hand on my arm, making me jump. "I'm sure he'll reach out to you real soon, Nic."

"Who'll reach out?" Garret booms from the doorway.

"Nic's boyfriend," Sophie squeezes my hand once. I get the vague feeling that she's reassuring me that she will keep my secret from her husband.

He grunts and moves toward the fridge. "Aren't you a little young for boys?"

"Nic used to be asexual," Chloe blurts.

I kick her under the table hard enough that she jumps.

She scowls at me. "What? You told me you thought you were before Aiden."

"What's asexual?" Tate asks.

Garret chokes on the soda he'd just tilted to his mouth.

"It's somebody who doesn't get married," Sophie puts in swiftly and sets a giant bowl of pasta and tomato sauce on the tiny table.

Tate looks from his mother to me. "You're not going to get married?"

"I...don't know." Weeks, I'd withstood Agent Hanson's interrogation and I'm crumbling like parmesan cheese in front of a six-year-old.

Tate thinks about that a second then beams at me. "Then, I'm asexual, too!"

More choking from Garret. Sophie pounds him helpfully on the back before taking her own seat next to me.

It's a tight fit, the table clearly meant to hold four, not seven. Garret takes up a massive amount of space. In addition to the pasta, there's a pitcher of water, a bottle of wine and garlic bread in a basket. Total carb-fest and nary a green thing in sight. I reach for the basket when Sophie snags Tate's hand and then takes mine. "We always start off dinner by saying grace. Would you like to say grace, Nic?"

"Ummm," I shoot a panicked glance with Chloe and Angrboda. Grace? So not in my wheelhouse. "That is...?"

"Don't put her on the spot, Soph." My rescue comes unexpectedly from Garret. "It's Tate's turn anyhow."

Tate bows his head. "Thank you for this food we are about to eat, for our family and for our new friends." He

128

speaks solemnly, as only a small child taking his task seriously, could.

"Very good." Sophie beams at her son and I feel my throat close up. I pull my hand out of hers and reach for the water pitcher.

"This smells amazing," Angrboda pours herself a glass of wine and then passes it to Chloe.

"I'm surprised you have any room," Chloe shoots the giantess a sidelong glance. "What with all the snacking you did on the way here."

Angrboda shrugs. "I have a wicked appetite."

"So Nic," Sophie passes me the bread. "Your aunt says you have a lot of hobbies."

I take a huge bite and then point to my full mouth, stalling for time. Hobbies? Since when is vigilante justice and wielding fey magic a hobby?

"Nic was in a rigorous physical training program," Chloe says. "And she knows all about ancient weapons."

"You do?" This comes from Jedda. I'm not sure how much the miniature Seelie king knows about me or our situation, but his default setting appears to be interested observer. Smart.

I nod, unwilling to give the fey royal any further insight. He may only be a child, but Wardon was a boy once, too.

"She also reads the classics," Chloe says. "Especially mythologies."

"Like Greek? Roman?" Garret asks, again surprising me. "That was my major in college."

"Really?"

He nods. "I always thought I'd be a professor in some dusty ivy covered school. Instead, I wound up caretaking a campground in the OBX. I can show you my collections after dinner if you would like."

"Sure." I push some pasta around on my plate. "I'm mostly interested in Norse mythology. Know anything about that?"

Garret strokes his goatee. "Not as much as some of the others. The Nordic names always put me off, extra j's all over the place. I always did find that Loki character fascinating though."

"Funny, me too," says Angrboda, who'd born Loki three illegitimate children.

Chloe raises an eyebrow and the giantess shrugs. "You live, you learn, am I right?"

The rest of the meal is just as stilted. A good Christian family breaking bread with a heathen giantess, a Norn and a teenage serial killer.

Stranger things have happened.

As soon as the last plate has been scraped clean, Chloe jumps up. "Nic, you look a little flushed. How about a walk?" I can tell by the light in her eyes that she's discovered something.

I look to Garret, who shrugs. "The library will still be here in the morning."

"Bring a coat. It's cold out." Sophie calls from her stooped position over the dishwasher. It's such a mom thing to say.

"I don't have one." Only the one Chloe had lent me in the car.

Sophie waves to the nook by the door. "My heaviest is in the hall closet."

Angrboda follows us out onto the deck and down the steps that lead to the secluded beach. The sand is wet from the snow which melted on contact but the wind is icy.

When we are a good distance from the house, I turn to face them. "What did you find out?"

Chloe gestures to Angrboda. "You better tell her."

"Tell me what?" I wrap my arms around myself as a sudden gust makes me shiver.

"I found out something, something about Agent Hanson." Angrboda looks at me thoughtfully. "She's gone rogue."

I frown. "Why would she do that?"

Chloe shakes her head. "No, you don't understand, Nic. She's been rogue ever since she took you. It wasn't just a job to her."

I frown. "What do you mean?"

Angrboda shakes her head. "You killed her husband."

GUILT IS THE NEW BLACK

S leep eludes me.

I'm not sure if it's because of my earlier nap, the nightmare about Underhill, Astrid's death or what Chloe and Angrboda had discovered about Agent Hanson.

Tim Hanson. I remember him. He was one of my early victims, before I'd refined my process. A good-looking man, dirty blond hair neatly combed, trim physique. Nice clothes, reflective sunglasses. Not your stereotypical pedophile.

He'd come after me when I was ten.

Or rather, I'd gone after him.

Children had disappeared from a park in Tennessee. The aunts had positioned me there, to see if anyone approached. I'd been wearing a little cotton sundress and Mary Janes, the picture of innocence.

At first, he'd looked like just another dad sitting on one of the benches around the play area. But unlike the other parents who'd been on their phones or chatting, he just sat and watched.

It had taken three trips to the park before he approached

me. He was careful, probably trying to assess who'd dropped me off. I sat on a swing, idly twirling.

"You here all alone, angel?"

His voice made all the small hairs rise up on the back of my neck. Some instinct long dormant deep inside me whispered, *one of mine.*

When I nodded, he held out a hand. As instructed, I took it. To anyone else watching, we would look like a father and daughter heading home for dinner. Chloe and Addy had been parked in Addy's Subaru across the street. I knew they would follow.

He'd driven me to a foreclosed house. Perfect for his purposes. When the door shut, my heart raced. Remembered flashes of the man who'd accosted me in the Black Forest surfaced.

I had a script I was supposed to follow. I was supposed to wait for proof of his intentions.

"If he drives you to the police station, don't attack him." Addy had reminded me. "And don't strike in public. Wait until he takes you somewhere secluded and makes a move."

I didn't want him to make a move. My stomach was filled with knots of anxiety and I thought I might throw up.

"Come here, angel." He removed his sunglasses and I saw the intention in his eyes.

I struck. My lips to the exposed skin of his hand.

He hadn't attacked me, not like some of the others. But I'd known he was evil. And I hadn't wanted more memories to haunt me. The ghosts of his hands on my body, like I could sometimes feel that other man's.

But I'd miscalculated. The memories that haunted me were of the light leaving his eyes, his body tumbling forward, crashing to the ground.

Of my stomach emptying itself while Chloe and Addy rushed through the door.

Of the house burning down around him.

The sound of raised voices pulls me from my reverie.

"Garret, please. She just got here," It's Sophie's voice.

I get out of bed and press my ear to the vent by the floor. Their bedroom must be right below mine.

"What if she's on drugs?" It's Garret, obviously talking about me. "What if she's some sort of criminal?"

I stuff a hand in my mouth so I don't laugh aloud. *If only you knew, Garret.*

"Keep your voice down," Sophie hisses.

"I'm telling you something isn't right with her."

No, it isn't. I finally see what I inherited from Garret —instincts.

"Her eyes are so cold. And at dinner? She barely held my gaze. And the others…. Soph, I don't want them here around you and our son."

"She's my daughter," Sophie snaps. "*Our* daughter. I won't turn her away when she's in need. If you're so worried, take Tate and go to your mama's house."

"I'm not leaving you here." It's a growl of protectiveness, one I am all too familiar with.

I wonder if Garret would like Aiden. If they will ever get the chance to meet.

Sophie's tone changes and I hear the steel as her words continue. "Nic is my daughter. If things had been different, we would have kept her. I know Chloe. She's a good woman."

No, but she just plays one *really* well. Better than I do.

"You've seen her a handful of times for a day. Exchanged a few letters. That doesn't mean you know her."

"I do. She didn't have to keep in touch. The adoption rules were absolute. Yet she sent me a letter and a photo every year. When I was attacked, she helped us hide. She was here when Tate was born." I can hear the tears in her voice. "If you're so worried Garret, take our son and leave. I will never leave a child of mine at risk. But I am staying here with my daughter."

Tears slide down my face. The only person who's ever been so vehement in looking out for me is Aiden.

I have a mother. A mother other than Underhill.

Addy and Chloe raised me, loved me. Did what they needed to in order to keep my secret. But for the first time, I understand the concept of unconditional love.

Would Sophie fight so hard with her husband if she knew what I've done?

"Don't cry," Garret soothes. "Everything will be fine."

"Please don't push her away." Sophie words are so muffled I can barely make them out. "Not now that I finally have a chance to get to know her."

I move away from the wall and curl back up in bed. Good people. These are good people. And as much as I know Chloe and Addy love me, it's somehow different to know that somewhere along the line, I come from good people.

That maybe deep down, in some shadowy corner, I have the capacity of being good, too.

My body shakes as I recall Astrid's acceptance of what I could do. I told her I was a vigilante, like her friend, Declan. Is that the truth though?

Agent Hanson had been married to one of my victims. Had she known he was a pedophile? A murderer? The authorities had found the bodies of the missing children in the basement of that same house where he'd taken me. She must have known what he'd done. Known, yet still blamed me. She wouldn't just shrug and move on to the next task. Finding me was personal for her.

Tomorrow I would rally my ragtag forces and come up with a plan.

135

Because what Garret—my father—says is true. I am a magnet for trouble.

We can't endanger these decent people any longer than necessary.

A‌IDEN STUDIES his sister's sleeping face in the firelight. *Harmony is my sister.* He still can't get his head around that.

Or that their mother had abandoned her to Freya's tender mercies.

Then there's the existence of other wolves.

Pack, his own beast insists. It is more content than it has been since the last night he'd been with Nic.

He glances around the cave. It's deep, with ventilation in the ceiling to let the smoke escape. The fire burns low. He gets the impression that if not for Harmony, they would have doused it completely.

The rest of the pack had bedded down for the night, all in wolf form. All save for Liam, who'd gone for a run.

Aiden stands and heads out into the night. The moon is out, full and fat above the trees. An owl hoots and there is a rustle of something small in the underbrush.

Nic had come here as a child. He'd hated that she'd been alone. The pack had protected her for him. Fenrir might be an evil vindictive monster, but his sons and daughters are a decent sort. He owes them.

So how can you consider bringing them through the Veil? What waits for them there but death?

"Aiden?" It's Liam, naked in the moonlight. "Is everything all right?"

Much like the fey, the wolves don't seem to concern themselves with nudity. "Fine. Just wanted to see if I could catch her scent."

Liam nods. "She's important to you?"

"More important than I ever thought possible." He shakes his head. "She's saved me so many times. Even from myself."

Liam looks out into the darkened trees, his expression troubled. "Do you really think we will have a place in this magic land?"

"If the right side wins? Yes."

The dark brow above his green eye tilts up. "And if the other side wins?"

He holds the young wolf's multihued gaze. "There won't be any land left, for any of us."

Liam nods. "I appreciate the direness of your situation. But I'm Alpha here. I need to do what's best for my people."

Aiden gestures to the cave. "They don't live like people."

Liam bristles. "No, they don't. The old ones have a hard time acclimating. It's simpler if we stay to ourselves and live like the animals we are."

He'd once thought the same way. "And does that fulfill them?"

Liam stares at him, a dominance challenge. Aiden doesn't twitch.

It is the Alpha who looks away first. Voice tight he says, "You could challenge me for leadership. Your wolf is more dominant than mine."

Aiden's inner beast snarls in satisfaction that the other would admit it so freely. *They are ripe for takeover. Be their leader and dispatch them as you will.*

Aiden ignores the beast. "Why would I want to do that?"

Liam's green eye seems to glow. "To get your way. Train the pack to fight and wield magic. Might makes right, doesn't it?"

Though his beast is still willing to fight, Aiden knows he is a lone wolf. "I don't want to be Alpha, Liam. From what I can tell, you've done the best that you could for your people with the few resources you had."

Liam turns away and Aiden spies the series of scars down the wolf's left flank. "Are those from the accident?"

Liam stiffens. "I don't talk about my scars, not even if you were a beautiful woman. And let's face it, uncle. You aren't."

Aiden doesn't bother to suppress a grin. "Fair enough. I've done nothing to earn your trust and you've done everything to earn mine because you looked out for Nic when she needed it. I'm asking for you to help her again. And let your wolves help themselves. The pack is strong. They can fight for a better life. You know there is more now, Liam. Can you really justify keeping them in fur and sleeping in a cave?"

Liam growls low, but it breaks into a smile. "Fine. I will consider it. Good enough?"

At Aiden's nod, he stretches. "Now if you'll excuse me, I want to get a little sleep."

Liam shifts in that slow, painful way of his and pads inside the cave.

Aiden stands and stares out into the trees. He closes his eyes and breathes in, searching for her scent. He finds it nearby, though it is old, almost stale. He shifts to sparks, the wolf's instincts demanding he find its source.

The trees grow close together, their bark almost black. He flits over the land until he spies a small clearing. His body reassembles on the ground and Aiden takes in his surroundings.

It's a house, a stone cottage though it is crumbling to the ground. The scent of Nic is stronger. Along with a whiff of fear.

This place, where the fate Lachesis had abandoned her at six-years-old. If not for Liam and his pack, she would have starved to death long before the hiker had attacked her.

He stares at it for countless time. Imagining what caused that terror.

"I should never have left her," he growls at the same time as his wolf. His hands clench into fists. His eyes growing stronger in the low light of the moon.

"You didn't have a choice." Another voice says from beside him.

He turns to see Harmony step out from between the trees.

"I thought I'd find you here." She looks to the cottage and pulls a face. "Ick, not exactly a summer vacation spot. Is it?"

"No." He lets out a shaky breath. "I know this place. Have heard about it from Nic."

Without conscious thought his feet carry him to the crumbling structure.

He can hear Harmony following closely behind him, but she doesn't speak. His mate's scent grows stronger, along with the echo of fear. She'd been left here. Her memories wiped by one of those cursed fates. He steps past the door which is hanging on its hinges. Vines snake up through the stones, the mortar crumbling, the roof all but a distant memory. It had been over a decade, but somehow, he knows the structure hadn't looked any better during Nic's sojourn here.

"She was attacked." He stoops down and picks up a small, rag doll that has buttons for eyes. "That bitch left her alone here and she was attacked by a full-grown man."

Harmony's hand brushes his arm. "She survived."

He turns to face her. "Did she? There are times I wonder."

She shakes her head. "Isn't there enough suffering in this world without you going out to look for trouble?"

"I left her with them, the Fates." He shakes his head.

"It was a smart choice."

"You don't understand. I could have stayed with her, used magic to keep her hidden from Brigit. But I was so angry about what she'd done." It's the first time he admitted it out loud. That he had chosen to leave his unprotected mate when she'd been most vulnerable.

Because he hadn't been able to stand the sight of her.

"What did she do?" Harmony asks.

"The seer doesn't know all?"

She waits patiently and he feels like a prick for lashing out at her. Time has barely scabbed the wound. "Nicneven deceived me. Forced my hand and tricked me to get her way. I left her alone and she and our babe died. And then when Laufey brought her back, merged her soul with that human child, I had a choice. To stay with her and protect her myself or find someone else to do it. I chose to leave her. If I'd known she'd be different...."

Harmony moves to stand in front of him. "Aiden, you may have been born of the gods but your heart is human. I don't think it's a coincidence that you didn't love Nic until she became human, mate or no."

He pulls in a deep breath and stares down at the doll in his hands.

"She forgives you, for all of it. She loves you."

He frowns. "It's odd, to hear you defending her."

Harmony shrugs. "I figure you're going to be with her whatever I say. I want you to be happy, brother."

His eyes fill with tears. "Thank you."

She squeezes his shoulder. "I wish I could have known you sooner."

"As do I, little sister. As do I."

She smiles but then her face goes blank, eerily so.

"Are you all right?"

She doesn't answer. He drops the doll and reaches for her,

intending to shift them both to sparks and take her back to Liam's den when she blinks.

"Was that a vision?"

She nods. "Yes. I know where Nic is. We have to hurry before it's too late."

EVIL INSIGHT

"Well well, what do we have here?" Pharaildis smiles at the bedraggled pair of females Rodrick's fey guards deposit at her feet.

"Exactly what is your problem?" The giantess Laufey shoves the Unseelie who'd been manhandling her to the side with enough force that his body leaves a dent in the hewn stone of the dungeon wall.

Pharaildis raises an eyebrow? "Were my guards too rough?"

Ignoring her, Laufey kneels over the body of her lover. "Fern, darling? Can you hear me?"

Fern doesn't respond.

Pharaildis crouches beside the giantess. "Tell me where he is and I'll heal her."

Laufey glares up at her, hatred burning in her leaf green eyes. "I will never tell you and you won't lay one of your perverse fingers on her."

Underhill sighs and then rises to her feet. Why must they always be so difficult? She moves around the pair bleeding on the floor as if they are nothing but mongrel dogs. "I have no quarrel with you, giant. Nor with her. I only want what is mine."

"My grandson isn't yours." With great tenderness, Laufey brushes hair off of Fern's cheek. "And neither is Nic."

Pharaildis pauses at that. She hadn't anticipated such resistance from the giantess. Though her encounters with Laufey and her kind had been limited in the past, they'd always been mutually beneficial.

She raises a brow at the giantess. "Do you really want to see the fey continue to rule this realm?"

"Better than having the dead overrun it." Laufey gestures to the window. "It's nothing but a blackened husk of what it used to be. You were the first dreamer here, Pharaildis. You know what this land could be. And yet you desecrate what you once held sacred."

Rage, hot and quick, surges through Pharaildis at her words. "They did this to me. Those accursed Fates. I have one of them lurking just beyond that door." She stabs a finger at the adjacent cell.

"You're not the first to have a beef with your destiny." Laufey lifts her chin. "I sympathized with you when you were imprisoned here. It was neither just, nor fair."

Her gaze falls to Gleipnir, the unbreakable chain that binds Pharaildis's ankles and tethers her to the fey realm. "You killed your lover when he spurned you. Given the chance, I would have done the same."

Pharaildis's hands clench into fists. "History has it wrong. John the Baptist was a letch, no better than any mortal. He came to my bed, made me promises. And then when he found out about her, he abandoned me. When I called for his head, those...Norns dump me here like refuse to serve the fey. I have spent hundreds of thousands of years, trapped and alone. Powerless in the dark. I will get my vengeance. I will be set free."

Something like sympathy flits across the giant's face. "It isn't just. But neither is it just that you punish them all for the acts of a few. The One True Queen is destined to end your reign of terror and blood."

Pharaildis lashes out with her stolen fire. The giantess throws up a magic shield and the flames wrap around her and her lover, incinerating the guards behind them. Their screaming echoes off the solid walls of the Unseelie catacombs.

Breathing hard, Pharaildis lowers her hands. "I have no interest in justice any longer. I will catch your grandson and when I do, I will use him to set Loki free. And you my dear giantess, will help me do it."

"Never." The hardness is back in Laufey's eyes. "I will never help you on this quest."

Calm suffuses Pharaildis once more. She holds the winning hand. "You will. Or, you will watch your lover die."

I SURGE up out of my latest nightmare, clutching the bedspread and panting. I grunt as all the aches and pains from the car wreck make themselves known. My healing has slowed along with all my other abilities.

A knock sounds and a moment later Chloe slips inside.

"I had a dream about Laufey and Fern." I say.

"Are they all right?" Chloe sits on the end of my bed.

"They were." Though I don't know how long they'll stay that way. I think back to everything I'd seen. "Tell me about the prophesy of the One True Queen."

Chloe's red gold eyebrows shoot up. "Where did you hear that?"

"It was in my dream. Angrboda said it, too. What does it say?"

"In essence, the One True Queen will rule the entire Unseelie Court. She is destined to repair the Veil and unite the two halves of the courts into one mighty kingdom."

She sighs. "And, if she joins with the One True King, the

Seelie and Unseelie Courts will come together as one. But it's never been possible before."

"Why not?"

"Your magic is based on the air. In order to rule year-round an Unseelie Queen must be able to wield fire as well."

I put a hand over my stomach. "Fire, like what she will inherit from Aiden?"

"Exactly. That's why Brigit had you murdered in your last life, to avert the prophesy of the One True Queen. It wasn't just jealousy—the One True Queen can sit on both thrones and overthrow the previous ruler. Brigit wanted to keep her power. And Underhill will be even more ruthless if she knows you are with child."

So Addy didn't fight to get me free only for my sake. She used the deception so that this baby would be born safe. "She knows."

Chloe grasps my hand. "Underhill will be hunting you now. You and Aiden both."

I toss the covers to the side. "We need to get out of here. It's not right to put them in danger from not just the FBI, but Underhill as well."

"Nic, think this through. The pocket realm is safe. No one can enter without a giant and there are less than a dozen on this side of the Veil. The baby is draining your magic. Your only defense is your goodnight kiss." She gestures to the scrapes and cuts on my arm. "You're not even healing properly. You need a safe place to convalesce."

"Look me in the eye and tell me that Sophie, Garret and Tate will be all right."

"I'll do everything in my power to ensure their safety." Her gaze shifts to the side. "Addy is stronger with mystical protections."

I reach out and clasp her hand in mine. "I'm sure she'll get free. Knowing Addy, she's looking for a way to free the rest of our forces before she makes her move."

Chloe nods, though doesn't hold my gaze. "You're probably right."

Another knock on the open wood doorframe. "Nic? Are you hungry?"

I gesture for her to enter. "Come in, Sophie."

She does, offering a hesitant smile as she sees me sitting up in bed. "You look better today."

"I feel better." I smile in appreciation.

"Chloe tells me that you are a vegetarian."

Technically I am but the smell of something delectable, which I fear is animal based, reaches me . "Um, well usually. But... not entirely?"

Way to be decisive, Nic.

"No need to explain." Sophie comes into the room and shuts the door. "I had unusual cravings during my pregnancies, too."

Chloe blinks. "You told her?"

Sophie shook her head. "She didn't need to. If you've ever tried to hide a pregnancy, you know the signs. So, pancakes or waffles with your sausage?"

Pancakes make me think of Aiden, how he'd made some the night he'd agreed to drink the unbinding syrup and severed the oath he'd made to me. How would things have been different if he hadn't done that?

I can't think about Aiden without feeling sick again. Gods, how will I tell him? Will I get the chance to tell him?

"Waffles," I say. "Can I help with anything?"

She shakes her head. "Be ready in a few."

We listen to her footsteps recede.

Chloe rises from the foot of the bed. "See why I always told you that you have good in you?"

"I do." There is a stray thread at the corner of the

bedspread and I fidget with it. "Chloe, do you know where Aiden is?"

She glances away. Confirmation.

"Tell me."

"Right this moment, I don't know. But he was in Asgard."

"Asgard? The realm of the gods?" As far as I know, Aiden hasn't been back to Asgard since he was changed and his father had been imprisoned. "What's he doing there?"

Chloe looks pained. "Don't ask me, Nic."

I narrow my gaze on her. "I don't like your tone. Tell me, is he in danger?"

She shakes her head, red gold curls bouncing. "No. In fact the gods are worried that Underhill is hunting Aiden so she can release the trickster."

Then at least he would be safe. Unless that cursed pantheon turned on him again. "I'm worried about these dreams, about what they mean."

She frowns. "What's the common thread you're seeing?"

"My mother."

We both know I'm not talking about Sophie.

"You're in charge Nic. But you have the heirs to three of the four thrones. From the message the ghost sent, the fourth, your pal Taj, is in the Vanir lands."

"We can't trust Nightweaver. She's reporting back to Underhill."

Chloe's eyes go wide with alarm.

Uh oh. "Have you seen her? Did you tell her where we are?"

She shakes her head. "No, but if she does discover this pocket realm, Underhill will recruit a giant to come in after us."

Shit. Shit shit *shit*. "We need to leave before Nightweaver comes back."

Chloe throws her hands in the air in obvious frustration.

"And go where? Underhill is out of the question. As soon as we leave here then Agent Hanson will be up our asses. We don't have a lot of options, Nic."

She's right, I know it and yet after watching Astrid die, I don't want any more innocents getting caught up in my nightmare.

My aunt rubs a hand over her face. "Think about what I said. Addy didn't sacrifice herself so that you and your baby wind up in Underhill's clutches."

With that she leaves me to dress.

AFTER BREAKFAST I follow my brother out onto the beach. Heavy clouds are stacking up to the east and the wind is sharp off the water. I'm happy to be outside though where the breeze can kiss my face and I can breathe in all the scents of the season.

My season. At least it had been.

"Why do you look so sad, Nic?" Tate tilts his head to the side.

"I have some friends who I miss is all." Nahini, Jasmine, Freda. Aiden.

He nods as if this explanation is sufficient. "Want to see my fort?"

"Sure." I allow him to take my hand and lead me to a copse of scrubby bushes, where a scraggly looking treehouse is perched.

"Wow, that's pretty cool." I smile at the *no girls allowed* sign. "What do you have against girls?"

"That's just to keep mom out. She always wants to tidy up."

He drops my hand and starts to clamber through the brush.

"Be careful," I say.

"Of what?"

"Snakes?" I suggest.

"They're all in dens for the winter. It's okay. I do this all the time."

Still, nervous knots twist low in my belly as I watch him disappear into the tangle of nature. If I had my magic…no. I need to get used to living without it. I am no longer a queen, no longer able to wield the power of the Shadow Throne or harness the gifts of the Unseelie Court. I'm just plain old Nic. Soon to be an unwed teenage mother with no high school diploma.

Statistics are a bitch.

"Come on," the small head pokes out through the open door.

I am wearing jeans and a sweater borrowed from Sophie along with Chloe's trench coat. I don't feel like getting snagged in that there briar patch. "What happened to no girls allowed?"

"You're not a girl," he waves off my protest. "You're my sister."

My heart clenches. Claimed as family, like it isn't a huge freaking deal. Before I can think better of it, I say, "Okay, I'm coming in."

Carefully, I make my way up the bramble path and into the fort. It's not exactly structurally sound but it's all Tate's. I can appreciate that. "Did your dad help you build this?"

He gives me a gap-toothed grin. "Yup. He showed me how to hammer the boards together and everything."

"Tools, very cool."

"Have you ever built anything?"

I think about it for a beat. "No, I'm not much of a builder."

"I can show you."

"Nic? Where are you?" Another voice calls from nearby.

I poke my head out the window and see Angrboda striding across the seagrass from the house. "Here."

Turning back to the small boy I say, "I gotta go. Thanks for showing me your fort."

"Wait, I've got something for you." He fishes inside an old metal lunchbox until he comes up with a pretty white and pink seashell. "Here."

I take it from him, a small smile on my lips. "Thanks, kid."

I take care climbing out and wipe my eyes when I reach the edge of the brambles at the same time as the giant.

"Have you been crying?" she asks.

"The wind is in my eyes."

She doesn't call me on the obvious lie as we fall into step along the line of frigid sand. "I wanted to tell you I've put out feelers for where Astrid came from and that boy you mentioned, Declan?"

"And?"

She shakes her head. "Nothing so far."

I blow out a breath. "I hope Agent Hanson doesn't know about him."

"I don't think they do. I've been monitoring their communications since they came for you."

I don't ask how, unsure if I want to know all the ways giants go about obtaining information. "And?"

"No one has called in an escaped fugitive. That facility you were housed in? It's supposedly undergoing renovation."

Which explained all of the construction equipment I'd seen when we exited the building. "Any idea where Hanson is now?"

"No. In fact, I'd wager she's holed up somewhere in the mountains, waiting for you to show up at the farm."

My head pounds. "What if Aiden comes back? The farm is the first place he'll look for me."

"Váli isn't stupid," she reassures me. "His wolf instincts will let him know you're not there."

"Chloe mentioned he was in Asgard." I pose it casually.

"That's right." Her tone is neutral.

"Is he with Freya?"

"I don't know."

"Don't spare my feelings, Angrboda. I already have Chloe doing that. I need real talk."

The giantess lets out a sigh. "Yes, he was with her, but not by choice."

"She's holding him captive?"

"Him and his sister."

I frown. "Aiden doesn't have a sister."

"Up until yesterday, you didn't have a brother." She gestures toward the fort.

I take a deep breath. "Why does Freya want him now?"

"He's the key for unbinding Loki. Underhill knows it. Fenrir knows it. And the gods know it."

I brush off a stump and sit. "Tell me about Fenrir."

She paces in front of me, her agitation plain. "What do you want to know?"

"I guess, how is he in Gretchen? Is Gretchen really a person or has it been Fenrir all along?"

She nods, her eyes taking on a faraway look. "Fenrir is bound by Gleipnir. You've read as much in the stories, I presume."

At my nod she continues, "Right, so what the stories don't mention is that Fenrir is bound inside a mortal for the span of the mortal's life. He's there, like a passenger, though he can snag control for short bursts. Do things the mortals will have no memory of. But the Gleipnir will eventually reign him back in. Until now, he has been unable to make himself known to his host or anyone else."

That explained how Fenrir had killed our spy, Isolde, but Gretchen had no memory of doing so.

"What changed?"

"Gretchen crossed the Veil. In doing so, Fenrir moved to the foreground, essentially taking over. The girl you know is now the passenger with the wolf calling the shots."

I let out a breath. "Is there any way to separate them?"

"Not without unbinding my son." She taps one of her long nails against her teeth, an annoying habit. "But there may be a way to put Fenrir back in his less active role. If crossing the Veil unleashed him…."

I follow her line of thinking. "Then bringing him back to Midgard might restrain him again. Any idea how we can coax him back here?"

She shakes her head. "It will have to be done forcefully and by stealth. You can't go, neither can I. Chloe can't interfere and Jedda is at risk as well."

I nod and then look at her, this giantess who has risked so much to help me. "In case I haven't said it yet, thank you. For coming to get me."

She looks away for a moment, then meets my gaze. "Figured I owed you after sending those Valkyries through and bartering magic with Wardon. I never should have trusted Freya."

I stop in my tracks and grip her arm hard. "Trust her how?"

Angrboda flinches. "She said she wanted to protect Váli, that he wouldn't return to Asgard unless you were dead. I felt I owed it to him, since my relationship with his father is what tore his life apart."

My mind whirls at this reveal.

"I only knew you by Nicneven's reputation though. The Ice Bitch never would have accepted him as her mate the way you've done."

"You're right, she wouldn't have. But Aiden and my friends mean everything to me." When I consider how cold and lonely my existence had been before them, I shiver in revulsion. "I didn't know what I was missing. I let my good-night kiss become my whole identity instead of just one part of the badass babe I am."

She grins at that and we fall into step, heading back toward the house. The worn cedar shingles have taken a severe beating from the costal winds, but the lights glowing from within make the space inviting.

A thought surfaces. "Freya appeared to me. Told me I had to kill Underhill with my goodnight kiss and *Seelenverkäufer*. Do you know anything about that?"

Her jaw drops. "Nic you can't."

I shake my head. "I was told my goodnight kiss could kill anything if I was intent on it."

But the giantess appears spooked. "Yes, but you wouldn't just kill Pharaildis. You'd take her place as the new Underhill."

"Nic?" Garret removes his reading glasses when he spots me in the doorway. "Come for that tour I promised?"

Truthfully, I don't know why I've sought him out.

Maybe because being near him, unlike Sophie or Tate, doesn't make me feel guilty. Garret has my number—knows I am no good.

Or maybe it's something to do with the man himself. The calm energy that radiates off of him. He's a barrier, I realize. As much as the giant sandbar that is the Outer Banks is a barrier between the peaceful tranquility of the inland waterway that is Sophie and Tate and the turbulent sea of my life.

Sophie and Chloe are baking, Tate is watching cartoons and Angrboda and Jedda have taken off for lessons in what I can only assume is magic they don't want the mortals to witness. Garret seems like the best source of distraction to keep me from losing my mind.

I don't want to be alone after hearing that the only way to kill my mother and stop the end of the world is to take her place in an immortal prison. I hated being locked up. And I remember all too well Pharaildis telling me what it was like to be her. To desire nothing, not food or drink, sex or sleep. She is endless and it had driven her mad.

But do I fear my fate enough to let the rest of the world die?

"Nic?" Garret asks again.

"Yeah." My voice is rough. "Show me what you've got."

He looks so normal, sitting behind a battered rolltop desk with papers strewn every which way. Clutter is a foreign concept to me. In the farmhouse there's a place for everything, even trash. Organized and precise. This place is as chaotic as the inside of my skull. The wall behind Garret's head is all glass though, allowing him a premium view of the sound. The late afternoon sunlight reflects off the water with a golden glow.

He smiles and gestures for me to come in. "This is something of a novelty for me. Sophie isn't interested in my dusty old tomes and Tate's too young. Let's see, where should we start?"

His boots hit the floor with a dull thump and he rises to his full height, his head nearly brushing the exposed beam of the low ceiling. I take a seat in the wide captain's chair on the opposite side of his desk and watch him peruse his overstuffed shelves.

"The classics of course, *Bullfinches Mythology*. That covers Arthurian legends and the Age of Chivalry. The Iliad, The Odyssey but also some snippets from the Norse pantheon. Beowulf, I believe. Have you read it?"

"I have." Chances are there's nothing in Garret's library that could expand my understanding of the nine worlds more than my recent experience. "You said your focus was Greek and Roman. Do you know anything about Celtic mythology? Fairies and the like?"

His dark eyes light up. "You like fairy tales?"

"Why not? I'm living in one."

He laughs, mistaking my truth for sarcasm. "You know I do. I always found the tales of the Tuatha de Danann most imaginative."

That isn't one I know. "Tell me about them."

Garret pulls a gray book from the shelf. Its spine is broken and the cover is battered and looks fragile in his large hands. "The people of the goddess Danu were a fierce tribe said to have supernatural powers. They invaded what we now know as Ireland, appearing from the mist as if from nowhere."

At his words, all the hairs stand up on my arms. "They came out of nowhere?" Or had they come from beyond the Veil?

"Well, more likely, the legend is puffed up to make them sound more invincible than they really were. Many believed they burned their boats to keep them in the new land. Did you ever hear the one about the chicken and the pig at the bacon and egg breakfast?"

When I shake my head he says, "It's one of Sophie's favorite expressions. There's different levels of involvement going onto the plate. The chicken is involved, the pig is committed."

Maybe it is my new appreciation for breakfast meat but I find myself returning his grin. "So, by burning their boats the Tuatha de Danann were committing themselves?"

He nods. "No going back. So anyhow, the Irish inhabitants weren't too thrilled by the invaders as native peoples usually aren't. But whether by magic, superior strategy or just sheer numbers, the Tuatha de Danann overthrew them and ruled in their stead.

"They ruled from," he frowns and turns a page before continuing, "1897 BCE to around 1700 BCE when the tribe was defeated by another. Legend has it that they were permitted to stay in Ireland but only if they stayed underground."

I suck in a deep breath. "Under the hill. Underhill."

"Right." He closes the book and hands it to me. "The original fairies."

Or maybe not. Maybe just a faction that had left the courts and tried their hand at living on this side of the Veil. I hold the book with both hands. "Thanks. I'm sure this will make interesting reading."

"Anytime." Garret pauses and I wait, wondering if he is going to ask me to leave, in spite of Sophie's wishes.

He studies me for an endless moment. "I didn't know about you until after she gave you up."

I wondered how long he'd wanted to say that. Probably from the moment our eyes had met. "I figured as much. From what Sophie said."

"It's probably better that I didn't know." He turns to look out at his magnificent view. "I wouldn't have taken it well."

Which I interpret to mean he would have asked Sophie to terminate the pregnancy. Great. First Underhill had tried to kill me in utero by drinking water from the poisoned spring Hvelgermir and now Garret's saying he would have ganked me, too. *Feeling the love, people. Really.*

He turns back and winces at the cold expression on my face. "What I'm trying to say, very poorly, is that I don't, I won't—judge you. Because I've made my share of mistakes."

His gaze goes to my belly. I raise a hand reflexively to cover it. I don't know if Sophie told him or he figured it out for himself. Somehow, I believe the latter. Sophie seems desperate to earn my trust.

"My baby isn't a mistake," I say. An accident perhaps, but I've come to believe in destiny. Aiden and I were careful, just not careful enough.

One of his thick caterpillar-like eyebrows goes up. "So, you were trying to get pregnant?"

"No, that is…," I bite off the words, *not this time.* "Aiden's coming back to find me. We're going to be together and raise this baby, together."

Garret doesn't say a word. He doesn't have to. I can sense the disbelief coming off of him. And the pity.

"Thanks again for the book." I leave before I can do something really stupid, like burst into tears.

Stupid hormones.

Lying down on the bed, I can't seem to keep my eyes open.

Not another dream. My soul is weary and I think any more will drive me mad. It's my final thought a second before sleep claims me.

THE GIRL CALLED Pharaildis finishes the dance with a flourish of her hips, her face hidden behind her Veil. Most of her father's guests clap and remark at her grace and beauty then return to their banquet. She straightens and moves to the doors that lead to her private chambers. She can feel the man's eyes upon her body, the way he follows her every step. She loves the attention he devotes to her every performance.

Almost as much as what comes next.

A tray with a light repast has been set on the table in her room. Ignoring the food, Pharaildis instead goes out to the patio and stands beneath the glow of the moon. Her fingers grip the railing and she leans over, staring down at the winding dirt street below, empty of all activity in this late hour.

"You were beautiful," the man says from behind her. "But then you know that, don't you?"

The corner of her mouth pulls up and she turns, greedy for another look at his bearded face. "It is always nice to be appreciated, my lord."

"I am no lord." He smooths a hand down her cheek, his gaze hot. "This is dangerous."

"It doesn't have to be," she catches his hand and brings it to her lips. "We could be married. Leave my father's palace. Go live out our lives somewhere else, somewhere we aren't known."

"You don't know what it's like out there, love. What people are truly like."

She turns away, angry and frustrated. "No, because my father doesn't let me leave this palace. I was born into captivity and in captivity I will remain."

His hands settle on her hips. He pulls her back against him until she can feel the evidence of his desire. "It's not all bad, is it?"

She reaches an arm behind her head as his lips lower to the side of her neck. "I want more, John. Eventually my father will marry me off to someone else. You know he will. And if he finds out that you've touched me—"

"Ssshhh, lovely. Do not trouble your mind with such things." He turns her in his arms and lowers his mouth to hers. His kiss is hot, insistent and after another moment, she yields to him completely. There in the moonlight she finds satiation if not satisfaction.

"A POCKET REALM?" Liam shakes his head. "Never heard of it."

"It's a place that runs parallel to this world, at least in natural architecture." Aiden explains.

"And they are only accessible by magic," Harmony adds. "Giant's magic."

Liam scratches his chin stubble. "Which is why you need a giant."

"Right," Aiden says.

Liam makes a show out of checking his pockets. "Sorry, fresh out."

Harmony rolls her eyes. "His sense of humor is irritating."

"What do you want me to do? I can't conjure a giant from thin air," Liam grumbles.

Aiden squeezes the bridge of his nose. "Like dwarves, giants make it a habit to visit Midgard, this world. You said you came from the Eastern part of the United States, correct? Then you're our best shot at finding one near the location we're heading to."

"You think I know how to find a giant in Washington D.C.?"

Aiden opens his mouth to explain but Harmony holds up a hand. "First, we need you to get us there. We need airline tickets, passports. Anything a human would require for international travel."

"Again," Liam shakes his head. "I can't—"

"I can," Owen says from behind his shoulder. "I know someone. There's a woman in the village."

Hope leaps in Aiden's chest. "And she has access to a plane?"

The wolf shifts his weight, clearly uncomfortable under Liam's scrutiny. "Yes."

"And how exactly do you know this?" Liam turns and narrows his gaze on his packmate. "Haven't I forbidden all contact with mortals?"

Aiden sees the guilt on the wolf's face, but also the glint of steel in his eyes. "You know," Aiden says thoughtfully, "I bet if we asked around, most of your wolves have mingled with the mortals. You all started out as humans. You're all related. And you all have animal lusts."

Liam casts him a murderous look, but even he flushes slightly. "It isn't safe for us to take bedmates."

"That doesn't mean no one has. You've been here for a

long time. Surely others of you have connections that we can use," Harmony interjects.

A female wolf steps forward. "I know a man who can get the documents we need."

"I don't remember agreeing to help." Liam growls.

"Alpha—" the woman protests.

"No." Liam's tone is final. "I won't risk the pack."

"If what they say is true," Gray says quietly, "the pack is already at risk."

Liam looks as though he's been chewing on rancid meat. "And this is what you all want? To cross this Veil into a world we don't know? To fight for the fey who mean nothing to us."

Owen shakes his head. "I do not wish to fight. But I think I speak for many others as well when I say I also do not wish to linger in this place like a bad smell."

"We want to live as people again," another wolf says.

Aiden steps forward. "You aren't people, or rather, not just people, not anymore. I can't promise you lives like you knew when you were mortal but I understand how important it can be to embrace both sides of your heritage."

Harmony flashes him a dazzling smile.

Liam searches the faces of his pack, his face going at last to land on Gray's. "This is truly what you all want?"

"You're a good leader, Liam. A better protector than I ever was," Gray says. "Come with us."

But Liam shakes his head. "Someone needs to stay here, to find the ones who haven't found the pack yet." He turns to Aiden. "You will watch over them?"

A lump forms in Aiden's throat. "I will do everything in my power to protect your pack, nephew."

Several wolves decide to stay with Liam, but the majority want to come with them. With each name Harmony adds to the list of those who will need forged documents, Aiden feels the weight of Liam's burden as their wellbeing is transferred to him.

There are other details as well. Since most of the pack have been living as wolves, many have no clothing. Harmony and a few of the females venture into town to procure at least enough clothing so that the wolves won't be discovered and Owen leaves to arrange for the flight.

"Will you at least come as far as Washington with us?" Aiden pulls Liam aside to ask. "To help me find a giant? It's territory you know better than I."

Liam nods. "I suppose I can do that. How do you know a giant from a mortal though?"

"By scent. You know the difference between a wolf and a mortal by scent, right?"

At Liam's nod he continues, "So, giants smell like magic. The fey do as well, but only if they have worked magic recently."

"But if I've never smelled magic how do I know what it is?" Liam frowns.

"Take Harmony's scent." Aiden tries to verbalize the olfactory patterns that he associates with his sister. "She can wield fire magic. When she does, one can smell the spice, the char of burning. Do you remember how Nic smells?"

Liam nods and Aiden's wolf doesn't like the way the other's eyes alight. "Like winter apples."

"That crisp whiff of ozone, like a first frost, that is her magic. A giant will smell even more potently of the same sort of things. Many times they smell like fresh churned earth, or a dousing of spring rain. In the past they blended in better, but those sorts of scents often stand out in a city."

Liam frowns for a moment. "There was an old man who lived down the street from my parents. He always smelled of sawdust and pinesap. I always assumed he worked with wood, like in construction or something."

"A loner? Kept to himself?"

"How did you know?"

"Giants tend to like their privacy."

Harmony approaches, bags of clothing in each hand. "Owen says the plane is ready to depart in one hour."

"That doesn't give us much time." Liam looks around at the wolves shifting into human form, some for the first time in years.

Harmony pulls Aiden aside. "Are you sure this is the best course of action?"

He frowns down at her. "You're the seer. You tell me."

She stares out into the trees. "I can't see anything right now. That's what scares me."

She'd comforted him so well at that cabin and he wishes to return the favor. "Harmony, you don't have to come. If you'd like to stay here, or even go back to Freya…."

She holds his gaze. "You'll let me go?"

Aiden swallows. "If Liam can let his pack make the decision to leave even if they are safer here, I can't justify keeping you against your will."

She tilts her head. "Tell me why you dislike Freya as much as you do."

His jaw clenches. This isn't a topic he wants to discuss with his sister, but she deserves the truth. "Before father's punishment, before the wolf, we were…involved for a time. When she brought me to her temple in Asgard, she made it clear that she wanted that involvement to continue."

Harmony stares at him. "You mean sexually involved? You were still a boy."

"Age is just a number." How many times had Freya said that to him as she groped and fondled him? Hollow words to stop his protests when things had moved too quickly.

Anger graces his sister's face. "Bullshit. She lured you to

her bed. What would you have thought if some god had done the same to me?"

The snarl slips past his lips before he can call it in.

"That's what I thought." Her gray eyes fill with sympathy. "I will stay with you, brother. While I will always appreciate what the goddess did to save me, I can't stomach the thought of going back to her now. In fact, if I did go back, I might kill her."

He lets out a breath he didn't realize he'd been holding. "We'll find Nic. And we'll take back Underhill. Together."

SALT OF THE EARTH

I've fallen into a pattern of sorts. A holding pattern. Get up, breakfast with the crew. Skulk back to my room. Sophie and Garret go check on their properties while I entertain Tate and Jedda. Although usually they're the ones entertaining me. Tate is quick and Jedda has a sneaky sense of humor.

Chloe and Angrboda often leave to keep tabs on Hanson and see if they can get any information from beyond the Veil. When they return, we congregate back in the house and pretend like this is a normal way of going on until Chloe or the giantess can catch me up.

I want to scream, to explode. To freaking *do* something.

I haven't spied Nightweaver. Is the former Valkyrie hunting for me even now?

Is Underhill?

I have to take her place. To be a prisoner beyond the Veil. The same punishment that has driven her mad and filled her with hate and bile the likes of which the worlds have never seen. What the fuck is wrong with the gods and the Fates, punishing Loki and Pharaildis the way they do? Why not just

165

kill them and be done with it? Did they really think that torturing them for eons would end well?

"Nic? Is everything all right?" Sophie raps lightly on the cracked paint of the wood doorframe.

I look up from the book I wasn't reading. "Yeah."

"I'm going to bake some cookies."

"Okay," I say slowly, wondering where she is going with this. "Not like you need my permission."

Her teeth sink into her lower lip. She's nervous, I realize. "I was wondering if…you want to help."

I blink in surprise at her suggestion. Usually when I offer to help, she turns me down, tells me to rest up. "Okay, sure."

"Good." She flashes me a quick grin. "Garret took Tate and Jedda out for the afternoon. I figured since we're the only ones here we could talk."

Talk. Now, I get her nervousness. Like some serious talk about how long my needy pregnant ass will be holed up in her house.

"If you want me to go," I begin, even as I wonder where I can go.

Her eyes widen and she blinks. "No, that isn't what I meant at all. It's just, do you have a plan?"

"Not exactly." I get up out of bed. "Let's go make those cookies. It's Chloe's life rule. When in doubt, eat something chocolate."

She smiles and then proceeds me down the stairs.

I sit myself at her cozy little table and watch as she extracts chocolate chips, flour and sugar from a high cabinet. The butter and eggs are already sitting out on the counter. I raise an eyebrow when she pulls out a wooden spoon.

"No electric mixer?"

She shakes her head. "Don't even own one. Besides, I like mixing by hand. It's how my grandmother taught me to bake. All the gadgets remove the love from the process."

"They taste as good to me."

"Just you wait and see." She smiles in that secretive way.

Once the batter is mixed, I grab a tablespoon and start plopping cookies onto the baking sheet.

"You can trust me, you know." Sophie's tone is mild. "Anything you tell me will stay strictly between us."

I stare at her, this older version of me. Odd to think I will never have the laugh lines around my eyes and mouth the way she does. Or the threads of white that shine a little more brightly under the fluorescent lights than the white-blonde strands.

"I'm waiting," I say as I plop another cookie onto the tray.

One blonde eyebrow goes up in inquiry. "For?"

"Aiden, mostly. It doesn't feel right to make plans without him. It's his baby, too." I know he has to be out of his head, wondering if I'm all right. If only we'd been able to cement our bond.

She studies me for a time and it's an effort not to shift under her scrutiny. "Does he know you're pregnant?"

A sigh escapes. "Not unless someone else told him."

She turns and places the first tray of cookies in the oven. "It took me a long time to work up the courage to tell Garret about you."

This surprises me. The two of them seem to have such a close relationship. The kind where partners confide in one another and share all sorts of intimacies. The kind I've never understood. "Why?"

She taps her finger idly on the side of the bowl. "Well, for a start, I didn't think he would stick around. I mean, I'd already done the hard part."

"You mean giving birth?"

"I mean giving you up." She shakes her head. "It felt like I was handing over a piece of myself to strangers and trusting them to do what is right for you. I would lie in bed at night and just...ache. Knowing a part of me was missing."

Tears sting behind my eyes though I'm not sure why. I can never let this woman know that one of those strangers had left me for dead at six. "You didn't trust him after he knocked you up? Garret I mean?"

A chuckle escapes. "It's not as black and white as all that. I didn't blame him or anything. Neither of us had expected to be more than a summer fling. My dad was still alive and I was stuck here. He had a life, a future at a big fancy school."

"So, it was shitty timing?" I wonder if the powers that had placed my reincarnated soul inside Sophie knew she would give me up. Had intentionally driven Garret away so she wouldn't have a choice.

And then I want to kick myself. Of course, they knew, they were the freaking Fates, always dicking with our reality. Even if they hadn't actively kept Sophie and Garret apart, I had every confidence that Addy had foreseen the outcome.

"You could say that. Garret, well, he's adjusted now but there was a time where he stuck out like a sore thumb. A tourist and a city boy all in one."

I was having a hard time picturing Garret walking down a busy city street. Obviously. Sophie knew him better than I did. "So, when did he come back?"

Her lips curve up and her eyes are distant, as though she's lost in remembering. "About three years after I signed the adoption papers. Garret was relentless in pursuing me. He sold his fancy sports car for a beat-up old truck so he could help me transport fish from my father's boat to the market. He just wouldn't go away. We fell into this rhythm that has become our life. Working side by side, taking comfort from each other. And by that point, I was afraid of his reaction when he found out."

Her face is so easy to read, every feeling she's experiencing written right there. I can see why Garret couldn't forget her. No games, no pretense.

It's easy to let a person like Sophie love you. Easier still to love her back.

Sophie lets out a sigh. "When he asked me to marry him, well, I knew the time had come. I couldn't spend the rest of my life with the man and not tell him that we already had a child together. Even though I knew I had to tell him, I dreaded his reaction."

I realized I was holding my breath. "How did he take it?"

She grimaces. "I have never seen him so upset, not before and not since. He went away for a full month and I was sure I would never see him again. And then one day, he came back and offered me this." She plucks her diamond solitaire out of the lopsided ceramic dish. That must be Tate's work.

I look at the ring. "So, he got over being mad?"

She shakes her head. "No, he never has."

I frown. "I don't understand."

"Garret is mad at himself. Because he couldn't protect me." Her smile is inclusive. "Or you."

I look away, deciding not to tell her that he'd essentially admitted he would have pushed for an abortion. Let Sophie keep her Prince Charming up on his noble steed. No need for her to wallow in the muck of reality with the rest of us.

"That's why we waited so long to have Tate. Neither one of us was really sure how to move past what had happened, what we'd missed with you. I guess we just had to get used to each other. And accept that we had changed and grown. That we were growing stronger together."

A lump forms in my throat. "It was like that for me and Aiden at first, too." I confide. "He had to convince me he just wanted to be with me. It was hard to accept."

"But eventually he won you over?"

I nod and then whisper the truth that has been eating me alive. "I'm scared to tell him."

She doesn't ask why or pry any further as we fill up the second tray.

I work some cookie batter out from under my nail. "Did you ever think...that is...did it ever occur to you to look into getting me back?"

She lays her hand over mine. "If I thought there was a way, Nic, I would have come for you. I guess what I'm trying to say is that though maybe our timing wasn't perfect, you were conceived in love. You were wanted very much. You still are."

This time the tears escape unchecked.

The timer buzzes. Sophie turns away and retrieves the first cookie sheet from the oven, giving me a moment to cobble my wayward emotions back together. Stupid fricking hormones.

When at last I feel like myself again there is a cookie sitting on a paper towel in front of me. A glass of milk standing beside it.

I take a bite and smile even as the melted chocolate burns my tongue. "You're right. These do taste better."

AIDEN HATES CITIES. Too many people, too many scents comingling. He stares out the window into the little enclave neighborhood that is just commutable enough to DC to make it expensive as hell.

"This is the place." Liam shuts the engine off and turns to face Aiden. His green eye glows brighter even in full daylight.

"You're sure?" From her perch in the backseat, Harmony hands him a pair of sunglasses to cover the discrepancy. She pulls the hood of the thick parka up to shield her purple face from any prying mortal eyes.

Beside her sits Autumn, one of Liam's wolves. She is a silent presence, but less threatening than Gray or any of the other large male wolves, making her perfect backup for this particular mission. "You're absolutely sure that a giant lives in there?"

"That's the house. It looks the same as I remember it." Liam frowns. "Like exactly, even that gutter that's detached over the garage."

Aiden risks having his olfactory senses overwhelmed and cracks a window. Inhales and cringes. Garbage, rot, chimney smoke, diesel, someone who didn't invest in deodorant… *there*.

"That's a giant's scent all right." He points to a brick ranch that sits by itself at the end of the street. "And glamour so thick it's shellacked over the place."

The four of them exit the rented Camry and walk up the slushy drive to the front door.

The glamour ripples but holds.

"Do you think he'll remember you?" Aiden asks Liam.

Liam shrugs. "We weren't exactly close."

"One way to find out." Aiden raises his knuckles and raps sharply three times.

A pause. He repeats the knock.

"I don't want any!" A gruff voice calls from inside.

"Friendly, isn't he?" Harmony's tone is dry.

"Mr. Carmichael?" Liam calls out.

Bulbous fingers appear around the lace edges of the curtain and one beady bloodshot eye stares out with menace. "Whose asking?"

Liam waves. "I don't know if you remember me, I used to live in that house over there." He points to a white Tudor-style.

"And?" The giant doesn't sound impressed.

"And we need your help," Aiden cuts in. "We're trying to get to a pocket realm."

The hand disappears.

"Too aggressive," Harmony chastises him. "Giants can't be pushed around."

Aiden ignores her and pounds on the door. "Mr. Carmichael!"

A chain rattles and then it's thrown open.

The full sight is…off-putting. In addition to the rheumy eyes covered by skin that droops like a basset hound, the man's ears stick out. The obscene features continue with a large, bulbous nose complete with a forest of untrimmed nostril hair peeking out. Scruffy salt and pepper whiskers cover a saggy chin. He's wearing a stained white t-shirt and denim overalls, with one button unfastened so the look is decidedly off-kilter. His feet are bare despite the cold and his toes are just as ugly as the rest of him.

This is not a being who craves company.

The giant stares at the three of them with displeasure. "And what's in it for me to help you get to a pocket realm?"

Aiden steps forward. "Whatever you want. Please, it's important I get there as soon as possible."

The giant scratches his liver-spotted scalp. Aiden had to give the beast credit, his glamour is repugnant and impeccable. No one who beheld this creature would ever think he could wield magic.

"I don't know. My help don't come cheap." Something in his tone indicates that they just need to find the right price. Then double it.

"If money is what you're after, I assure you—" Aiden begins but Harmony puts a hand on his arm.

"He's not after money. He wants something else. Something of great value." Her gray eyes narrow.

Holding onto his patience by a fraying thread Aiden says, "Whatever the price."

"I want a guard wolf." His eyes go to Autumn with avarice. "To keep the riffraff away and protect my interests. Maybe a pretty buxom one who'll sleep at the foot of my bed at night."

Autumn gives him the finger and the giant chuckles.

Liam growls low in his throat. "Get bent, old man."

"We're not trading you a living creature." Aiden forces himself not to snap.

"Too bad. Maybe I'll call up that nice woman at the FBI and see if she'll reconsider." The dirty, scratching nails move down to Carmichael's chin.

"What woman?" Aiden and Harmony speak as one.

A flash of crooked, yellow teeth. "Oh, so that caught your attention. She offered me a girl, a little Norn, though she didn't know what the creature actually was. Of course, I have no use for a wise woman. I need someone to help protect my treasure." Again, his greedy gaze goes to the she-wolf.

Liam growls again but Aiden holds up a hand. "We're not giving you a wolf, but perhaps I can offer you something better."

"Better than a pretty red-haired she-wolf?" Carmichael's bloodshot eyes look skeptical. "Whatcha got in mind?"

Ten minutes later it was done.

"I can't believe you gave him a dragon's egg." Harmony shakes her head. "An egg you *stole* from Freya no less."

"Call it compensation for the forced detour." Aiden holds up the pink potion that Carmichael assured him was the key to the pocket realm in the Outer Banks. "Are the wolves ready to travel?"

Liam nods. "They're gathering there. I'll drive to the airport, and you can take the car from there."

Harmony and Autumn could. Aiden would be shifting to sparks to get himself across the barrier as soon as possible.

Two exits from the airport, Liam curses. "We're being tailed."

Aiden checks the rearview mirror. "You sure?"

The wolf's jaw clenches. "It turned out of the development with us and is hanging back just enough to be conspicuous."

"Where?" Aiden turns in his seat and spies the black sedan. "Harmony? Any insight?"

She shakes her head. "This isn't part of my vision."

"Try and shake him." Aiden grits his teeth as Liam spins the wheel and cuts down a side alley.

The black sedan follows. The driver fishtails in the middle of the street. The sound of blaring horns and squealing brakes fills the cold winter air.

"Oh, he's not even trying to pretend," Liam grunts.

Aiden rolls his window down. "Head out of the city. Don't meet up with the others unless you're sure you've lost them."

"What are you going to do?" Harmony asks.

Aiden retrieves the vial from his jacket pocket and thrusts it at her. "Stay safe. And whatever you do, don't let this fall into the wrong hands."

He dissembles into a shower of sparks and drifts out the window.

COMEUPPANCE

A ngrboda and Chloe return to find me poring over
family albums with Sophie.

"That was your wedding dress?" I ask, astonished to find it was a pair of cutoffs, a white tank top and a veil.

She shrugs. "I'm not much of a dress girl."

"Funny, neither is Nic," Chloe winks.

"Anything?" I ask when my aunt plops down into the chair next to me.

She helps herself to a cookie and shakes her head, red gold curls bouncing. "Diddly freaking squat."

A knock sounds on the door.

"Are you expecting someone?" Angrboda asks Sophie.

Sophie frowns. "Garret won't be back with the boys until after dinner."

"Nic, stay where you are." Chloe advises me as she moves to the door. "Angrboda, watch them."

A small shiver runs through me. It's not cold. In spite of the relentless wind, the house is warm and comforting, the

fire crackling in the grate. No, it's more a frisson of antic-
ipation.

And suddenly I know who is there.

"Don't!" I rise up out of the chair, knocking the album to
the floor.

Chloe turns to look at me a second before the door is
kicked in by none other than Agent Hanson.

Beside her, her wrists in cuffs stands Laufey, Aiden's
grandmother. And as a giant, she's a key to the pocket realm.

"I only want the girl." Hanson has her weapon drawn.
"Give her to me and no one else will get hurt."

I fight the terror that is clawing at my insides. No, I can't
go back. I *won't* go back.

"Not happening," Chloe snarls. Her eyes begin to swirl.

Before I can blink, Hanson fires her faux Taser weapon
right at Chloe. Light fills the small space crackling blue and
purple streaks. My aunt shudders and collapses to the
ground.

"Quick, out the back," I shove Sophie in front of me
towards the kitchen door. The tranquility of the domestic
scene is shattered with the arrival of one determined FBI
agent.

"I'll cover you," the giantess shouts over her shoulder.

Is Chloe dead? No, that's not Hanson's style. She likes to
play with her prey. If Agent Hanson has the means to fell my
aunt, Sophie and I don't stand a snowball's chance in hell.

Sophie stumbles and I pull her upright. I will get her out
and then double back with Angrboda to rescue Chloe. I'll be
damned if I let that bitch take my aunt.

A growl sounds from my left, and I turn just in time to
see a large black wolf streaking past us down the hill.

I freeze in my tracks. *Aiden?*

It can't be. Yet it is, because a moment later, as he runs

past us toward the black sedan in the driveway, the vehicle fireballs.

"Come on." Another man has appeared from gods alone know where. He's roughly my age with shaggy dark hair. "He told me to get you out."

"My aunt." I gasp as I look up into his different colored eyes. "They have her."

He curses and then begins to…melt. That's the only way to explain his change, with his skin sloughing off and hair sprouting from where it had been.

Within moments he stands before me on four paws. Only the eyes are the same.

Another werewolf?

"Nic!" Harmony, clad in a thick purple parka, races toward me. "You need to get out of here. There are more on the way."

"I can't leave them." Aiden is here, and Hanson has that Taser thing. The sound of weapons being discharged and a snarl from a werewolf. Energy gathers, like an electrical storm. I see Hanson and her team drag three unconscious forms across the frozen ground to her truck. One human, one giant, one wolf.

"No." Power the likes of which I'd never known surges inside me. An eerie wind begins to blow off the churning sound. It pushes my hair back and whips sea spray. It's not the sentient wind from Underhill, not the North wind that I know and love. It is raw, deep and powerful.

And from some dark corner inside me, there is a burning. I stare at the house, door hanging off its hinges, one wall blown out from some sort of magical discharge. Pictures from Sophie's album scattering in the gale. My hatred for Hanson feeds the flames. The inferno erupts from me in a great torrent.

Fireballs explode from my hands, streaking down to ignite the other two vehicles.

"Nic?" Sophie calls my name but I barely hear her. I am beyond hearing. Aiden is here, he came for me. Chloe helped rescue me and if that vision I'd seen of Underhill is true, Laufey was only helping the FBI because Underhill had her lover. I won't let these people take my friends and family away.

They are mine.

It is then, in the heat of battle, that I feel her for the first time. The One True Queen. It isn't movement I sense but intention.

Ours. she whispers.

More power surges through me. It's as though I am a conduit of fire, a lightning rod pulling the blaze from all over the nine worlds to this space and time. The flames meld into streams of fire, bending from the house and encircling the group. My toes don't touch the ground as the wind propels me down the hill. Still more flames spurt out of my hands, causing the conflagration to rage higher and higher.

No more.

I see Hanson first, crouching over Chloe's slumped body.

She looks up, and her lips part, but she recovers quickly. She props my aunt in front of her as a shield.

When I speak I don't recognize my own voice. "Release them or I will kill you all."

Though I see the eyes of several of her task force members go wide, Hanson doesn't flinch. "You had your chance to talk to me and you squandered it. Now I'm going to cut your friends open and see what makes them tick."

"Nic." The cry comes from far behind me. Sophie, scared for me.

She should be scared *of* me. They all should.

I hold out my hand and skew a fireball directly into the

chest of one of the unprotected FBI agents. He shrieks and goes down, rolling in the snow to extinguish the flames.

"Lower. Your. Weapons." Each word speeds from me like a bullet.

This power coursing through me….it isn't mine. Nor does it belong to any of the Unseelie Court. No, this is magic much older and stronger. God power, from the Trickster born of flame and wielded by a fey. My magic is still out of reach, but my daughter's….

Agent Hanson's eyes go to my midsection and I see the unholy light in them. "That child. It's not you, it's the babe."

I see the wolf twitch. Aiden's awake. This isn't how I wanted him to find out.

No time, there is *never* any time for us. The rage I feel is endless, spiraling down into the dark. My gaze turns to the woman who'd tortured me, held me captive. Held Astrid captive.

And now she's dead.

Because of people like Agent Hanson, full of fear, wanting only to spread their misery.

I raise my hand, ready to kill them all where they stand.

"Nic, what is this?" Behind me I hear Sophie pleading. They'd take her too. The woman who gave me life, who'd opened her home and her heart to me.

It's come down to us or them. And it isn't going to be us.

AIDEN LOOKS up and sees Nic hovering above the ground. Her toes are pointed down several inches above the sand. Fire is reflecting in her icy eyes, rage deeper than the water at her back.

Beside him, her aunt moans. On her far side, Laufey's chest rises and falls. They are still alive.

His shock at discovering his grandmother in the vehicle that had been tailing Liam's had nearly made him materialize in the car instead of on its roof. When Laufey had opened the doorway to the portal realm, he'd gone right through, trusting Harmony and the werewolves to follow.

He'd hung back, ready to strike. Never imagining that the FBI would have the means to take down one of the Fates, even temporarily. And whatever that weapon was, it made his knees buckle and his mind check out for a few minutes.

And he'd woken to chaos. And talk of a...baby?

He shakes his head, his ears ringing from the explosion from when he destroyed the SUV.

No, it can't be.

But Nic, the reincarnated queen of the Shadow Throne, is wielding fire. And not fey fire. God's fire pouring out of her.

The change in her scent. It is an addition, but not of another male. Of a child.

She's carrying my child.

But they hadn't...it couldn't be.

Yet in his heart he knows the truth.

Fear pierces Aiden's heart even as the wolf surges to the surface, making a grab to be in charge. *Protect her. Protect them.*

He will. The rest will be sorted out later. He tries to focus all his energy on shifting back to human.

"Nic," the small older woman says from behind his fearsome mate. His eyes turn and looks at the mortal. "Nic, don't hurt them, baby. Please."

"They want to kill us," his mate spits. "It's us or them."

"If you kill them, they will never stop hunting you," the female says. Her voice is choked with emotion. "Please, Nic. I just got you back."

Aiden shakes off the last of whatever that magical stun weapon did and shifts. There are gasps from the outmatched federal agents. Calling his own fire, his palms alight and they fall back. He moves swiftly to the center of the circle, where the agent, Hanson, is fumbling with her weapon. He kicks har arm from behind and the thing goes flying. Angrboda dives for it and plucks it up.

He releases the flames and grasps the woman in charge around the throat. With the enemy secure, he turns to face Nic. "She's right, love. You can't kill them all. They aren't yours."

She lets out a shuddering breath, shaking her head so her blonde hair falls in waves, covering her face. "You don't know, Aiden. You don't know what they did to me in that place. They killed Astrid!" Pain rips at her voice.

The wolf bares his teeth. It wants the taste of this woman's blood.

No. Aiden's will is stronger than the wolf's. He has a mate to protect, and a child on the way. He will not let the wolf out.

Sucking in a deep breath he says, "We're not going to let her go. We're going to take her with us."

"Take her with us." Nic repeats a second before her eyes roll back in her head. Abruptly the flames die out and she falls to the ground.

"Take me where?" Agent Hanson tries to pry his grip from her throat. He grunts as her elbow digs into his solar plexus, but doesn't let go.

His eyes are on his mate.

"You wanted to see where the magic happens? Be careful what you wish for mortal." Angrboda steps forward, weapon aimed at the band of mortal soldiers. "You just, might get it."

With the threat contained, Aiden rushes to Nic's side. Her eyes dart behind closed lids.

Trusting Liam and the other wolves to watch the feds, Aiden carries Nic into the house through the hole in the wall.

He puts her down on the couch. Chloe is brought in by Angrboda who then returns for Laufey. The other woman trails behind him as though in a daze.

"You must be Aiden." The mortal's smile is shaky, but after just witnessing what happed in her back yard, he couldn't blame her. "I'm Sophie, Nic's mother."

Any other time, that announcement would have shocked him. But he is too focused on his mate.

"What's the matter with her?" Sophie puts a hand to Nic's forehead.

"Magic overload," Angrboda's voice is harsh as she settles his grandmother on the rug beside the Fate who had once tried to kill her.

"She's an immortal queen," Aiden says.

But the giantess shakes her head. "She's not a fire wielder by nature. All of that magic came from the child."

"Can you help her?" Aiden asks.

"I'll do my best." The giantess begins chanting under her breath.

Sophie pulls him to the side. "Will she be okay?"

"She's strong." His gaze is focused on his mate, willing his own strength into her to help her heal. "Thank you for keeping her safe. For making sure they are all safe."

She smiles, but her expression is worried. "The FBI?"

"We'll take care of them, Ma'am." This from Liam who stands poised in the doorway. "A word, Aiden?"

"Not now." The growl escapes before Aiden thinks better of it. The wolves have been a tremendous help, he needs to muster some gratitude. But his mate is in his sight and she is pregnant with their child. Nothing can force him from her side.

Instead of leaving though, Liam enters through the damaged siding. "Some of the pack are feeling a little...

nervous about the feds. We don't like the idea of killing mortals, regardless."

"We're not going to kill them," Aiden says, his attention still fixed on Nic. She looks so small and delicate, not the being of immense power he'd witnessed earlier. She reminded him of his father, eyes wild, flames spurting to the sky to illustrate her wrath.

"Taking them to Underhill will be killing them," this from Laufey, who is struggling upright.

He kneels by her side. "What are you doing here?"

She stares at him, her expression bleak. "Had to come. Underhill has Fern. The dead are everywhere."

Aiden pulls in a deep breath. He knows how much his grandmother loves Fern. The same way he loves Nic.

"How is she?" This from Harmony who appears by his side.

Nic's mother does a doubletake as she spots his sister's purple face. Her lips compress, but then her eyes return to where Angrboda is standing to her full height.

"It's done," Angrboda sighs as though exhausted. "She's sleeping now. I'd suggest moving her to a proper bed and letting her wake up on her own."

"I'll show you where she's been staying," Sophie puts a hand on his bare arm. Later, he will probably regret introducing himself to Nic's mother while naked, but at the moment he can't be bothered to give a damn.

In one fluid movement, Aiden scoops Nic into his arms and carries her up the pokey staircase to the room on the top floor. It's cramped but clean and smells of her. He sets Nic down on the candlewick bedspread.

"She knew you'd come for her," Sophie says.

He turns to face her, Nic's mother. "I'm her mate."

She tilts her head to the side. "Do you know what they did to her in that place?"

He swallows and shakes his head. "If I could have taken her place there, I would have."

She lets out a slow breath. "I guess that answers my question of whether or not you'll protect her."

"I live and die for her."

"Don't leave her again. I'll bring you some of my husband's clothes." The mortal says and leaves them alone.

Aiden kneels down beside the bed. So long. He'd waited so long just to be near her again. To be free to love her.

"I'm sorry." He holds her hand brings it up until he can rub his face against it. "I wish I had known about Gretchen, about Fenrir. I should have stayed close to you."

Her breaths are even, her posture relaxed. She doesn't move, not even when his hot tears splash her knuckles.

"I've missed you more than you will ever know," he breathes and then, tentatively slides his hand to her midsection.

A shock goes through him as he feels the life inside her. Winter apples and crackling embers. The One True Queen of the Unseelie Court.

His daughter.

"Hi," he whispers to the life there. "It's your dad."

"Gods, that sounds weird," a soft voice murmurs.

His head jerks up to find her ice blue eyes fixed on him. "Nic?"

Her hand strokes his hair. "You really are here."

"I really am." Grasping her hand, he pulls it to his cheek so that he can nuzzle her.

Her lip trembles and she shifts as though intending to rise.

Alarm fills him at her abrupt movement. "What are you doing?"

Her only answer is to slide off the bed and into his waiting arms. Her body shakes with full spasms as her emotions drain out of her like water through a sieve. He holds her close and breathes her in, not knowing what to say, only sure that nothing will ever come between them again.

UNTIL I HEARD Aiden talking to me, or more accurately, to my stomach, I thought I was having another of those lucid dreams. His scent, that unique combination of cedar, sage and wildness that only Aiden possesses lures me into his waiting arms.

His breaths are ragged as he buries his nose in my hair. "I'm sorry I didn't get here sooner."

I can't speak yet. Words, those tricksy adversaries, elude me. He knows about the baby, about Hanson.

Aiden pulls back just far enough so he can see my face. His eyes flash emerald fire. "What did she do to you?"

I shake my head, not wanting to talk about it.

"Nic," he breathes.

"It's over," I murmur. "I just want to focus on you. I've missed you."

His expression is tight and I can feel his wolf prowling beneath the surface but he just pulls me in tighter.

Now that I've started though, I find there is more I need to tell him, more that can't wait. Into his shoulder I make my apology. "Aiden, I'm sorry. I know you didn't want…that is I didn't plan…."

He stiffens, then sets me back so we are once more looking eye to eye. "What is it, Nic?"

"The baby." Tears are brimming, those hormones getting the best of me once again.

"Hey," he cups my face in his big hands. "Nic, I know you didn't mean for this to happen. Neither of us did. I was there, remember?"

His tone is amused, of all things. I stare at him, unable to comprehend this change of heart. "But you told me you never wanted kids. You were adamant about it."

"I know. I didn't. Not with her." He cups my face in his warm, rough palms. "But you aren't her. You're mine. And this baby will be ours."

Ours. The word sends a hot wave through me that spreads from my heart to my fingertips. It's similar to the way I used to feel about the monsters I had hunted. Possessive. Greedy.

Looking into Aiden's eyes, for the first time I feel hope. Maybe I can do this after all. As long as I have him, anything is possible.

GAME PLAN

"We have to go back," I say to the group gathered around Sophie's kitchen table.

Blank stares from every direction. Sophie's blue eyes are huge as she takes us all in. No doubt we are a motley crew of misfits. Werewolves, giants and serial killers, oh my!

I'm not as confident as I want to be that this is the right move, but after catching up with Aiden, I know there is no alternative. I am a wanted felon on this side of the Veil.

"It's suicide." Angrboda peels the label off a beer bottle. "There aren't enough of us to combat the Draugar."

"I have to agree," Chloe says. She appears better, though there is a large bump on her forehead that she holds her own beer bottle against.

I turn to face my wolf. "Aiden?"

"Where you go, I go. And so will the pack." He chucks a thumb out to the missing side of the house where the majority of the wolves have congregated besides the burnt carcasses of the SUVs.

Pack. While I'd been tortured and experimented on,

Aiden had gone and found himself a pack. And a sister. Lucky for her purple hide. If not for that connection, I would have murdered her for handing Aiden over to Freya. I glare at the seer with dislike.

She glowers back. "You really think we all deserve to die? The fey realm is two worlds out of nine. I say let Underhill have it."

Aiden shakes his head. "It isn't practical. Pharaildis won't stop with killing the fey."

I add my support to his observations. "How long until she finds a way to free Loki? Between herself and Fenrir, Underhill controls the entire Unseelie Court. She wants to kill Aiden. She wants to kill my child to prevent the prophesy of the One True Queen. I won't let her just go ahead with her plans."

Laufey's eye is swollen but she nods. "We can't just abandon our friends and allies. And yes, while I mostly mean Fern, don't forget she holds Soladin, Nahini and the other Fate as well."

"But every dead soldier on our side adds to her army," Angrboda points out. "I say we stay here and try to live in peace."

"Peace?" I gape at the giantess. "Did you not see how they came down on us today like fire from the sky?"

"That was a few mad mortals. You're talking about going up against every being that has ever died beyond the Veil."

"Trust me, there are plenty more like Hanson." I suck in a deep breath and put my hand over my belly. "I'm past the point in my life where my only goal is to stay out of prison. Freedom comes with a price and I am willing to fight for it, for ours and for all the fey."

"As am I," Laufey stands.

Angrboda shakes her head.

"We could really use your help," I say to Chloe.

Her teeth sink into the flesh of her lower lip. "You know I can't interfere with Fate, but I'll do what I can."

"Angrboda?" I face the mother of Fenrir.

The giantess looks around the table, then throws her hands up in the air. "Fine. I guess I'm outnumbered. But don't say I didn't warn you."

"So here's the plan," Aiden folds his hands on the table. "We go in, snag big brother and drag his—er, Gretchen's—carcass back across the Veil."

"Um, isn't Fenrir like royalty?" Liam asks.

"An Unseelie Queen," I say with a nod.

"With magical powers?" Another werewolf, a redhead wearing one of Sophie's long dresses, asks.

It's Aiden's turn to nod. "That's right."

"So, if he's a queen with magic powers, how exactly are we supposed to abduct him?" The eyebrow over Liam's blue eye juts up.

"I know the Underground Palace better than anyone in residence," Aiden says. "The corridors which are collapsed, the ones that have been abandoned, the ones that are undoubtedly guarded. We'll send in a small team to overpower him. All we need to do is avoid Underhill's notice."

"Oh, is that all," Liam snorts.

"I'm going to lure her out," I say.

"No," Aiden snarls.

Which is exactly why I didn't tell him in private. A wolf guarding his pregnant mate who was just sprung from jail is not prone to reason. If I'd told him upstairs, I don't doubt he would have locked me in the room until the meeting was over.

"I have to. She banished me so I'm sure she has some way to track me. I won't do anything foolish—I'll just stay long enough to draw her notice."

Aiden looks ready to argue when Angrboda steps

forward. "Váli is right. You and the babe are far too valuable to risk. I have also been banished, so I will trigger the alarm."

I hold her gaze for a long moment. I see many emotions flickering in the depths of her eyes. Regret, determination, anger.

"All right," I acquiesce. "Chloe and I will wait at the farm." Now that the FBI is out of the picture, it should be safe enough.

The backdoor opens and Garret strides in followed by Tate and Jedda. "Sophie? Are you all right? What the hell happened to the house? And what are all those naked guys doing on our prop—" he looks around at the crowd gathered in his home.

I get up. "Garret, I'm so sorry."

Aiden reaches for my hand and tucks it inside his palm.

Garret's blue gaze goes to the connection and his eyes narrow. "Is this the guy? The one who left you?"

I bristle at the tone. "This is Aiden."

Aiden releases me and reaches out, extending his free hand to shake Garret's. "A pleasure, sir."

Garret offers him a quicksilver smile, takes Aiden's right hand in his left. His other hand balls into a fist. Then there is a crunch. Aiden staggers back, blood gushing from his nose.

"Aiden!" I fall to his side at the same time as Sophie cries out, "Garret!"

Garret ignores both of us, his eyes blazing blue fire at Aiden. "You just count your lucky stars that I'm not armed. That's my daughter and I want to know right now whether your intentions toward her are honorable."

I stare at him, open mouthed.

"Sir, they are, sir." Aiden sounds like a first year cadet instead of a millennia old god.

Garret goes on as if Aiden hadn't answered. "Because if they aren't, I'll hunt you down like the mangey beast that you are. Now, if you'll excuse me, I think I need a drink." Shaking out his hand, he strides into the other room.

Sophie hands me a dishtowel and then hustles over to Tate and Jedda. "Come on boys, bath time." She hurries them out of the room.

"Holy shit." Liam is gaping at the scene. "Dude was lucky you didn't really show him your inner beast."

"I thought you said he was bookish?" Aiden winces as he touches the bridge of his broken nose.

"He is. And I was sure he didn't like me."

Liam snorts. "Yeah, but he's still your dad."

"What are you still doing here?" Aiden snaps at Liam. "I thought you were going."

The other wolf shrugs. "No hurry."

"Well, I guess that means the meeting is over." Angrboda stands up and gives Liam a hearty once over. "If we're going to die tomorrow, I want to find some company for the night. Too bad you're family."

"Yeah," Liam says faintly as he watches Angraboda walk away. "Too bad."

"Dude, quit gawking. She's like your grandmother," I snap.

Liam shakes his head as though to clear it.

"Are you all right?" I hold the cloth gently to Aiden's nose.

"It will be. My pride took the worst of it." He chuckles. "Sucker punched by a mortal. A bookish mortal."

At least he isn't angry. "I guess that's what dads are like."

"I'm just glad he doesn't have any magic, or I'd be nothing but a twitching pulp on the floor."

The others trickle out to make their preparations for our journey.

Aiden removes the towel. The bleeding has slowed and he's healing before my eyes. Tossing the bloody towel in the trash, he offers me his arm. "Take a walk with me."

I clasp his hand. "Want to get out of here before Garret comes back?"

His green eyes are sincere as he holds my gaze. "I just want some time alone with you."

We step out onto the moonlit path and down to the beach. He raises his face to the shining fullness above.

"I guess I need to get used to thinking about the big picture." I slide a hand over my belly.

His smile is soft. "I still can't believe it."

"Me either. I thought Hanson was messing with me at first."

Aiden studies me. "Are you sure you're all right?"

"I will be. Losing Astrid was the worst part." Briefly I tell him about the Norn girl. "Nothing good happens to people who befriend me. Sarah, Astrid, Gretchen."

"Gretchen isn't your fault. From what the wolves tell me, Fenrir is placed randomly in each lifetime."

"It's so odd, to think that Fenrir lives inside of her." I shake my head. "Is it coincidence that he was born into a mortal in the same time in the same town as me?"

"I doubt it." Aiden pulls me into the shadow of the barn. "Nothing is coincidence. Someone somewhere is pulling the strings."

I run a hand along his jawline. "Don't let them catch you, Aiden. You're just as valuable as I am now."

He pulls my knuckles to his lips. "I won't get caught. Not by Underhill or the fey."

"And don't get distracted either." As much as it pains me, I know I can't send him after Fern, Addy, Bard, Nahini and Soladin. "This is about dethroning Fenrir and taking the power out of my mother's hands. With three of the four thrones out of her grasp, she's trapped."

"I won't." He hesitates. "Have you thought about what we do when we get Gretchen back? We may have neutralized the FBI special unit, but that doesn't mean there aren't threats to us here."

"I'm going to help her start the life she wants," I say. "She can get out of town, go to college, and do something great."

"And you think she'll keep our secret?"

"It won't matter. By the time we let her loose, we'll be back on the other side of the Veil. One way or another."

He scrutinizes my face. "You sure you don't want to stay here?"

It's the first time either of us has mentioned it. In many ways, life in Midgard is simpler. Hide in plain sight, pretend to be normal.

"I tried to run away from my responsibilities before. It didn't end well."

We are both silent for a time, enjoying the chill breeze and each other. I want to tell him about what Angrboda said, about me needing to take Underhill's place, but I find I can't bring myself to do it. Instead, I focus on something else.

"Chloe told me you were in Asgard."

"Not by choice." He holds my gaze. "You know I was trying to get to you."

I did. "You said Harmony helped Freya capture you but you never said why."

"Freya," he spits the goddess's name like a curse. "She wanted...well it doesn't matter now. She's not going to get it."

He looks to me and I feel that tug, the connection between us burrowing deeper than I ever believed possible.

"No more secrets," I whisper.

Aiden scrubs his free hand over his face. "She said she wanted to have my child. To protect her from Loki's wrath."

He's mine. A spear of that same possessive energy burns through me. The goddess had been with him, and wanted to take back what was mine.

"Nic?" Aiden let's go of my hand and I see that mine is engulfed in flame. "It's okay. I didn't touch her."

"I'm going to kill her," I murmur. Not with the heat I am feeling but with cold detachment, with surety.

"You can't. If Underhill is successful, the gods of Asgard will all be needed at Ragnarök."

I say nothing. Where there's a will, there's a way and I have some magic on tap, thanks to our baby.

"How do I control this?" I ask holding my hand aloft like a torch.

Aiden studies my hand. "Try and picture dousing the flames in your head, like you're coving the fire with a jar."

I concentrate, but the flames burn brighter. "It's not working."

He covers my hand in his again, the two of us burning together. "This power is different from mine. It's tethered to you but also to the child. And she can feel what you feel."

Without warning he sinks down to his knees and presses his face against my stomach. "Hey now, little one. It's all right. I'm going to take good care of your mommy and you."

The flames wink out.

Aiden looks up at my hand and smiles. "Have you thought of any names yet?"

I shake my head.

He rises to my feet and then takes my hand again as if nothing had happened. It's these moments with him I love best. The times when I can forget the things I've done and the destiny lurking around the next corner. It doesn't matter that he's a wolf god and I'm an uncrowned fey queen. We're just Nic and Aiden, strolling in the moonlight.

I stop and pull him close. "Promise that you'll take care of her. Genetics are against her, with Pharaildis on my side and Loki on yours. You're the only good influence she will have."

"She'll have you," he murmurs with total sincerity.

I love that Aiden sees me as good, even though I'm not. "How can you possibly say that after all the things I've done to you? All the pain and the suffering I've caused. Don't you know the Unseelie are wicked by nature?"

He shakes his head. "No, they aren't. You aren't. I see you and where you come from." He gestures back to the house. "All good things. No amount of Loki's DNA can fuck that up."

I let out a relieved breath, the first one since I found out I was with child. "I don't know what kind of mother I'll be."

"The best kind." He grins. "Because unlike my mother, your priorities are in order."

I've never heard him talk negatively about Sigyn before. "What changed your mind?"

"Harmony." He picks up a rock and bounces it in his palm, then chucks it out into the sound. "I guess I never felt worthy of her love. Nari was gone and I'd killed him. So there was no going back for me. I accepted that she stayed by Loki's side even when he treated her like dirt because she didn't think I was any better. But to have a newborn babe and give her over to Freya...?"

"That's messed up."

His expression is grim. "She's a coward. That's not loyalty. She's no better than Lachesis leaving you alone without your memories. Call a spade a spade. It's neglect and abandonment."

I've never heard him talk this way before and tilt my head to take him in. In the short time we've been out, his nose has healed completely and he is just as physically flawless as he was the first time I saw him. But there is a change that goes beneath the surface, a new light around him. "You seem...different."

He threads his fingers through mine. "I feel different. Better. Whole."

I smile. "Because we're together?"

He shakes his head. "I mean that's part of it, but it's more than that. You are my world, and our daughter will be too. But Nic, I feel…content. I'm at peace with myself and with the wolf."

Acceptance. I smile and squeeze his hand. "That makes me so happy to hear, you have no idea, Aiden. I want you to smile more, to laugh more."

"As my lady commands," he bows low over my hand.

"None of that," I wait until he stands upright then press my lips to his. He tastes of coffee and cold air and Aiden. His unique scent of cedar and sage mingle with the wildness of the man I love. The wolf I love.

He holds me close, allowing me to play, to kiss and touch him as I will. So new, these feelings are still so new for me, for us. The building heat, the surge of need to get closer, to be closer. Yet they are right.

"Nic," he breathes. "That's a gallows kiss."

I pull back. "Maybe it is. Maybe I'm worried."

He traces my lips with his fingertip. "You, my brave beautiful mate, have nothing to worry about. Nothing will keep me from you. Not your mother, my father, not even the end of the worlds."

I swallow and nod. "You promise you'll come right back?"

He nods. "Right back. But that's not for several hours yet. Do you have any ideas on how we should pass the time?" His grin turns wicked.

I look around and raise my eyebrow. "Here?"

He shakes his head and snags my hand in his. I feel my body coming apart a bit at a time as he shifts us to sparks. Then we are drifting up and up and up into the air, back to the house and in through the open window to my attic room.

We come together, minus any sort of clothing.

"Do you want to get punched in the nose again?" I hiss. "You are courting Garret's wrath."

"I'll risk it." He pulls me in tighter. "For you, I'll risk everything."

His fingers tunnel into my hair and he cups my head, holding me in place while he slowly explores my mouth.

My skin tingles at every point of contact. I touch his body in a sensual exploration. His hands shift lower. I shiver under his touch, goosebumps rising along my arms and legs.

"Cold?" he murmurs.

"It isn't that. I'm just so aware. Physically, I mean."

His eyes are burning green flames as he leads me over to the bed. "You know now that I am going to have to take shameless advantage of that admission."

"Rogue," I tease.

He laughs. "I love this."

"What?" I tilt my head.

"Seeing you happy." The skin around his eyes crinkle. "Maybe even because of me."

He's so strong, almost indestructible. He knows who I am, what I can do and yet he admits that vulnerability to me.

But I've changed, too. "You definitely have something to do with it." I frown, trying to put into words what it was like being separated from him for so long. Somewhere along the way I've changed for this man. Maybe because of him. I never used to be a person who teased. Who cared.

"I KNOW, Nic. I felt your absence acutely." He takes my palm, raises it to his lips then places it over his heart. "Every beat is tainted without you."

With the worlds coming down around our ears and my life in turmoil, there's nothing to anchor me.

Except for Aiden.

His touch is soft as he sweeps one fingertip over the column of my neck, down through the hollow of my throat. My head falls back, my eyes sliding shut at the contact. This is what I've been craving, been yearning for every night. More of this.

More of him. My Aiden.

He takes his time, tracing my collarbone first with his fingers, then with his tongue. "So beautiful," he murmurs before delivering another light lick.

My fingers tunnel in his midnight hair to hold him close and keep him exactly where he is. For all time. "Make love to me," I breathe.

He pulls back. "You're sure?"

I roll my eyes. "It's not like you're going to get me more pregnant."

"That's not what I mean." He threads his fingers through mine. "I wanted to wait until you were really ready."

"I am really ready," I tell him. "Give me a night to remember, Aiden."

"The first of many," he growls.

And then does.

Through the Man's Eyes

"Why do you have to go already?" Nic asks as he climbs from the bed.

She is beautiful there in the dawn light, the sun's early rays bathing her white blonde hair in their glow. The ends are darker, where the dye has grown out. He can't help but reach out and run his fingers through the spun silk.

"I didn't mean to wake you. I just heard someone—"

Three quick knocks on the door and then a tentative voice calls through the door. "Nic?"

"Just a second, Sophie." His mate struggles out from under the sheets and plucks a t-shirt off the ground.

"Find your pants," she hisses at him.

Aiden glances around, finding the rumpled denim. Nic makes an impatient gesture with her hand, until he is covered.

"You could open the door, you know. She already saw all there was to see."

She wrinkles her nose as if the thought of her mother beholding his nude body is unthinkable.

The zipper is stuck and he grates, "Half the pack was naked on her property yesterday."

"So not the point. She's my mother." Nic shakes her head. "We're going to have to agree to disagree about the nudity thing."

"Just as long as I get to see you unclothed whenever possible."

The corner of her mouth curls up as if his honest statement pleases her.

"I can come back," Sophie's tone is hesitant.

Nic opens the door. "Hey, Sophie. Sorry, I know I owe you an explanation. Do you want to come in?"

"It's okay Nic. I think…whatever it is that's going on is a bit outside my comfort zone. So please don't try to explain."

Nic squeezes the doorframe so hard her knuckles turn white. "We're leaving today. And we'll get the house fixed."

"Don't worry yourself, honey." Sophie shakes her head and then holds out a stack of men's clothes that smell of her husband. "Those…men are asking for Aiden. I figured he was with you."

He nods. "Liam is probably ready to go."

Nic doesn't speak, her expression inscrutable. His wolf shifts, sensing his mate's unhappiness.

"We'll be down in a few minutes. Thank you for the clothing." Aiden reaches out and takes the offering from Sophie.

After her footsteps retreat, he drops the pile on a nearby stool then moves to wrap his hand around her nape. "What is it?"

She looks up at him, pure torment in her eyes. "I want to go with you."

His heart hurts. "Nic, you can't. You have been banished. She'll sense if you cross the Veil."

She waves her arm as if he can erase the logic of his words with that single gesture. "I just got you back and I have been doing nothing for what feels like an eternity."

"You aren't doing nothing." He places his palm over the small swell of her belly. It's hardly noticeable, even to his keen senses. "You're protecting our child."

"You're the protector, not me," she grumbles.

He pulls her in close and buries his nose in her hair. "You know if we had any other choice I wouldn't go. The wolves don't know the Underground Palace the way I do. We're more likely to succeed if I lead the charge."

She presses her face into his bare shoulder and mumbles, "I know that."

What else can he say to reassure her? "It'll be a quick operation, with Angrboda spearheading the distraction." They'd gone over the plan the day before. Everyone has a role to play.

"I know that, too."

"And you know I'm coming back. That I'll meet you at the farm?" With Agent Hanson's team being dropped in Underhill, Nic was eager to return to the place she felt the most secure.

"Yes." She pulls back until she stares up into his eyes. "But Aiden, I'm scared."

That admission…. He never would have believed the icy girl she'd been when he first met her, the stone cold killer, would admit to her feelings of helplessness and terror.

He never would have thought she would accept him. Or that he was eager to meet their child.

But first they had to secure her a place.

"Tell me what you fear."

She places her hand over his on her abdomen. "Everything that's coming."

Because of the child. The danger on both sides of the Veil. Because no matter how much he wants to reassure her, there are things out of his control.

"So am I," he breathes, pulling her close again. "But we won't let her win, Nic. We both have too much to fight for. To look forward to. I have a house to build you."

For a moment she looks as though she wants to say something. But then her eyes close and she nods once. "Okay. The sooner you go, the sooner you'll come back."

And really what more is there to say?

He presses his lips to her forehead. "Time to kidnap a werewolf."

PARTING WAYS

Angrboda uses her magic to slip Aiden and the wolves out of the pocket realm and into an in-between. Since she is planning to appear in a different location to draw Underhill's attention, they will have to cross back over through the Tear.

It's a sound plan. Yet I can't seem to shake the worry knotting my gut.

Someone knocks on my bedroom door and Chloe sticks her head in. "You ready to leave?"

No, but I'd promised Garret and Sophie that we would all be out of their hair as soon as possible. Giant contractors have already been called to repair their house and we need to be gone before they arrive.

I worry my lower lip. "Do you really think it's safe for us to return to the farm?"

She nods. "The mortals are all under Angrboda's thrall. They won't reveal anything."

It had been the giant's idea to enthrall Agent Hanson and the rest of the FBI. They would serve the creatures beyond the Veil for a year and a day—Underhill time— and be returned after our fight was over.

I swing my feet down and reach for my borrowed shoes. "I'll be ready in a minute."

Chloe wrinkles her nose delicately. "It smells like werewolf and nookie in here."

"Feel free to show yourself out."

She sighs and then turns to go.

"Chloe?"

"Yeah, babe?"

I hesitate. "Do you think…that is, should you mindwipe them? Sophie and Garret, I mean."

They'd witnessed a lot. I didn't want to leave them as a loose end, or have anyone come after them for information on us.

Chloe holds my stare. "Do you want me to mindwipe them?"

"No." Having been mindwiped myself out of my first six years of life, I knew how upsetting the experience could be. "But maybe that's why I should. To keep them safe."

She comes back into the room and shuts the door. "Maybe you need to give them the choice. True, they will be safer if they don't know who you are and what you can do, but I don't know if that necessarily means they will be more content. You're their daughter, Nic."

I nod. "Okay, I'll be down in a few."

"Laufey and I will wait in the car."

I take one final glance around the room. This could have been mine, if things had been different. Somehow, I doubt my life would be on the same path if I'd been raised by kindhearted Sophie and honorable Garret. I wouldn't be the same person I am now.

Chloe and Addy had encouraged me to kill, to use my gift

to make a difference. Here, I would have maybe hurt an innocent by accident, maybe even Tate.

Everything happens for a reason.

I leave the door open and head downstairs. Sophie is at the stove. She is wearing a cream-colored sweater and black leggings. Her hair is tucked up into a messy ponytail that bobs as she moves. "I'm just making you a fried egg sandwich for the road."

"Thanks," I say even as my stomach knots. No way can I eat anything, but I've discovered that Sophie cooks to ease her own tension and worry as much as to feed the people around her. She's been practically chained to the stove since the day before.

She turns to look at me, her expression sad. "You don't need to leave."

"I do." I swallow past the lump in my throat. "You don't know what it's meant to me that you took us all in. I can never repay you."

A clomping of boots on the stairs and Garret appears. His goatee is neatly trimmed and he is tucking his plaid shirt into well-worn jeans.

"Is that boy gone?"

I assume he means Aiden and I nod. "He is. Listen, there's something I want to ask the two of you."

Garret pours himself a mug of coffee and settles in across the table. "Go ahead."

"Chloe has a way to erase your memories."

"Like what the giant did with the FBI?" Sophie's eyes are round.

"No, that's a thrall. The person under it won't remember what they're doing after it ends. A mindwipe erases memories that have already formed," I let out a sigh. "It might be safer for all of you if you don't remember any of this happened."

"No," Sophie is already shaking her head. "Absolutely not. I want these memories."

"Garret?" I turn and face my sire. "How about you?"

"I'd like to forget a lot of things," he makes a face at the hole in his wall. "This entire living situation has been strange. But I don't want to erase knowing you, Nic." He pats my hand.

A lump forms in my throat and I remember the way Garret had decked Aiden, his misplaced gesture to protect my honor

"What about Tate?"

They share a look and I can see the worry for their youngest child in their eyes.

Garret appears uncomfortable. "It might make it easier for him."

"Once the memories are gone, can they ever come back?" Sophie asks.

I shake my head. "I still remember nothing before my sixth birthday."

She swallows. "No, then. He deserves to know. He can keep a secret. Besides, who is he going to tell here?"

"Okay." With nothing else to do, I stand and pick up the paper sack containing our breakfast sandwiches. "Thank you for everything—"

The words are barely past my lips when both of them pull me into a tight embrace.

"You come back anytime," Sophie whispers. "Whatever you are, whatever you are running from, know you will always have a place with us."

Garret grunts in a way that I take as agreement.

Tears track down my face. Stupid hormones.

I sniffle and then pull away. "Take care of each other."

"And I want pictures when that baby is born," Sophie scolds.

I smile and nod. "Agreed." I'm not sure how I'll send pictures from across the Veil, but wouldn't that be a nice problem to mull over?

Through the Man's Eyes

THEY APPEAR in the collapsing tunnel outside the kitchen of the Underground Palace. Aiden, Liam, Owen, Autumn and Gray. All but Aiden and Liam are in wolf form.

Liam's multihued eyes dance with excitement in the dim light. Aiden doesn't speak, just inhales and moves down the hallway to the servant's stairs that lead to the bedchambers.

It is dark in the catacombs, but that isn't saying much, since direct daylight never strikes the halls. Aiden moves closer to Liam so he can whisper low. "Royal bedchambers are on the top floor. We need to subdue him and get him back down to this location without alerting anyone else."

Liam nods and gestures for Aiden to lead the way.

The air is thick as though being bogged down by fear and pain. They pass the empty throne room, and Aiden shivers as the Shadow Throne seems to reach out for him. Fickle damn magic in that chair. He never would have believed Fenrir could have taken it.

He pauses and draws to a halt.

"What is it?" Liam asks.

Aiden strides forward. The magic he's feeling isn't coming from the Shadow Throne, but from the Fire Throne. He frowns. All the magic is coming from the one seat.

"Aiden," Liam hisses.

Shaking his head, Aiden follows them through the room and to the secret spiral staircase that leads directly to the queen's chambers.

There are several sentries on the landing, which the wolves dispatch with ease. He and Liam catch the armor-coated bodies before they can hit the ground.

He sucks in a breath as one helmet clatters down the stairs, raising enough of a racket to wake the entire castle. But after several breaths and no one comes to investigate, he knows Angrboda has done her job well.

Then he is at the door, the familiar chamber he'd shared with Nicneven for centuries. The door is solid oak with intricate patterns of air magicked into the wood. He tries the latch, isn't surprised to find it locked.

He nods to the others and then shifts to sparks, squeezing his form a bit at a time through the keyhole.

Aiden takes stock of the space before reforming to unbolt the heavy door. The fire dances in the grate, the covers on the bed are piled high, and soft snores emanate from within the space.

He comes together and unbolts the door. It's Liam who carries the potion Angrboda concocted to subdue Fenrir. Aiden gestures the wolf forward and takes the potion from him. Maybe this will go smoothly if they can just—

Fenrir's eyes flash open.

They stare at each other for an endless moment before his half-brother leaps forward, crashing into him. The bottle goes rolling across the moonstone floor. Thankfully, it doesn't shatter.

Snarls erupt from the human girl's mouth as she bares her teeth at him. "I'll rip your throat out."

She's strong, stronger than Aiden. But unlike him, Fenrir can't transform.

Aiden dissolves into embers, until Gretchen's body is face down on the floor. The wolves charge and Liam vaults over them to pin her flat on the floor. She thrashes, swearing and feral.

Aiden recombines and picks up the bottle. "Flip her over. Hold her mouth open."

Liam does as instructed and Aiden crouches low and tips the contents to Gretchen's mouth.

She spits some of it out but he dumps the rest in as she sucks in a breath. Liam pinches her nose until she is forced to swallow the liquid.

"How long until it takes effect?" Liam asks as the girl tries to bite his hand.

"I don't—"

Gretchen falls limp.

"That long." Aiden smirks and then helps his nephew up.

Liam stares down at her, shaking his head. "Nice to see you again, da."

Aiden hoists her over his shoulder. "Come on, let's get out of here."

THE FARM LOOKS DIFFERENT. Like something I've seen on television before and is somehow less impressive in person. There is no smoke curling from the chimney, no signs of life at the veterinary clinic.

"How are you holding up?" Chloe asks Jedda who is settled in the back seat with a book.

"Fine, your ladyship."

"I love his manners." my aunt winks and then pops the door. "Come on. I'm sure all the food in the fridge is bad by now, but I can probably scare us up some veggie chili."

"I'll be along in a second," I say.

She studies me carefully, but in the end nods and guides Jedda inside the farm house.

I head into the barn. It is not much more than an old hay barn, hasn't worked as more than a garage for years. I let out a breath at the familiar smells. Clean, fresh air. Freedom.

I would have done anything to get it.

Scratch that, not anything. I'm not my mother.

Putting one foot in front of the other, I climb up into the hayloft and sit facing the west, to the setting sun. How much time has passed in Underhill? How long will Aiden and his friendly neighborhood wolves be gone?

"I was wondering where you'd gone." A voice says from the corner.

I look up unsurprised to see Nightweaver. "Have you been here long?"

She shrugs. "Time really isn't relevant to me anymore."

I hear that. "What do you want, Nightweaver?"

"Freedom."

A chill goes through me. "What do you mean?"

She tips her head to the side. "You needed me for a single purpose, to find the spirits of the Wild Hunt. That was long ago, yet you've kept me tethered to them."

"You know the rules. Once a soul is claimed by The Wild Hunt it belongs to the Hunt for eternity."

She hisses, her hideous birdlike face pulling up in revulsion. "You aren't even a queen any longer, not even a fey. The Wild Hunt belongs to another. And yet I made a vow to serve *you*. Release me."

"You also made a vow to Underhill."

She stares at me, her dead gaze unblinking.

I swallow and then shake my head. "I'm sorry, but I can't."

"You won't. Selfish fey bitch. You're no different than you ever were." Mist rises up through the barn and she vanishes out the open window.

I put my head in my hands. Maybe Nightweaver is right. I could let her go. What is one spirit compared to all the rest of The Wild Hunt? But if I release her, I have no one to tell me what's going on across the Veil. Nightweaver is my only connection and spy or no, I refuse to give that up.

A chill travels up my spine and I look to see another ghost lingering in the space. It's the FBI agent who'd shot Astrid. "What are you doing here?"

He shakes his head, his mouth opening and shutting like a fish out of water.

I blow out a tired breath. "Okay, pal here's the skinny. You're dead, I killed you and your soul belongs to The Wild Hunt. They are across the Veil in a land called Underhill. You follow?"

He scowls but then nods.

"What's your name?"

"Hank. Hank Yates."

"Well, Hank Yates. You work for me now."

He didn't like that. I can see the flare of resentment on his face.

"I have one job for you. About three miles in that direction," I point to illustrate. "There is a tear in what we call the Veil. Go there and tell me the instant anyone crosses through it onto our side, okay?"

He looks as though he's going to argue, but then dissipates. Nahini told me it's difficult on the new ones. That they don't understand where they are or how they are different. They don't know why they are compelled to obey me.

I lie back in a pile of hay. It pokes through my sweater, making my skin itch but for the first time in weeks, I am where I belong.

"Nic?" A voice calls my name.

I sit up and then look around, utterly disoriented. "Hello?"

A head pops through the opening by the ladder. Jedda has shed his glamour and again has taken on the silver-blue skin that is so reminiscent of his father. "Chloe said I should come get you. That dinner is ready."

"Thanks." I stretch muscles stiffened by the cold. "Any word from the other side?"

Slowly he shakes his head.

I follow Jedda down the ladder and into the house. It smells of hot spices and dust, a side effect for having stood empty for the better part of a month.

"There you are. Dinner's on the table."

"Where's Laufey and Harmony?" Their car had been right behind ours.

"Went for a walk." Chloe turns to the fridge and extracts a bottle of wine.

"Chloe?" I ask, eyeing Jedda. I'm not sure how much I want to say in front of the boy king.

"What is it?" She tips the entire bottle into one huge glass.

"Nothing." I tuck some hair behind my ear and concentrate on getting some food into my system.

"What are you going to name your baby?" Jedda asks.

I pause with the spoon partway to my mouth. "You know, I haven't really thought about it."

"How about Addy?" His question is innocent but a cold shard spears into my heart. "That's your other aunt's name, right?"

Chloe and I exchange a look. "It is," I say at length.

Jedda nods. "My father said it is important to keep names within families so that the beings who matter know where they come from."

"How about Addison Sophia?" Chloe says softly.

I smile at the suggestion. Addison Sophia Jager. Because I want the baby to carry Aiden's last name. Rutherford is just something my aunts made up to help me fit in.

"I'll suggest it to Aiden."

The next time I saw him. Which I hoped would be soon.

SNAG

"I t's gone," Liam breathes as he touches the wall that had been an in-between.

Cold chills travel down Aiden's spine. "Underhill must have moved it. She knows we're here."

The wolves stare at him, waiting. He doesn't know what to tell them. If Underhill didn't know where they are, she'll soon find out. There is only one path left to them.

"We'll have to cross through the tear," he says. "Follow me."

Taking off at top speed, Aiden runs down the hall to the kitchen. The pack is hot on his heels. They burst through the kitchen, startling cooks into dropping their spoons and leaping onto counters. Most of the servants are enthralled humans, like the FBI. But some are low magic fey who work for the scraps that fall from the royal tables.

"It's him," one fey woman cries. "The one Underhill has been hunting!"

Shit. Aiden picks up speed. Liam is less than a pace behind, the three other wolves flanking them.

"Take her." Without slowing, Aiden shoves Gretchen into Liam's outstretched arms. "I'll try to lead them away."

Fey lights flare up in the darkness outside the underground palace.

"Stay with us!" Liam yells. "Aiden, it's too risky!"

"I won't let them catch me." He's the one they want, there's no doubt in his mind. He shifts to sparks, flitting up over the underground lake, rising higher and higher through the gossamer strands of reflective webbing and into the fresh air beyond.

Even with Underhill's ability to change the landscape, he can still feel the tear to the east. The wrongness of it, the sucking void of darkness. He heads north, planning to double back once he is sure Liam and the others have had enough time to pass through to Midgard.

Up and up he drifts into the night sky. Behind him, all sorts of winged creatures take flight, following, tracking him. Their wings blot out the moon as they swarm behind him.

He dives down into the icy mountain peaks, his sparks barely clustering together enough to keep him intact. One hundred feet from the snowline, then fifty, twenty. At ten feet he shifts again into his wolf form, his pads hitting the snow with enough force to make the peak shake.

Aiden runs. He charges down the hill, ducking into the trees to keep the winged fey at a disadvantage. Spells are hurled in his direction, bright balls of light igniting like fireworks in the blue-black haze of the night.

He runs harder, zig-zagging across the ground. The evergreens thin out into an open space. There are more trees dead ahead if only he can reach them.

He hears the crack first and thinks the fey have brought down trees to block his path. And then the ice beneath his paws splinters. He tumbles into the frigid water.

The cold penetrates to his marrow. He struggles and

fights, but his head dips down beneath the water, then bumps up against the intact ice at the far side of the fissure.

He tries to shift but the wolf's panic bubbles up. The beast hates water deeper than his knees. He bucks and struggles, trying to fight his way free.

We're both going to die if you don't stop, Aiden tells the beast.

The wolf relents enough and allows him to shift.

The sparks lift up again. All the water stays in the pond.

"Gotcha." A gossamer net falls over him.

The chains force another shift on him. He crashes to the ground in his human aspect. Naked and freezing on the ice.

A face looms over him.

Rodrick.

"Somebody wants a word with you."

ANGRBODA LANDS in her giantess form on the far side of the tear.

The land beyond her writhes with bodies of the dead. Some intact, others with visible mortal wounds. Still others nothing more than bones. It is the magic which animates them the evil magic of the runes.

The giantess pulls her ax from across her back and releases the hold on her glamour. She grows larger, towering over the army of corpses.

The dead don't move forward, don't move at all.

As if they are waiting for something.

"I told you never to come back here," Underhill murmurs.

Angrboda stares down at the small female figure who strides out from the ranks. She's a beautiful woman, with hair the color of midnight under a new moon. Her dark eyes though, are as dead as her army.

"You won't win, Pharaildis."

"I already have, Hag of the Ironwood. I have Loki's son."

Angrboda swallows. Váli and the others are lost.

She turns, planning to leap back inside the tear and warn Nic, but with a snap of her fingers, Underhill alters the world around them. The plain disappears. Instead, they stand in a frozen wasteland.

"What do you want?" Angrboda faces the threat.

"From you? Nothing but your death."

"You'll have to do better than this puny army," Angrboda grows larger still, letting her powers have free reign. For a moment she basks in the free magic, there for the taking. Midgard is nothing like this.

But Underhill's smile never fades. "Goodbye, Hag of the Ironwood."

She strides off through the dead, who close ranks around her.

And then they too begin to grow. With each step, their height increases until they become taller than the trees, the mountains.

Taller than her.

She swings her ax, connects. But weapons can't kill what is already dead. Desperate she strikes out with her magic, blasting those nearest her away.

She is grabbed from behind, tossed down hard enough to make the ground tremble.

The ground shakes as the swarm over her tear into her. And carried on the wind is her former lover's mad laughter....

I awake, the scream bursting from my lips. No. *No.* It can't be real, it can't.

Yet it felt real.

My palms are saturated with sweat and my hands tremble. Throwing off the covers, I head into my bathroom and turn on the light.

My blue eyes look haunted.

These hallucinations can't be real.

Yet what had Harmony said about the gifts of those who've been snatched away from the clutches of death? They manifest in different ways. Dreams were how I'd remembered my past life. And Nahini said those threads could lead to the future as well.

I'd had one every time I'd slept, except when I'd slept in Aiden's arms.

Aiden. If that dream was real and Nightweaver had really betrayed me, Aiden and the wolves are in danger.

I splash water on my face, then pull on an oversized bathrobe and head out into the main sitting room.

Chloe is curled up on the couch, her gaze locked on the fire. "Couldn't sleep?"

"More bad dreams," I tell her.

"You want to talk about it?"

I shake my head. "What good does talking do?"

She looks at me for a long moment, then gets up and moves to the kitchen.

"What are you doing?"

"Making hot cocoa."

"Why?"

She looks over at me. "Because if I learned one thing from your mother, cooking something is better than doing nothing."

A fist pounds on the front door so hard it rattles in its frame. I leap up but Chloe is faster.

"Where is he?" I ask when I see Liam standing on the far side of the door, three wolves at his heels and Gretchen slung over one shoulder. "Where's Aiden?"

Out on the front lawn, his wolves are shifting in that horrible melting way of theirs.

"We got separated," Liam gasps. He carries an unconscious Gretchen into the room and lays her on the couch. "Did it work?"

Chloe shakes her head. "No way to know until she wakes up."

"You left him?" Damn it, I knew I should have gone with them.

"He gave her to me and just did that fire thing he does." Liam swallows. "I have no way to keep up."

"It wasn't our fault," Gray comes through the door, snagging a blanket off the bench seat. Unlike Aiden, most of the werewolves had been human and possess a sense of ingrained modesty. "Underhill changed the in-between. We had to cross through the tear."

I shudder at the memory of crossing through the rip in the Veil, the angry jagged pieces populated by the souls of the damned. "I'm going after him."

"Nic, no," Chloe is on her feet. "Aiden can take care of himself."

I ignore her, stepping into my boots. "He's public enemy number one so far as Underhill is concerned."

"Until she finds out that you are there!"

"Then I'll have to be sneaky." I storm into my room searching for my trusty backpack. Without paying too much attention to what I grab, I fill it full and then head for the door.

"Think about this a minute," Chloe begs. "We can put out a call for help. Freda and the others—"

"There's no time. You know as well as I do that time moves differently over there. She intends to kill Aiden and free his father."

"And what about your baby?" Chloe snags my arm on the front porch. "What about little Addison Sophia? You're not just risking your own life now, Nic. You have her to think about."

I swallow. "I know that, Chloe. Believe me, I do. And I am thinking about her and how much I want her to be born, not die in the womb like my last child."

Her eyes fill with tears. "Nic."

I yank myself free. "Listen to me. Underhill isn't going to hold Aiden captive. She is going to cut him open and use pieces of him to unbind his father. I've seen it, she tried to do it to Addy while she was disguised as Aiden."

Chloe pales.

When she doesn't respond I add, "Think, Chloe. If Loki gets free, there will be nowhere safe. The end of the worlds."

Chloe grumbles something under her breath. "Fine. But you're not going alone."

I gape at her. "What?"

She pulls her coat off the hook at the back of the door. "You heard me. You and Addy think you can just leave me here keeping the home fires burning like some 1940s housefrau? No way. I'm done sitting on the sidelines. And if the universe doesn't like one fate messing with the timeline, it will hate two."

I stare at her. "This could mean your life."

She gives a rueful shrug. "Then that much more chocolate for the rest of you. Come on. Let's go."

THE TRUCK FISHTAILS on the gravel roads as we race for the tear. My stomach lurches and my dinner threatens to make a comeback.

Chloe murmurs inaudibly under her breath. I don't know if it's some sort of spell or incantation, or maybe just a self-directed pep talk. My own thoughts need to settle.

Crossing through the tear is dangerous and not just because of the mental and physical strain. It's a fixed point, one that is easily monitored from both sides.

Which is why I sent the newbie ghost to keep a lookout.

"So, what's your plan?" Chloe asks.

I shake my head. "Find Aiden and get to him before my mother guts him like a trout."

She wrinkles her nose. "Okay one, that's icky. And also, that doesn't sound like much of a plan."

"You're right." I glance over at her. "But it's the best I've got."

We pull into the woods alongside the tear. I shift my vision to the spirit plane. The tear has grown even larger since the last time I saw it. It stretches from five feet above the ground to a mile above the surface of the earth.

"Shit," Chloe says as we see the magnitude of it.

"It shredded Nahini's horse." I say, still hearing the deafening screams as the creature was pulled apart. "But the wolves made it through."

"It might be less severe over there." Chloe sounds doubtful.

"Why is it getting worse?" I ask.

She shakes her head. "No idea. But when it reaches the ground level on this side anyone or anything can cross."

Meaning the Draugar. The dead might walk right on through and start terrorizing the good people of Western North Carolina.

I swallow and secure my backpack over one shoulder. "Let's go."

"You must go back!" A voice calls, startling us both.

I turn and behold the two women, side by side. Aiden's sister, the traitor Harmony.

And the goddess of love and beauty herself.

My lip curls in revulsion. "Goddess or no, if you stand between me and Aiden I will end you. Freya."

She stares down at my belly as though she can see the pregnancy within. "You can't cross, not while you are with child."

"Then I'll find another in-between. Midnight isn't far off.

219

The largest in-between in the world." One I had crossed though before.

"No, Nic. You need to listen." Harmony holds out her hands, palms facing me. "I promised him I wouldn't let you go after him, no matter what."

"And you think this is the right way to go about it? Go running back to the goddess to tattle on me?"

Freya lifts her chin. "The dead swarm over the fey lands without cease. There is nowhere to hide. You are marked. If you cross, you will be overwhelmed and torn apart." Her gaze holds mine. "Just as Angrboda was."

I sway on my feet. "It was real?"

The goddess tilts her head, studying me. "You know it was."

Angrboda's...dead. The giantess who was literally larger than life, who risked her neck so I wouldn't have to go....

My throat feels raw as if I've been screaming. The world tunnels and I shake my head, trying to fight off the dizziness, the overwhelm.

"Nic?" Chloe's hand is on my back. It is only then that I realize I've fallen to my knees. "What have you done to her?"

"Nothing. I am here to protect her and Váli Sigynjarson's child," the goddess says.

Shoving my grief into one of those small compartments I used when hunting to suppress fear or doubt, I slam the lid then struggle to my feet.

"You tried to seduce Aiden," I growl up at the goddess then turn to face Harmony. "Did he tell you that? She was trying to seduce my mate. Isn't it enough you snared him when he was a boy?"

Harmony's purple face pales in the moonlight.

"As if you didn't hurt him even worse than I have done."

That's it. I am sick owning Nicneven's mistakes. "Not in

this life. It took me awhile to accept him but now that I have, I will never let him go."

The goddess's hands ball into fists. "How dare you speak to me in such a way. I am a goddess of Asgard."

"Clearly you have your own agenda." I say. "Tell me what it is."

Freya glowers down at me. "I wanted his child for the prophesy. My seer predicted that the One True queen will stop Underhill's reign of terror and free the fey. What better queen than the daughter of two gods?"

"Except that he doesn't want you." I'm done arguing with her. "He needs me, I can't just sit here while he's captured."

"Listen to me. You must stay behind." Freya's hair whips in the wind. "You are marked. She will come for you if you cross. And if Underhill manages to kill you or your child, the fey's final hope dies with you."

"She wants to *murder* him. Murder my Aiden." Terror coils in my gut at the thought she already might have done it. "He's been through so much already. Overcome so much. And you're asking me to abandon the man I love?"

"Not forever," Harmony gestures to my belly. "You felt the power of the One True Queen. Just wait until she is ready to fulfill her destiny."

"He would come for me," I tell them all. "He wouldn't wait."

"But he wouldn't expect you to come for him, especially not if doing so would put your baby at risk," Chloe murmurs. "They're right, Nic. You must wait."

"How long?" I look to the seer. "How long do you want me to do nothing?"

Harmony takes a deep breath. "When your child comes of age, she will be the savior of the land under the hill."

I shake my head. "You're talking years? Aiden doesn't have years."

"He might get free," Chloe pushes my hair back over my shoulder. "He has allies there. Nahini and Bard, Soladin and Fern. And don't forget Addy. You can't count her out yet."

Years. They wanted me to sit around in the relative safety of Midgard while Underhill is torn apart. While my mother plots to bring about the end of the world.

"What if I'm too late?"

"Time moves differently beyond the Veil." The goddess says. "I can slow it to a crawl. Years here will be no more than a handful of hours to Aiden."

"Nic," Chloe says softly. "That's better than anything I could do. You can have the baby and when she is ready, she can rule."

When I have the baby, because Aiden wouldn't be here for the birth, to see her come into the world. See her first step, hear her first word.

"We're supposed to be together, to raise her together." I cover my stomach with my hand.

"So stubborn," Freya snaps. "You get to have your cake and eat it too, Nicneven. Why do you hesitate?"

"Because I love him." I glower up at the goddess. "This is what you do when you love someone—whatever you can."

She doesn't respond aloud. I wouldn't call her expression regretful, but she does appear a bit more contrite.

"Nic," Harmony reaches out a tentative hand as if she wants to touch my stomach. "That's my niece in there. I couldn't protect Váli, but I can protect her. Please, help me do that."

"I won't abandon him." The words clog my throat.

Chloe puts her hand on my shoulder. "I can't see the future, not like Addy. But she's right about your banishment. You might not even make it through the tear, the force could shred you both. Or you could land surrounded by a thousand Draugar."

Just as Angrboda had. Underhill knew she was coming because she was marked.

I stare up at it, the gap between our world and the fey realm beyond. "You're asking me to walk away from all of them. Addy, Nahini, Bard and Soladin. Aiden."

Chloe shakes her head. "Not forever. Didn't Freda teach you never to go into battle unarmed? You have no magic."

"The fire—"

"Is the power Underhill holds. She can turn it around and burn you to ashes." Freya smiles as though contemplating my immolation. "Not that I would mind seeing that, once the One True Queen is secured."

I clench my hands into fists. Deep down, I know they are right. I have no magic, no army of the Wild Hunt at my back, not even my sword. I'm a pregnant teenager in desperate need of her baby daddy.

Am I risking our child for Aiden? Or for myself?

All magic comes with a cost. The price of freeing my wolf might be me and our baby. And I know Aiden wouldn't survive that loss.

Not again.

"She might not have him yet. And even if she does, maybe he can escape." Chloe picks up on my hesitation. "He has resources, you know."

Aiden wouldn't wait for me to escape. But they are right, he wouldn't expect me to make a suicide run that will end in all of our deaths.

Haven't I learned that life is precious? That I need to fight to survive? Crossing the tear unarmed, risking my life and the life of my child with no plan, is foolish.

Tears blur my eyes as I turn away from them, from the tear. Tossing the truck keys to Chloe, I head up the hill, blundering through the dark.

"Nic?" Chloe's voice is full of worry.

"Leave her, Norn," I hear Freya say. "She's accepting her fate."

I WALK BLINDLY for hours through the woods, stumbling over roots and rocks, pushing tree branches out of my way. At first, I have no destination other than away from the tear in the Veil that I am so desperate to cross.

But after a time, I begin to recognize my surroundings and head with a more purposeful stride.

I stare at the spot, the clearing on the bluff overlooking my farm. The site of our first date. Seasons have come and gone since Aiden brought me here, took me through the design of the house he was going to build. A place he said I'd always be welcome.

If I close my eyes, I can still hear the excitement in his voice. He'd come here to watch over me and had dreamed of a day when we could live together in peace.

My breaths tear from me, the frigid night air turning each exhale smoky. How much time is passing in Underhill? How much more will he suffer?

It was almost better when I was being held by the FBI. Though they'd tormented me and kept me locked up, I could still plan. It was supposed to end with me going after Pharaildis, dispatching her once and for all.

But that was before the baby. A sob rips from me.

"How can I do this without him?" I ask the night.

There is no answer other than the bitter caress of the North wind.

SHATTERED

Aiden comes to with his face pressed into a familiar moonstone floor. Rodrick must have knocked him out. His clothes are sopping wet, plastered to his body. The sound of splashing water filters into his mind and he frowns and then looks up.

Just as Underhill emerges wet and naked from the queen's private bathing pool.

"It really is you this time, isn't it?" Not bothering to dry herself, she reaches for a silk dressing gown.

Slowly, he sits up, keeping a wary eye on the fire blazing in the hearth.

"I see you've undone the Kiss of Madness." Covered, she moves past him. Flames lick out from the fireplace and encircle his neck. It doesn't scorch his flesh, but he doesn't think her intent is to harm him.

Not until it serves her purpose.

The fire leash yanks him from the bathroom and into her dressing room. She sinks into a large padded chair before an ebony framed mirror. The wet silk clings to her curves. "Pity I can't give it to you again. My daughter would surely love to know you were out of your senses when you help me free your father."

"I won't—"

She smiles at him. "You don't have a choice. You and Nic left me with no choice. All I want, all I've ever wanted, is to be free of this place. I was going to do it with power, destroy the Veil so the worlds could unite. But you've spirited the kings and queens away. Now, I have to end it all to have the freedom I crave."

"You'll die, too."

Pharaildis shrugs as if she can't be bothered with the trivial details. "Escape is escape. Do you know I tried drinking the most toxic poison known to mankind? I'm surprised it didn't kill the child."

Aiden's eyes go wide. "You tried to kill your own baby?"

Underhill reaches for a crystal goblet and pours herself a healthy glass of fairy wine. She studies it intently. "You never think about the small pleasures until they are gone."

Aiden can't tell if she is addressing him or simply musing aloud.

"Food, wine, sex. Such simple joys. Hedonistic. And essential to maintain one's humanity. Without them you become…something else." Her eyes snap back to his and she sets the glass aside. "Nicneven's never been more than another shackle around my ankle."

He lets out a breath. "You don't know what you've done to her. What that water did to her. It changed her fate. Your actions have damned her not only in one lifetime, but in two."

She rises and reaches for a black gown. "She was never meant to exist in the first place. Why should I care if she's suffered? No one cares about my suffering."

"Nic cares." He swallows. "She wanted to free you. She still can. You long for death? I know what that feels like. She can grant it to you and no one else needs to die."

She releases her hair from its clasp and the dark river of night spills down her back. "Oh, I don't want to die alone. I want to punish the fey. All of them. For what they've caused me to endure. How does the saying go? Tis better to burn out than fade away?"

"There are innocent souls," he pleads.

Her dark blue gaze glitters. "Like that of your child?"

A growl rips out of him, the wolf rising to the fore. "You leave her out of this."

Underhill smirks. "Unlikely. Even if she is the one prophesized to combine the thrones of the Unseelie Court, it will take years for her to come of age. The end begins nigh." With that, she rises from her seat and crosses the moonstone floor. With a wave of her hands the outer doors open and Druagar shuffle in. "Guards. Load him into my carriage."

Aiden is dragged from the room, shaking, panting. He has to go, to get back to Nic. He promised.

Dawn bleeds through the bedroom curtains when I see Gretchen's eyes crack open and she squints. "Nic?"

"Hey," I rise from the chair I'd parked next to the bed and reach for the water glass. On the far side of the room, Liam rises from the crouch he's held since I came in here to keep watch over Gretchen.

"Where am I?" She blinks owlishly.

Instead of answering, I hand her the water. "What's the last thing you remember?"

Her brow furrows as she drinks. "I took your backpack and the truck to a spot in the woods. Harmony sent me after Aiden. She said I needed to cross the Veil with him."

So nothing about crossing, Underhill or any of it. It really had been Fenrir in control. I let out a relieved breath and meet her worried gaze.

"Gretchen, that was over a year ago."

Her lips part in shock. "What? Have I been in a coma or something?"

"Not exactly." I lean forward to take the glass from her shaking hand.

"Don't get too close," Liam cautions.

I glare at him. "She's human again. At least as human as she ever was."

"What?" Gretchen asks, her head whips back and forth between the two of us. "What do you mean, human as I ever was?"

Having spent several hours watching her sleep, I've gone back and forth trying to decide how much to tell her. Then my gaze falls to her necklace. "Sweetie, how long have you had that necklace?"

"It was a Christening gift from my grandmother," she says. "Why?"

"It's a long story and you need rest. The point is, Underhill is not the place for you."

She glances around my room and shakes her head as though to clear it. Suddenly, the wind rushes into the room, an icy blast of air. Liam leaps up to shut the window.

"Um, Nic?" Gretchen holds out her hand, the one containing the glass of water.

It's frozen solid.

"Yeah," I sink down into the chair. "I guess I should start at the beginning. The thing is, there is one Unseelie queen in this room. And it isn't me."

Gretchen listens as I catch her up on all the big bad wolf had done in her absence. She shakes her head when I tell her that the wolf destined to swallow the world lives inside her, but she doesn't deny it.

"And who is he," she leans close to ask me, gesturing toward Liam.

Of course with his acute hearing he catches every word. "Technically, I'm your son."

Gretchen's jaw drops.

"From your last incarnation," he adds as though that will answer all her questions.

I glower at the wolf and then snap my fingers to break Gretchen's stare. "It's going to be okay. Really. But you need to learn how to control your abilities before you hurt someone by accident."

She nods. "Okay."

"For now, do your best to keep calm. We'll figure it all out." I squeeze her hand and then move to leave, gesturing for Liam to proceed me out of the room. He doesn't. Freaking stubborn werewolf. At least he falls into step behind me and shuts the door to my bedroom.

Laufey rises from the barstool where she'd been grinding some sort of red root into a fine powder with a mortar and pestle. "How is she?"

"Overwhelmed."

The giant nods as though that's what she expected to hear. "And how are you, little mama?"

I almost snap at her to not call me that, but I catch the tender glance she shoots toward my belly. This child, for better or worse, will be part of her family. With both Aiden and Fern out of reach, the baby I am carrying is the only close connection she has.

Liam shoots his thumb toward the door. "I'm going to be out in the barn."

I nod and wait for him to depart before I settle in a seat next to her. "Honestly? I'm scared out of my mind. Nothing that has happened has terrified me as much as the thought of raising this child alone."

Laufey taps the powder out onto a sheet of parchment paper. "You won't be alone. I'll be here, as will your aunt, and Harmony, if you let her. And now you have the mortal host of Fenrir as well."

True, but none of them were little Addison Sophia's parent. "Freya told me she would slow the passage of time in Underhill. Can I trust her?"

Laufey snorts. "About as far as you can throw her. But in this matter, I do believe she will keep her word."

"Why?" I ask.

"The fey are the largest group of worshipers Freya has. Gods derive power from their worshipers. She has too much at risk."

Which explains why the gods of Asgard allowed the fey to take temporary refuse in the Vanir lands. Was everyone driven only by self-interest?

I put my head in my hands. Life was simpler when I just killed the bad guys.

Over on the stove, the kettle begins to sing. Laufey rounds the counter and then shuts the burner off. She dumps half of the powder into the bottom of a large mug and then pours the boiled water over the top, before sliding it to me. "Here, breathe that in. Just don't drink it."

"Why?" I stare suspiciously into the mug. "What's in it?"

"Something to easy anxiety. Carrying around so much stress isn't good for the baby."

I want to argue that it seems nothing I've done so far has been good for the baby, but think better of it. Instead, I wrap my hands around the mug, soaking up the warmth and breathe in the deep woodsy fragrance.

Slowly, the muscles in my shoulders unknot, as though the fragrant steam has grown a set of fingers and is picking them apart a little at a time. The mountain of worries fades into the fog. My eyelids grow heavy, the physical exhaustion settling in.

"You should get some rest," Laufey says when I am practically slumping on the stool. "It's going to be a difficult number of years for you."

Nodding, I murmur a thanks and trudge upstairs. Chloe is down at the vet's office but I lie on top of Addy's bed anyway.

Please gods, I beg a second before sleep claims me. *No more dreams.*

Of course, the bastards don't listen.

"How can I be sure it's mine?"

Pharaildis's expression falls. She'd been so pleased to discover she was with child. So happy. Never in her wildest imaginings would she have expected to see that look of revulsion on her lover's face.

"Surely you must know." She reaches out a trembling hand, needing to touch him. "There's been no other."

He catches her hand in his before she can make contact with his chest. "No, I don't know. I sneak into and out of your rooms easily enough."

"I was virgin," she protests. Tears threaten, but her pride is great enough that she refuses to let them fall. "The night we first lay together."

He shakes his head, denying her claim.

"Please, John. It's not so awful. We can be married."

"I have a destiny," he insists. "You're asking me to deny my calling."

She pulls back, stung. "I would never,"

He grips her wrists, hard. "Get rid of it."

She blinks, sure she had misunderstood. "What?"

"Find a wise woman and have it taken care of."

That he would suggest such a thing... "John, please. This is your child. Our child."

Pain explodes across her cheek and it takes her a moment to realize he'd backhanded her.

"If you name me, I will deny you." He turns and strides from her room.

She sits numbly for a long time. No tears will fall. Not for her foolish heart, which has been broken into a thousand jagged little pieces. Not for the life growing in her womb, the life her lover ordered her to snuff out. She is too angry to cry. At John, but mostly at herself.

A knock sounds on the outer door to her chambers. "My lady? Your father wishes for you to perform at the gathering tonight. Are you all right?"

"I'm fine." Pharaildis meets the serving girl's dark eyes. "Tell him I will be there soon."

She takes her time, dressing in her finest outfit. Covering the ugly red mark on her cheek. Her body is still her own, still capable of graceful movement, of enchanting men. There is nothing in her head, the rage blotting out all around her but her purpose. She takes no notice of her surroundings as she strides down the halls. Ignores the admiring glances that follow her, the envious stares of the women as she takes her place.

"There you are, my dear." Her father smiles. "Would you delight us all with a dance."

She nods and then waits. When the music starts, she turns and sways, bends and explodes into sensual movement. Power and grace fills her. The room disappears, the people disappear as she loses herself in the dance. It is a dance to enrapture, a dance to consume, a dance never to be forgotten.

When she falls into her final bow, her father is on his feet. "Name your price. Name it and so it shall be yours."

She stands and stares out at the crowd, heart thundering.
"Deliver unto me the head of John the Baptist."
***

The hours grind into days and tumble into weeks. Winter turns to spring, to summer. My waistline disappears as Addison Sophia grows larger and larger inside me. I smile at her fist kick. She's a fighter, this one.

Like her father. The smile disappears.

No news comes from across the Veil. No sign of Nightweaver. No word from the Wild Hunt. Liam leaves us long enough to retrieve the rest of his pack from Germany and bring them to the farm.

"You don't need to stay." I tell the Alpha who has appointed himself as my surrogate big brother.

"You're pack too," he tells me. "We watch out for pack."

Try as I might, I have no memory of him or any of the others. The mindwipe is flawless.

Night after night, dreaming about Pharaildis and the man she called John, I contemplate letting Chloe mindwipe me again, if only to expunge the memory of the two of them. Every dream I have is tied to her. To my mother. Underhill is —and will always be—a heinous bitch. But she was once a girl with dreams. A girl who thought herself in love with a much older man.

One who, if the dreams are accurate, took shameless advantage of her vulnerability and her loneliness.

I'd seen her imprisonment. The dreamer tethered to the fey lands by the Norns. After ordering John's execution, she'd gone to sleep in her own bed and woken in the dark cavern in the Unseelie Catacombs. No trial, no chance to explain her actions, just imprisoned and abandoned.

She heard the fey voices, all of them, begging for magic, for power. Their voices stayed in her head, day and night, beseeching, demanding, raging when she didn't help them.

They didn't know her name. Didn't know she had once been a person.

The one from last night was the worst. I'd seen myself—or rather Nicneven—being born. She'd been imprisoned for months. The pains had come on her suddenly in the middle of the night, sharp enough to penetrate her depression. For hours she'd paced and cursed, the ground beneath her very feet quaking as it mirrored her pain. She'd cried out for her father, her dead lover, anyone to help her.

"I want her," Pharaildis whispers to the dark. She hadn't wanted the child at first, not the reminder of John and his betrayal. She'd drunk from the poisoned spring, hoping to end them both. But as the life inside her continued to thrive, she'd clung to the hope that the child would be her salvation.

"I need someone to help ease my suffering. Oh gods, please let my loneliness end. If she dies, let me die, too."

No one had come. Not the fey who wanted everything she had to give. In the end, she had crouched over her bed and pushed until the baby had slid free of her trembling body. She laughed and held her daughter to her breast and let the babe suckle. Exhaustion had pulled her under.

At the direction of the goddess, Freya, the fey had come to take the child while Pharaildis slept. When she awoke in her prison, she was alone once more.

I shake off the dream that isn't a dream. It had been her life.

Is it any wonder she's insane?

"Nic?" There's a knock on my door and Gretchen pushes it open. "I don't suppose you'll reconsider coming back with me?"

I roll onto one side so I can see her. "You mean school?" I gesture to my extended belly. "What's the point? She'll be here in a few weeks."

Gretchen moves farther into the room. "It's something for you to do all day other than worry."

"I'm not worrying." It's true, I'm not worrying. I'm waiting. Waiting for the baby to be born. I've come up with a new plan, a deadly one. I have confided in no one because I doubt they'll approve.

Once my daughter is born, I'm leaving. Crossing the Veil to save Aiden. When our lives are no longer tied together and she is no longer dependent on me, then we will part ways. She doesn't need me. Look how decent Pharaildis had been before John had used and discarded her. Look how much her actions had condemned not just her but me as well.

Gretchen is still lingering in the doorway.

"What?" I snap, then regret it. The mortal girl is having a hard time coming to terms with what lurks inside her. She doesn't have it any easier than I do. "Ignore me, Gretchen. I'm just…." I shrug, not knowing how to finish that sentence.

"Heartbroken?" Gretchen supplies.

"Yeah." Funny, not so long ago, I didn't think I even had a heart to break.

She moves farther into the room. "I know. But Nic, you can't just sit around here. What about when the baby arrives?"

"I have a plan." Permanent incarceration. Pharaildis must die and according to Angrboda, I am the only one who can kill her. It's my duty to take her place.

When I don't offer anything further, Gretchen rises and slings her backpack over her shoulder. "I'll be back by dinner. I think I'm going to stop by and see my grandmother first."

The only family member she'd bothered to contact. I wonder why she doesn't just go live with the woman and am absurdly grateful that she's stuck around. "See you."

I lie back down and wait for her to shut me back into my room.

"Hurry up, little one," I whisper to the baby inside me. "The waiting is killing me."

There's a forceful kick as though my daughter wants out too. I wonder what she'll look like. Will she have my fair hair and ice blue eyes? Or will she take after Aiden's line, with bright green eyes and dark hair? Will she be tall like him or petite like me and Sophie? Maybe some of Garret's DNA will creep in.

There's another knock on the door, this one more forceful.

"What?" Why can't they all just leave me the hell alone?

Harmony slips inside and tosses a pair of sneakers at me. "We need to talk."

I glare at the seer. Aiden's sister. Funny how I don't like her any more than I did before I found out about their relationship. "Go away."

"No. Aiden would hate to see you like this."

"Like what?"

"A borderline shut-in? A recluse? A hot mess minus the hot?"

"I hate your face," I tell her without heat.

Her expression turns serious. "I know what you're planning."

"I have a destiny." My tone is hollow.

"And it isn't to wallow in your own filth and make a suicide run at Pharaildis."

A tired breath escapes. "Freya said—,"

"Fuck Freya and whatever she said," Harmony snaps.

My eyebrows lift at that.

"You are the Risen Queen of the Shadow Throne. You will be the mother of the One True Queen. You can't throw your life away."

I sit up, staring at her furious purple face. "You know something."

"Maybe I do and maybe I don't. But the only way you'll find out is if you get up and brush your godsdamned teeth. Your breath smells like a cesspool. Meet me in the kitchen in five minutes or I will forcibly drag your pregnant ass out of here." She storms off, letting the door bang shut in her wake.

I study the sneakers a moment. She might be bluffing. I wouldn't put it past her to lure me out and tell me diddly freaking squat. But as I look around the dismal room, I know there's an undeniable truth behind her tantrum. Aiden would hate to see me like this.

"Hey, Nic." Chloe says when I emerge from the bathroom. "You hungry?"

I am busy pulling my greasy hair up into a ponytail. Blonde to my shoulders and then black below that. I really need to cut it. "Not right now."

"I'm making veggie chili tonight."

I stare at her. I wish I could give Chloe the reaction I know she wants. But it's not in me to feign excitement. Nothing is in me except a huge sucking void of emptiness. And the One True Queen.

Harmony trots down the stairs from Chloe's space, carrying my backpack. When she hands the tattered thing to me, I frown. "What's this for?"

"You'll see." Without another word, she strides out the door.

"See you later," Chloe says. I detect the worry in her tone.

"Yeah. Later." I follow Harmony out into the August sunshine.

The cicadas buzz and the humidity is oppressive. My center of gravity has shifted and I'm feeling off balance in more ways than one. The air is fresh though, much better than the stuffy interior of my bedroom.

Harmony heads down the hill to the lake. Not so long ago, the Wild Hunt had camped on its shores. Now, the surrounding area is still. Nothing livelier than the occasional croak of a frog or flit of a butterfly's wing. The cattails bend gently in the breeze.

Harmony strips off her shirt dress to reveal a bathing suit. One of Chloe's. It's a red and white polka dot two piece that looks bizarre next to her purple skin.

"I'm not swimming," I say.

"No, but I am." Braving snakes, the seer wades into the water and glides into an easy breaststroke.

I stare down at the pack in my hands. Curiosity drives me to slide the zipper and peek inside. I suck in a breath when I see the ratty sweats Aiden had clung to so stubbornly. The only thing I had given him to that point.

"Where did you find these?"

"They were in Addy's trunk. I think your aunt knew that maybe you would need them."

I hold them close and tears fill my eyes. Harmony concentrates on her laps and ignores my silent sobs.

The grief hurts so much worse than the night I decided not to cross the Veil. Isn't time supposed to heal all wounds? Mine is festering. One of these days the infection will likely do me in.

"Underhill has him," I say when Harmony comes to sit beside me. "Doesn't she?"

She nods, water dripping from her midnight hair.

"Will he get free?"

"Not until she takes the thrones." Harmony nods in the direction of my belly. "Freya has been good to her word. If you leave after she's born, you and Aiden will both die. The Veil will fall and the worlds as we know them will end."

I shake my head. "You're asking too much of me."

"He's not dead, Nic. He's not going to die, not unless you do something selfish."

"Selfish?" I round on her. "How can you say that? Do you think I want to be a prisoner, tethered to the fey land for the rest of eternity?"

She holds my gaze. "I think you would rather be a prisoner beyond the Veil than a mother on this side of it."

My lips part but I have no retort. No quip to show her how wrong she is.

Because every word is true.

"Our mother, mine and Aiden's. You met her?" Harmony asks.

I nod. "And your father."

"Then you've seen how devoted she is to him." The seer looks out across the water. "A fantastic wife and a horrible mother. When she had to choose, she chose him again and again."

I hear the pain in her voice.

"When I found out about Aiden and Freya...how she had seduced him...I felt sick. My entire life I thought that I was okay because even though my own mother hadn't wanted me, the most beautiful goddess in Asgard had my back. Freya was looking out for me. But she was using me. The same way she used my brother."

"Gods are selfish assholes," I mutter.

Her lips turn up. "They are. And if you leave, who do you think will step in and whisk the One True Queen away?"

My lips part. "You've seen this?"

She nods once. "And nothing beyond Freya absconding with my niece. The gods will let the worlds burn in Ragnarök. You and me, your child, Aiden...we are all just pawns to them and their whims."

I close my eyes. "How long must I wait?"

Harmony shakes her head. "Sixteen years, maybe more."

Sixteen years without Aiden. "I'm the only one who can protect her?"

She nods. "Freya is afraid of you. She won't try anything for fear of risking your retaliation."

That makes no sense. "Why though? I don't have fey powers anymore. I'm not an Unseelie queen. Why would an omnipotent goddess fear me?"

"Because you found a way in." Harmony holds my gaze. "You can get to her."

Freaking oracles and their doubletalk. "Into what? Stop talking in riddles."

"Your dreams. You can go both ways. See the past or the future. And you can see ghosts."

I shrug. "That and a few bucks will get me a cup of coffee."

Harmony starts braiding her long dark hair. "Freya's Valkyries walk the battle fields. They determine which soldiers will live and which ones will die. Which will be brought to Valhalla to live among the gods. Which others will go to the Veil. You captured one of hers and tethered the soul to the Wild Hunt. A Valkyrie belongs to you."

"You mean to the Hunt."

"No, Nic. You are the one who bound her. And through that creature, you have access to the goddess."

I stare at her. "How?"

Harmony drums her fingers on her bare knee. "The spirits you see. Your regressions into the past. They are all connected to your blood. The souls you claimed are connected to your kiss. I'm no expert, not like Nahini, but I do know that if you find those strings and trace them, they will lead you to other strings. Your seer gifts are different from mine. They center not only in the future, but in the past as well. You can see those connected to you and those who are connected to them."

"I still don't understand why Freya would fear me because of this."

"Don't you get it? You have knowledge through that Valkyrie. And knowledge is power, Nic. Especially when it comes to the gods."

I SEE the battered station wagon kicking up dirt on the road long before it comes to the house. After taking a much-needed shower I decided to fake being an active member of the household a little longer. I sit on our front porch, shelling peas that Laufey has grown in her massive garden. The garden is the one thing Aiden's grandmother had thrown herself into to bide her own time until we could go after Aiden and Fern.

"Who is that?" I ask Chloe.

With Addy gone, the veterinarian clinic is closed. We never get unannounced visitors.

Chloe shrugs and tosses a pea pod into a bucket we're using for compost. "No clue."

I set my bowl of peas on a wicker side table as the wolves emerge from the trees. Liam and company are on constant patrol of the grounds. Forever seeking to keep me safe. Or perhaps it isn't me. It could be Gretchen that they are guarding so fiercely. Fenrir, their progenitor.

The car pulls to a stop and a tiny blonde woman emerges from the passenger's side door.

"Sophie?" My deadly lips part in shock.

She grins at me, rushing up the stairs with both hands extended for an embrace. "Nic, baby, just look at you."

"She's the size of the house," Chloe snarks. "I hope you like peas."

"Yuck," Tate says as he scrambles from the car to join us on the porch.

"I've got brownies too. With chocolate chips." Chloe takes his hand and after collecting the bowl of peas in her free hand, leads him inside.

"What are you doing here?" I ask Sophie. "Isn't it dangerous?"

"If it's safe enough for my daughter and grandchild, it's safe enough for me," Sophie declares. "Besides, I didn't want you to go through it alone."

Garret stands off to the side, scanning the tree line. "Are those the same wolves?"

"Sure are." Chloe calls from inside. "Come on in. I'll get you some sweet tea."

Garret scowls at the pack, then puts one hand on my shoulder. "Good to see you, Nic."

"You too."

"Just look at you." Sophie places her warm palms on my enormous midsection. "Oh baby, you're not too far off are you?"

I shake my head, still unable to believe she was here. "How did you escape the pocket realm without a giant?"

Sophie holds up a piece of paper. "We got this in the mail last week. Along with this." She offers up a brilliant pink stone.

I take the letter and read it once.

In case you need to get out. If you are receiving this, I am gone. Take care of the queen. –A.

"Angrboda." My eyes mist over. The mother of monsters was still looking out for me and mine, even after her death.

"That's what we thought too." Garret rejoins us on the porch, handing a glass of sweet tea to his wife and the other to me. His gaze strays back to the wolves. "Are they friendly?"

"I wouldn't try to pet any," I warn. "But for the most part, yes, they won't hurt anyone unless they sense a threat."

Garret says something else, but I miss it as a sudden sharp pain seizes my lower back. I stagger and then stumble. The glass of sweet tea crashes onto the porch, shards of glass glittering in the late day sun.

"Nic?" Sophie's tone is full of worry. "What's wrong?"

"The baby," I gasp.

Another wave of pain and then a splash.

"Garret, get her into the house." Sophie barks. "Her water just broke. The baby is coming now."

I shake my head. "It's too soon." Oh gods, what if there's something wrong? What if I'm going to lose her? Earlier I'd been eager for this to happen but now…. Panic claws me as another wave of agony twists my spine. Blindly I reach for Sophie. "Mom, help."

Garret swoops in and lifts me up, heading towards my bedroom. "Call the midwife."

"Here," Laufey moves up the stairs. Her hands covered with garden soil. "Take her to her bedroom."

There is a flurry of activity. Harmony and Gretchen run around collecting towels and boiling hot water. Sophie strips my bed and remakes it with an old quilt while Laufey and Chloe walk me back and forth. My breathing is uneven, unstable. I'm already failing at this.

"I need to lie down," I grunt as the pain moves from my back to my center. The pressure is building and alongside it, all my worries mount. Is Addison Sophia all right?

They get me onto my back. Laufey slips my sodden underwear off. Sophie takes my left hand and Chloe my right.

"She's ready."

What comes next is a blur of endless hours broken by ebbing and flowing waves of pain. I stopped tracking anything. My limbs shake. Everything hurts. I want it to end. Am terrified of what the end will mean.

"Push, Nic," Laufey grunts.

I cry out, sure the pain will rend me in two.

"Push!" the giantess orders.

A scream tears from my lips. The pressure is absolute.

"How long?" I grit out between clenched teeth. We've been at this for hours, days. Years maybe.

"Until it's over," Laufey's gaze holds mine. "Chloe, prop her up."

My aunt climbs nimbly on the bed, wedging herself behind me to help brace my back. She takes both of my hands and breathes in my ear. "You can do this."

Fear fills me, more potent than any feeling I've ever known. I see the press of familiar faces merging and blending in a circle around me. They don't understand.

In its path of inner destruction, like a horseman of the apocalypse, rides absolute certainty.

I can't do this without him.

I shake my head and tears track down my face. "I can't. He's supposed to be here."

"It's okay, Nic." Chloe bathes my forehead with a wet cloth. "But you need to power through this."

A sob breaks the pattern of my breathing. If not for the enormous mound of my stomach, I would curl up and tuck my knees to my chin. But it's been months since I could do that.

"Baby, I know you're tired," Sophie says in a soft drawl. "You're at the end of your rope. It's not fair, none of it. But you must keep fighting."

The dream of Pharaildis, alone in her prison flashes through my head. She wanted me for her. The fey took me for themselves.

Just as they would take my baby. Without Aiden, I can't protect her.

"No," I shake my head.

Gretchen hovers at the side of the bed, looking like an anxious bumble bee, ready to fly off in any direction. "Aiden needs you to get through this."

"I can't," I yell at them. How to make them understand? I can't do this alone, can't protect her, teach her to be good.

Lachesis words from so long ago. *It's not in your nature.*

"Aiden—,"

"Get your shit together," a cranky voice barks. "It's time to grow up, Nic. You're about to be a mother."

My head whips to the closet door, to the figure that lurks there. "Addy?" Her image is that of a shade, transparent and colorless. "Are you dead?"

She laughs and it isn't a nice sound. "Not yet."

Behind me, Chloe starts to tremble. "Is it really you?"

"Yes, sister mine. I'm here. Waiting for your judgment."

Chloe asks, "How did you get here?"

"Magic." She toys with her long braid. "I'm with you in spirit."

"Are you with Aiden?" My lips quiver. "Is he all right?"

She hesitates. "He will recover."

Another sob, this time from the pain in my heart, not the wave of agony ripping me in half.

Her dark eyes begin to swirl with a silver light. "I can't stay long, but I want to tell you something. This child that you carry, she's the one who can fix it all. This infant girl will halt the forward march of destruction. And she will do it because you will teach her how."

I shake my head back and forth. "I can't. Not without Aiden."

"He's always been with you. You know this, Nic."

"I need him." The tears spill over and another ripple of torment across my belly.

Addy leans down until she is in my face. For an instant, she's the realist thing in the room. "Then fight for him. Fight for all of us. Do what you have to do now and take the fight to Pharaildis. Bring this child into the world and let her fulfill her destiny. So you can fulfill yours."

I swallow, and then nod.

She backs away a step.

"Addy?" I reach for her.

The ghostly image flickers. "We're here, Nic. We're all here waiting for you."

"Addy, I'm so scared." Terrified I'll screw it up. That I'll be worse than Pharaildis. She hadn't been a killer. Hadn't been a deadly Unseelie queen. Just a heartbroken girl.

And I'm worse. I'll turn my innocent child into a monster.

This isn't fair. None of it. I should be with Aiden. With Addy. They are my family.

Addy's shade smiles softly. "So was I. So were we all when we took you."

"How?" I swallow. "How do I do it?"

"Love her. Let her be who she is and just…love her."

Another contraction. A scream tears from me as the urge to push overwhelms everything else.

"That's it, Nic." Laufey meets my gaze and holds it. "I can see the head. You're almost there."

The pressure intensifies again. My midsection turns hard as stone. I scream and push with everything I've got left. No training on earth could prepare me for the fierce sensation. Chloe cries out with me. I squish Sophie's hands as tightly as possible. Addison Sophia makes her entrance into the world with a hearty wail.

"One more big one," Laufey prompts. "Almost over, Nic."

"You aren't alone," Addy adds. "Not now, not ever."

Sophie has her free hand on my belly, waiting for the tell-tale clenching. "One more big push. That's all, sweetheart."

"You got this," Chloe's voice breaks. "Nic, you've got this."

"Ahhhh!" The scream rips free as I push with all my might.

Laufey's weathered face splits into a grin. She lifts the small wriggling body covered with all sorts of grossness. I have never seen anything so beautiful in my life.

Gretchen is ready with a baby blanket, one of many. Outside the sun is high in the sky.

"Here you go." My friend hands me my daughter, a smile on her round face. "Mom."

My hands shake as I reach for her. Part of me is worried I'll drop the child.

The rest is sure I won't. Because I know deep down that I will *never* let her go.

"Addison Sophia Jager." I smile down at her. I count ten fingers, ten toes, no wings or wolf tail. No purple skin, though she does look a bit red from the exertion. We did it, together. The two of us forged our way through.

She looks human. Until she opens her eyes and they glow bright with emerald flames.

Chloe rests her chin on my shoulder. "My gods, Nic. She's magnificent."

Sophie's eyes glisten with tears. Addy is right, I'm not alone. I may not have Aiden, but I have help.

When I look up to tell her, Addy is gone.

GROWING PAINS

"**A**ddison!" I call out, striding across the field to where my three-year-old daughter is kneeling in the grass. "What's wrong, honey?"

"It's hurt." She's crouched beside a fox with a twisted leg.

"Stay back," I caution her. "Wounded animals are more likely to bite."

She ignores me, as is her way. Her blonde hair is much darker than mine, golden in color, the same as the hay in the fields. "It won't bite me."

I lunge for her but am too far back. She lays her hands on the fox's body. It makes a pained sound but holds still. A red gold light pulses out of her hands.

"Nic?" It's Liam, striding across the grasses. "What's going on?"

Suddenly, the fox leaps up. My lips part as Addison giggles and the beast darts away into the trees.

"She healed it," I say to Liam.

"Like new." In some ways he reminds me so much of Aiden, like the way he tilts his head, his gaze tracking the woods around us, searching for danger.

I stare as my daughter leaps up and then runs to find Jedda and Tate.

Her powers are growing by the day. How much longer must we wait?

Her laughter bubbles up and my heart clenches in a tight fist.

How can I ever risk her?

"MOMMY?" a little voice asks from the side of the bed.

I sniffle and wipe the tears from where they'd congregated on my lashes before looking over at my daughter. She looks so much like Aiden at times that it hurts. "What is it, imp?"

"I had a bad dream." Her flame green eyes glow eerily in the darkened room. "Is it okay if I sleep in bed with you?"

In answer, I lift the covers and scoot over, making room for her small form.

"Do you want to talk about it?" I ask.

Silently she shakes her head so her blonde curls bounce.

I stroke her hair.

"How about if I sing you a song?"

A slow and easy nod.

I'm not a natural, but I do remember a song a young girl sang to me once while I suffered in the deepest depths of despair.

Long ago and far away
In a field kissed with golden sun
A spright flitted from branch to flower
and there she met the one
Her love as fresh as a summer breeze,
her heart as big and warm

> *his eyes guileless and serene*
> *gave no hint to the coming storm*

> *Together they danced and laughed and played*
> *until the light faded from view*
> *For then he turned into a monster there*
> *and she his victim anew.*

HER BREATHS ARE slow and easy by the end of it, the cadence I've managed to pull off hiding the disturbing imagery of that song. Not exactly a lullaby, but it's a message I plan to instill deep in her psyche.

You never know what lurks beneath the surface.

For the longest time, I saw the world in black and white. Good or bad. Mine or not. Until my monster met its mate.

The tears begin anew. Gods, I miss him.

What had ever become of Astrid's Declan? With the FBI trapped in thrall, they would have forgotten about him. But I want to meet the boy my young friend had given her heart to.

Not for the first time, I wish I was a free agent, able to go out and hunt the way I used to. Not for victims, but for my friends and family.

For my mate.

"Hold on, Aiden," I beg the quiet shadows of the night. "I haven't given up on you yet."

HER GROWTH IS human and yet my daughter is distinctly *other*. I fill my days as best I can teaching her everything she needs to know. Where there are holes in my knowledge, Laufey and Garret are happy to fill in. I curse myself repeatedly for not finishing school, the way Gretchen had.

Had my laziness not held me back, perhaps I could figure out a way out of this mess.

The more I get to know Addison, the more I realize how broken Underhill is. Because there is no force stronger than the love between mother and child. If someone had taken her from me, nothing would have stopped me from getting her back.

All of her gifts are gentle and sweet. Healing wounds both physical and emotional. Her laughter is like the tinkling of bells. I have a hard time believing this child will claim both the Shadow Throne and the Fire Throne. The Unseelie court is cutthroat.

"She will rule with love," Sophie tells me as we sit on her front porch and watch Addison chase butterflies with a net.

I snort. "You've never met the fey."

She studies me and then leans back in her rocker. "No, but have you."

"Many of them. And they are all dangerous in their own way."

"Any animal will bite when cornered," Sophie says and continues to rock.

I think about Aiden's wolf. The beast who'd shredded his younger brother. Aiden hated himself and the wolf for centuries because of that. Yet from the wolf's perspective, he'd been cornered and lashed out at the nearest perceived threat.

Had Aiden not shoved him down so hard and let himself be captured and tormented, he and his wolf could have found a balance long ago.

251

I stare at Addison. Will she rule with wisdom and love? Will she want to rule at all?

"Mama?" Addison tugs on the hem of my shirt.

"What is it, imp?" I frown when I see the tears gathered on her lashes.

"Tate told me that grandpa told him that my daddy was a bad man, that he left us."

I grit my teeth together. *Damn you, Garret.* "Your daddy is not a bad man. You know he risked his life to save Aunt Gretchen. And me. More than once."

She lets out a little puff of air. "But why isn't he here with us? Doesn't he love us?"

My heart is breaking anew. How do you tell your six-year-old that her father is practically frozen in time? That he's done it for her and that someday she will have to return the favor?

I hate these moments. Not just because my heart bleeds anew from missing my mate, but because I'm so not prepared for them. "Addison Sophia," I say and crouch down beside her. "Don't you ever, *ever* think for one moment that your daddy wouldn't reshape the worlds to be with you. If he could be with us, he would."

"Then why isn't he."

Because he might be dead. Because we might be too late. But I can't let myself think that.

"Because bad people are keeping him from us."

"Auntie Chloe says you used to kill bad people."

I have never once lied to my daughter. Fey can't lie and turned mortals aren't supposed to be able to either. Physically I can, but from the moment Addison was born I knew I would never lie to her about any of it. "That's right. But killing is wrong and you should never do it."

She rolls her eyes and puts one hand on her hip, her sass coming back to the fore. "Of course not. That's your job."

A laugh bubbles out of me as I watch her skip off, curls bouncing.

SHE'S READY. I can feel it in to the darkest pit of my soul. Addison Sophia Jager has reached her full strength. She seems to glow with a gold and green light. Birds perch on her windowsill, waiting for her to rise along with the sun before they sing. With a snap of her fingers, she can set a bonfire fifty feet high. One sharp inhale will call a hurricane toward the coast.

Ghosts flock to her, the disembodied spirits looking for direction, for hope.

She's ready.

I'm not.

How can I let her go?

It's Freya who makes the decision for me. I'm in the middle of my sparring with Liam when she appears behind me. All the hairs rise on the back of my neck and I sense something is wrong even before Liam freezes mid lunge.

"It's time," the goddess says.

I whirl, blade high. I don't know if I can do any harm to the goddess but I'm willing to find out.

Her gaze bores into me. "She will meet her destiny and you will meet yours, Nicneven."

"My name is Nic. I want more time." More time to get to know my daughter, to prepare her. Sixteen years isn't enough. An immortal lifetime won't be enough.

"Take her to the Tear. It will be her test. If she can heal it, you know she is ready." The goddess vanishes.

I double over and only Liam's quick reflexes keeps me from falling flat on my face in the dirt.

"I'm not ready." Not ready to kill Pharaildis and take her place in an immortal prison. Not ready to lose my daughter.

Not ready to see Aiden.

"You don't have to take her." The alpha's tone is gentle.

I shake my head. "Freya was holding the timeline across the Veil to a crawl. If I don't take Addison now…." I trail off.

Shit. Shit shit *shit.*

"I'll drive you." Liam sprints for the truck while I go to collect my daughter.

"WHAT IS THIS PLACE?" Addison looks at the wreckage from the ranch house. After sixteen years, there isn't much that the wild mountains haven't reclaimed.

"It used to be an in-between. A direct line from Midgard to the heart of the Unseelie Court."

Liam, now in wolf form, whines from the bed of my pickup but I hold up a hand, indicating that he should stay put.

I study her face, so like my own. But those emerald eyes are her father's. "Are you getting any feelings?"

Addison's intuition can put even mine to shame.

Her blond brows draw together. "It feels…. wrong."

"This is where the Veil is torn. Do you remember how I showed you how to change your vision to the soul plane?"

She nods.

"Do it now." I do as well. Together we look at the massive void that eats soul energy.

A gasp escapes her. "Oh."

She's so innocent, my sixteen-year-old daughter. She's never killed, never done anything but heal. Sometimes I can't believe she came from me.

"What happened?" She studies the jagged tear, assessing the damage.

"Life and death came together. The forces of creation and destruction tore the Veil that separates our realm from Underhill. When it gets to ground level, anything can cross through. Including the dead."

"Draugar." She's a better student than I ever was.

"That's right." I hesitate. This next part is tricky. I think back to my aunts and Aiden, all of whom were there to help lead me to my destiny. "Addison, do you know how to fix this?"

She swings her gaze to meet mine. "Fix?"

"The way you repair animals?" She was a better vet even than her namesake. Part fairy queen who speaks with the beasts like a Spriggan, part goddess whose touch can heal any wound.

She frowns and then gets out of the truck. After a moment, I follow.

This is it, the test.

Sometimes the hardest thing to do is nothing.

She reaches out and closes her eyes. I stand next to her, ready to sweep her away from this place, to kill anything that threatens her. I sacrificed my heart to keep her safe. Have lived without it since before she was born. Only love, pure and true from a mother to a child, could turn the icy soul of a once selfish fey queen into the sort of mother who will always, *always* have her back.

Time moves differently on the other side of the Veil. If Addison can do this, if she can heal the tear I made before she was born, she's ready for what comes next.

My heart pounds. I don't know what to hope for.

At first nothing changes. I see her raise her hands as though measuring. Then that familiar light begins to glow.

My vision shifts to the tear, the jagged edges that flap in an ethereal breeze that my skin can't perceive but seems to suck at my black soul. All at once I know.

All of this was meant to be.

Addison is she—the One True Queen of the Unseelie Court.

Through the Man's Eyes

THE CARRIAGE RUMBLES past the sea of animated corpses. The landscape beyond their gnarled carcasses looks like the surface of the moon. No green anywhere. Nothing to sustain life. The dead outnumber the living fey a hundred to one.

Too late. Aiden feels it in his bones. They are too late to save the fey. He wonders if Freda and Taj got everyone out in time. He wonders if the gods allowed them to stay in Vanheim.

Will Nic sense it when he dies?

Underhill's gaze is lost in the bleak landscape.

"Is this what you wanted?" Aiden keeps his tone soft. "You loved this realm once. Were one of the original dreamers. And now it's in ruin."

"It is indeed a high price." Her tone is soft and utterly without remorse.

"My lady?" Rodrick clears his throat.

She holds up a hand before he can speak.

"Stop the carriage," she barks.

With a frown on his weathered brow, Rodrick calls for the driver to stop.

She turns to the window that faces west. Closes her eyes and waits.

Aiden stares at her intently. With his hands and wrists bound by *Gleipnir*, he can't move more than his facial muscles.

"She's repairing it," Underhill grates.

"Who? Repairing what?" The fey general looks around in confusion.

Pharaildis's eyes flash open and looks not at Rodrick but at Aiden. Her face is a mask of barely leashed fury.

Only Nic could have upset her so much. What is his mate doing?

It hits him like Thor's hammer. Pharaildis said she's repairing it. The prophesy. Somehow, Nic had found a way to mend the tear.

His shoulders sag as much as the restraints allow. She's safe and they have Gretchen. The Veil is intact.

"It matters not. Drive on," Underhill drums her long, bloodred nails on the door of the carriage. "By the time Loki is free, nowhere in the nine worlds will be out of our reach."

"You did it." I move forward and put a hand on Addison's shoulder.

She doesn't even appear winded. "Can we go home now? I promised Tate that I'd give him a rematch in blackjack."

A smile flits across my face and I cup her cheek. "Addison," I say.

Her green eyes are wary. She has my instinct for trouble. "What is it?"

I swallow. "I need to leave."

Her blonde brows pull together. "Leave?"

"I'm going to rescue your father."

Addison's lips part. "I want to help."

As I knew she would. "The best thing you can do, baby, is stay here."

She shakes her head. "No. Mom, I want to come with you. I'm the same age you were when you first went over there."

"I know you do. But this...this is my fight. Go home with Uncle Liam."

She shakes her head, her eyes sad. "You're not coming back."

I don't know how she knows this for a fact. She could have overheard me speaking to Sophie or Gretchen. Hell, for all I know her ghosts have been spying on me. "I will if I can, baby. If you don't believe anything else, believe that."

Liam has shifted to human form and pulled on his jeans and boots. He catches my gaze. "Nic, granted I don't know much about it, having only been over there once. But weren't you waiting for her to come of age so she could take the thrones?"

I shake my head. "No, I was waiting for her to be strong enough to protect herself. This is my fight, Liam. Addison Sophia Jager, I want nothing more than for you to have a beautiful, normal life. Fuck fate. Make your own gods-damned destiny."

Addison's green eyes shimmer with tears. "Mama. I don't want you to go."

I pull her into a tight embrace and press my deadly lips against her neck. "And I don't want to leave you. But I have to and you need to stay here and be safe. I know what I'm asking you. Nothing is the most difficult thing you can do."

Her shoulders shake. So easy with demonstrations of emotion, my beautiful daughter.

I look to the Alpha. "Liam, I am trusting you to keep her safe."

He puts one hand over his heart. "The pack will defend her to the death."

"Let's hope it doesn't come to that. Both of you, go now. I'll send word if I'm successful."

Liam's two-toned eyes glow but he wraps an arm around my daughter's shoulders. "Send word if you want us to back you up."

"I will." The lie falls easily from my lips.

I watch as the truck drives off. I imagine them going back to the farm. Chloe and Sophie, Laufey and Harmony will all be pissed that I left without saying goodbye. But I can't bring any of them with me. I refuse to risk any of them.

There is nothing they can do. I will be imprisoned or I will die. And I've always hated long goodbyes.

THE FINAL CROSSING

I check my watch. Twenty minutes until midnight. The grass has gone dormant for the season and leaves fall steadily from the trees. Midnight on Samhain. The night the Wild Hunt should take to the skies to bring in the end of harvest and the beginning of winter. This has always been, will always be my season.

"My queen," a familiar sibilant voice hisses.

I glance up into the face of the dead Valkyrie. "Long time no see, Nightweaver."

She stares at me impassively.

"Is Underhill expecting me?" I ask.

The spirit nods.

"You betrayed me." My tone is mild, almost indifferent. "I saw it."

"You don't know what you saw."

Her answer pisses me off. "You've been spying for Underhill."

Her head bobs easily. "As Nahini ordered."

My lips part. "Nahini ordered you to spy on me for Underhill?"

She drifts closer. "Your mother trusts me now. I know where the cave is, where she plans to bring your wolf. And I know that the Underground Palace is mostly unguarded."

I swallow. "Why should I believe you?"

"You shouldn't," the Valkyrie responds. "I hope you don't. Your death means I will be free to join the Veil."

At least she didn't lie. I consider her for an endless moment. "You said the Underground palace is unguarded? Does that include the prisoners?"

She drifts up. "Yes. And if you cross here, you'll appear in the Unseelie catacombs."

Dare I trust her after I've witnessed her actions? Though it galls me to admit, Nightweaver is right. If she is following Nahini's orders, I might have help.

I check my watch. One minute until midnight. Time to choose.

I just hope I won't regret it.

Through the Man's Eyes

UNDERHILL JERKS UP in her seat. "Stop the coach."

Aiden breathes in her scent at the same moment. Nic. She's crossed the Veil. Her scent is that winter apple fragrance he loves.

Alone. No hint of the wildness, the otherness.

The pup. His wolf is frantic but held by Gleipnir, there is nothing he can do.

"My lady?" Rodrick leans forward.

"She's here," Underhill mutters. "She's in the catacombs. Do you have any soldiers there?"

Rodrick's eyes ice over as the Spriggan connects with the few birds and beasts that still live. "No, my lady."

Cursing, Underhill rolls up her sleeve. "Give me your dagger."

The general hands his weapon over to her. "Be careful, the blade is poison—"

Underhill slashes down into the pale white flesh of her arm.

Rodrick's eyes widen at the sight, but Pharaildis isn't affected at all. She dips the tip into the bleeding gash and then writes in the air above her face. The letters formed in blood create angular carvings. Runes.

"What are you doing?" Aiden asks.

"Sending a welcoming committee."

Though he knows it is useless, Aiden struggles to free himself. "You can't kill her. She's your daughter."

"She's a traitor who will kill me. You said so yourself." Underhill mumbles something too low for even his wolf ears to discern. She slashes the air with the red dagger, carving patterns. The images linger, glowing brightly for a moment before her bloody commands fade slowly into the ether.

She meets Aiden's gaze and her lips curve in a satisfied smile. "She deserves what's coming for her."

I APPEAR in the same tunnels I'd traversed during my time in the gauntlet. The walls pulse with magic. Even without my queenly powers, I can feel it throbbing like a heartbeat. The womb of power for the Unseelie Court.

"This way," Nightweaver beckons me forward.

I have no weapons. Sixteen years I've been preparing for this fight and for sixteen years I'd imagined what I would bring with me, how I would lay waste to Underhill's forces.

But the only weapon I need is guile. I recall Loki's poem from so long ago. *Knowledge is power, unless you're not sane.*

Aiden's father isn't sane, but my mother is. She knows what she's doing and is doing it anyway. I will only win by outsmarting her.

The magic that makes Pharaildis Underhill comes from her knowledge of the fey. Though her magic is formidable, and her army is deathless, my strength and determination to end her reign of terror give me the advantage.

She has nothing to lose. I have everything to protect.

My sneakers make no sound as the ghost leads me through the craggy tunnels. Pixies flit from little cracks in the walls, sifting their magic dust across the floor. I dodge it where I can, not wanting to deal with the mind-altering effects of their magical byproduct.

The corridor splits into a Y.

"That leads to the throne room." Nightweaver indicates the left facing tunnel. "She likes to keep them close."

We turn right. The thrumming of the walls grows louder and we ascend a hill so steep that my calf muscles burn.

"I have no memory of any of this," I huff.

"She rearranges the palace. To keep those who still live unsettled."

Nightweaver does an abrupt about face and drifts through a solid wall. I stop. The dead often forget that things like walls will keep a living being out.

Nightweaver reappears. "They are just inside this chamber."

"I can't get through that way," I say to the spirit.

"Use your magic."

I don't tell her I'm fresh out of Unseelie powers. Instead, I shift my gaze to the soul plane to sense what's behind the wall.

All it takes is the hazy golden glow for me to recognize Addy.

"Find another way." I say to the Valkyrie.

"There is no other way," she insists. "Underhill moves the chamber around to create the door. She trusts no living guards on the prison."

Paranoid. Untrusting. I've come by those traits honestly.

Footsteps sound from down the hall. Slow, dragging.

"Draugar," I whisper.

"Run," Nightweaver says. "If they corner you in here, they will shred you to pieces."

I point at the wall, to the prisoners within. "Stay with them. Let them know I'm here."

I take off back the way I came, panting as I round one corner and head into a new tunnel.

And skid to a halt.

Three Draugar turn to face me.

The dead fey are hideous. Skin hanging, flesh shriveled like raisins. Their eyes have liquified, what little moisture is left runs from the sockets.

My Goodnight Kiss won't do a damn thing against things already dead.

"No," I back up, but more are coming. They move slowly, closing the net around me. With each step they grow larger, blocking out all the space around their putrid carcasses.

"Little queen," one of the creatures speaks in a sibilant voice. "Come to die?"

It shouldn't be able to talk, its vocal chords flap in the open air. Gruesome magic is at work.

My back hits the wall. Trapped.

"Up here!" A familiar voice calls. "Nic, hurry!"

I scan the area before glancing up. The ceiling is structured like a wasp's nest with holes obvious from the rock. A hand that looks more like a large dark paw protrudes from between the crevices just above my head.

I don't hesitate, leaping up and grasping the offered limb.

An arrow whizzes past my body. It connects with the nearest Draugar. The creature shrieks, then bursts into flames.

The large hand pulls me up into the dark space between chambers. Then something wraps around my midsection.

A pair of arms. Pale, slender, and overly affectionate.

I stiffen, but then light flares to my left and I can make out the delicate face, the pointed ears, of my assailant.

Or rather my savior.

"Jazz?" I whisper unable to believe it's really her.

"It's so good to see you." She grins up at me. She doesn't look any older than she had the last time I'd seen her. The smattering of freckles exactly how I remembered them.

"Looks like you needed a hand," A deep male voice says from behind us.

I turn, dislodging the nymph and then blink. "Taj?"

The Lord of the Land bows low. "Good to see you, Nic."

"How?" I shake my head, stunned. "How did you come to be here?"

"I told them it was time." Harmony steps forward.

"You told me you were taking a vacation."

She shrugs. "Vanheim is lovely this time of year."

If the seer hadn't just saved my bacon, I might hate her. That's when I see the final member of the party. The winged helmet, a long intricate golden braid. And in her warrior's hand, a familiar sword.

"Freda." Tears fill my eyes at the sight of her. "Where did you get that?"

"From me. I pinched it from the goddess." Harmony says.

"I wanted to come sooner." Freda says. "But we had no way across."

I shake my head. "How can I complain about your timing? You saved my life."

She nods. "And now we need to get our people back."

"How will we get out of here?" Jazz asks. "The dead are everywhere."

"Leave that to me, little one." Taj puts his hand to the rock. The fissure starts to tremble and shake. I hang on to Jazz with all my might so she doesn't slip through the opening below. It's a struggle to stay on my feet.

"What are you doing?" I shout at him.

Taj ignores me. His cat eyes are closed in concentration.

Shards of stone fall from the cavern's ceiling, impaling several of the Draugar. They squirm, pinned in place.

"You're going to land us right on top of them!" Freda shouts.

Just when I think that is his intention, I notice thick roots poking out from the new cracks. Like fingers gripping a windowsill, the roots widen the crevasse. Small stones fall as solid rock is infiltrated by the trees.

The shaking ends as abruptly as it began and the tree roots slither back, leaving a gap large enough for us to walk through single file.

"After you, my Queen." Taj says with a smile.

"I'm not a queen." I tell him. "Not anymore."

"Nic," Freda begins but I hold up a hand.

"I know. The Wild Hunt answers only to the Queen of the Shadow Throne."

"Who do you think ordered them here?" Harmony smirks.

My lips part in shock. "Don't tell me you let Gretchen come, too."

She shakes her head. "Of course not."

In Harmony's purple hand, a second flame leaps to life. "I brought her to meet with Freda and Taj in the Vanir lands."

"She told us to do whatever it took to secure the Underground palace." Freda nods. "She's not you, but I like her style."

I can't stop smiling. Not alone. I don't have to do this on my own.

"I need to get Addy and the others."

"I thought you'd say that." Freda points to a spot where the tunnel diverges. "This will bring us out above the prison."

"You're sure?"

She makes a derisive noise. "Who do you think you're dealing with?"

"Then I'll follow your orders, first of the hunt."

Freda hands me *Seelenverkäufer*. "This is one reunion that's long overdue."

I shake my head. "It belongs to The Hunt."

"It belongs to you, Nic." Freda pushes the blade at me again. "Go on, take it before it gets offended."

I accept the Soul Reaper and feel whole again with it in my hands.

"Where's the rest of the Hunt?"

"Waiting to cross." Freda makes a face. "We can send a ghost for them once the palace is secure."

"Then let's proceed." Taj cracks his knuckles. "Soladin has waited for me long enough."

Exactly how I feel about Aiden. "The clock is ticking. If we see any Draugar get them out, Freda. There is nothing you can do against the army of the dead."

Freda lifts her chin. "I will do as my queen commanded."

I open my mouth to argue then realize the futility of the gesture. "Fine, but if you die, I'm going to be really angry."

Harmony takes the lead, her hand wielding fire directly out in front of her. Jasmine goes next, followed by Freda then Taj and I bring up the rear. We walk for what feels like days, winding up and down through the caverns in front of us.

The hole made from Taj's tree roots widens out into an actual tunnel. There are no lights. The air is damp and chill and smells of old death.

"Quiet," Freda hisses.

I'm about to tell her that no one said anything when I hear it. A shifting sound as though someone is moving.

"Who's there?" I wield *Seelenverkäufer* out in front of me. Jasmine points one of her flaming arrows and Harmony holds out her flame filled hand.

"You...you're alive," the small voice quavers.

"Who are you?" I repeat the question, not fooled by the childlike appearance. The fey make a habit of putting on an innocent façade, the better to lure the unsuspecting to their dooms.

"I know her," Freda crouches down low, heedless of the danger. "Your brother is Alric the Spriggan, yes?"

"I'm called Rowena." The girl has a distinctly Eastern European lilt.

"What are you doing here?" There isn't much to recommend her hideout.

"I'm hiding from her."

"Her?" Harmony asks.

The girl's gaze darts around. "Underhill."

Then it clicks. Alric's sister was the potential heir to the Fire Throne. The one heart Underhill had left. Pharaildis would have ordered any threat to her power executed. Freda and I exchange an uneasy glance.

"How did you get down here?" Harmony asks.

"My brothers." Her gaze goes to the floor. "They were trying to get me out. But the dead got them."

Harmony squeezes the girl's shoulder. "I'm so sorry."

Tears fill Rowena's eyes but she brushes them away. "I've been hiding here ever since."

Jasmine steps forward and holds something out to the princess. "Here."

The girl hesitates, staring at the brightly colored wrapper. "What is that?"

"Chocolate," Jasmine says with a smile in my direction. "The best thing you could ever hope to eat."

Rowena sniffs it delicately and then takes a tentative bite. Her eyes light up.

A pang goes through me. This is Alric's sister. She'd been groomed to lead a court not banished to starve in the bowels of the world. I want to order Freda to take her back into the Underground palace, but that's no safer than our route.

"Which direction do the dead come from?" I ask her.

She points with the hand not holding the half-eaten candy bar. "That way."

I turn and spy an eerie blue light pulsing in the deepest depths of the cavern. "Stay here." I say to Taj, Jasmine and the girl.

"Nic," Harmony begins.

"It's important." I don't know how I know, only that I do.

We move farther towards the light. The incandescence grows brighter with each step. I suck in a sharp breath when I realize what it is we're looking at.

Underhill's lair, the heart of the hill.

And in the water that has never seen the light of day, float bodies. Countless bodies.

ANIMATED

I hold my breath, seeing the vacant looks in their sightless eyes. Focusing ever upwards on something they can no longer behold. Something that is the source of the light, glowing blue and gold and green which reflects off the midnight water.

"Nic," Freda hisses in my ear. "Look."

She points to our right. There is a sudden splash and we jerk back as two of the corpses drag another body forward. They are standing on some sort of incline. They roll the corpse down and it hits the water. They turn and pull forward another, repeating the process.

"It's an assembly line." At the far end of the pool, a hand flails. It grasps for something to hold, snags an outcropping and pulls itself from the water. Behind it another of the Draugar reaches out and grasps for something to hold while it clambers to be free.

"A what?" Harmony looks at me, confusion in her eyes.

I pull her and Freda farther away. "The dead. Those glowing marks above the water. Those are runes. They need to put the bodies in the bespelled water. Otherwise they won't animate. The Draugar drag more corpses into the water. They aren't just rising at the second of death. They need to be brought here."

"But why?" Freda hisses.

"Because the magic comes from runes." I stare at the glowing marks on the ceiling. One that means life, the other that means time. I turn to face the seer. "What do you know about runes?"

"Only that some of them were lost to time."

"Unless you are a fate." I say. "And I know just where we have one of those."

WE MAKE our way back to where we left the others and fill them in on our discovery.

"This is foolish," Harmony says. "What of Aiden?"

"If I'm right, we'll buy ourselves enough time to fix everything. But we need Addy to do it."

"It's an awful risk," the seer cautions. "What if your Fate won't help?"

"Oh she will. Everything Addy does is for a reason. Do you really think Underhill could have kept her here if she wanted to escape?"

The tunnel narrows again, and then opens back up. The constant stop-start of the pace is maddening. My task list is growing, but I know this is the right thing to do. Addy knows how the magic of the runes works. She can turn back the clock, the same way Underhill had once done for me. Our army can grow from a handful to thousands if only we can work the magic right.

"There." Jasmine points and I skid to a stop at a branch in the tunnels. The veins of moonstone glitters under the torch-light, enough to spy the enormous boulder Nightweaver had led me to earlier.

"Nic?" Freda asks.

I gasp. "Taj, can you move it?"

The Seelie king shakes his head. "No. My roots deflect off it. Only the power of Underhill can open it."

The air shimmers and as one we are surrounded by the dead of the Wild Hunt.

"First." Nightweaver inclines her head to Freda. "The Second sends her regards and suggests that if you can't go through the door, you ought to make a new one."

"A new one?" Freda looks blank.

I hold up *Seelenverkäufer*. "You mean we should make a tear through the stone the way we do the Veil?"

"That's not possible." Freda shakes her head. "The Soul Reaper cuts through spirit, not solids."

But my eyes are on the ghost. "I trust Nahini's judgment. Stand aside."

The others back away and I hold the sword with two hands. It thrums in my grasp. The buzz of power fills me, intensifying until the entire cavern seems to hum with light and intention.

I make a slice through the air. Though I am expecting the clang of metal on rock, there is no sound. Only a great bleeding gash that pulses with life magic. As one, the dead of the Hunt dive for it, stretching the cut open the way Taj's tree roots opened the tunnels for us.

The inside is dark as pitch.

"Harmony, the light." I snap.

The seer steps forward and extends her flames.

I spot Nahini first. She's chained to a wall on the far side. Her head is slumped forward as though she no longer possesses the strength to hold it up.

I cross over the threshold. A gust of air rushes through

the space, cooling the seared edges the ghosts and the blade left at the entrance to the cell.

"Nahini?" I ask.

Her dark head lifts, the beads on her multitude of braids clicking. "Nic? I knew you'd come. Is it truly you?"

She's not asking out of a sense of awe or wonder. We've been tricked too many times by shapeshifters.

"It's really me," I say. "Nightweaver can vouch for me."

Freda is hot on my heels, a small knife in her hands. She shoves it beneath the bolt that holds Nahini's chain. "Hold on. We'll have you free in no time."

I scan the dank space. It smells of unwashed flesh and waste. Bard is collared to the wall. Soladin is shackled at the far side of the space.

No sign of Addy.

I shift my gaze to the soul plane once more and spot her golden signature. Addy is sprawled on the unyielding ground, curled up in the fetal position, her silver and jet braid lying limp. I'm glad to see that she wears her own form again.

"Hey you," she whispers when I rest a hand on her arm and call her name. "It's about time."

Tears fill my eyes. "I've missed you. Come on, let's get you out of here."

"Can't," she coughs.

"Nic, hurry up." Harmony strides closer, bringing the light with her.

It's then that I see the blood.

Through the Man's Eyes

UNDERHILL'S CARRIAGE stops before the cavern. The Draugar line the path on either side, ready to close in at her command.

Rodrick tosses Aiden out onto the ground. He lands face first on the hard-packed dirt. His teeth sink deeply into his lower lip and he tastes blood.

"Why are you helping her?" Aiden spits at the fey general. "She's going to kill everyone."

Rodrick stares at him a beat. "Better serve the devil than get in her way."

"You know," Pharaildis murmurs as though to herself. "I should have just moved the castle closer to this place. Then again, you probably didn't mind the long carriage ride, did you, Váli Sigynjarson?"

"Don't call me that," he snaps.

"Afraid I will wield power over you." Pharaildis shakes her head. "Little wolf, I hold the ultimate power over you. The power of life and death."

He stares at her. "You are about to unleash a monster you can't control."

She scoffs. "I'm not afraid of your beast."

"I mean Loki." His gaze slides to the cave. "He's not stable. He wasn't stable *before* centuries of endless torture."

She shrugs. "Harbingers are never stable. I have the dead, I have the heart of the last queen of the Fire Throne. And I have you. All the ingredients for the perfect end of the worlds. Now enough stalling. It's time for a family reunion."

She waves a hand and the chain flies upwards into his mouth. He hisses at the lash of the metal against his tongue. But there isn't a damn thing he can do about it.

Rodrick propels him forward. They move down the torch-lined cavern. It is a descent into hell, into madness, each step driving him ever darker into himself.

The wolf in him struggles and fights but Gleipnir is inescapable. If Fenrir hadn't found a way free in all his centuries of imprisonment, there is no way Aiden will get loose.

The journey is agonizing. His heart pounds faster as they descend lower. He wants to run, knows it is futile.

Light flowers up ahead, a sickly greenish hue that dances on the walls. And then they are there. The place that haunts his nightmares.

He looks at his mother first. Her blonde head is lowered, all her focus on his father. She never looks away, never flinches from her task.

Not even when she gave birth to his helpless sister.

And beyond her, chained by his brother's entrails, is the mad god himself.

"I've been waiting for you," Loki sing-songs.

Sigyn turns to empty the bowl of venom. The snake coiled above Loki hisses. Green venom drips down on his father's face. The ground quakes beneath their feet.

Nic. he thinks. *Where are you?*

"How long has she been like this?" I snap.

"For days." Bard moves forward, the chains rattling on his ankle. "She moved out of reach of the rest of us. We called for help but no one came."

Days.

"Addy," I lean over my aunt and take in the horrific, gaping wound. It looks as though she's been burned with a blowtorch. The skin around the edges is chalky and flakes away and beneath I can see raw muscle and the white of her ribs "What did she do to you?"

"This wasn't Underhill." Fern crouches by Addy's side.

"Did to myself," Addy wheezes. Her hand flaps like a wounded bird.

I catch it in mine. "What?" Horror fills me at the thought.

"Can't interfere." She coughs and more blood spills out onto the stones. "Our law. It's a killer."

She laughs and the sound goes through me like a death knell.

So many things start adding up. Why Chloe had looked so sad when I'd mentioned a possible stay of execution for Addy. They'd killed a sister before, had destroyed Lachesis after the third Fate had abandoned me in the Black Forest. Had interfered with the course of my destiny.

Is it possible they had done so out of...mercy?

My aunt is dying. Before my eyes, her golden light dims. "What can I do to stop it?"

"Nothing, sweets. There will be another soon. One who will rise up and take my place."

Take her place? Who could ever replace Addy? I shake my head. No. This isn't possible. She'd lived for eons, has seen the secrets of the universe. She can't die.

"Take care of Chloe, Nic." Addy holds my gaze, hers swirling more slowly as if her magic is draining away with her life's blood. "She will need you. Help her find her way to the others. Don't waste your second chance, Nic."

Her voice trails off then rattles. "Hurts."

"Let me give you the Goodnight Kiss." I can spare her the pain at least.

"Won't work," her edge of steel is still there, in spite of the horrific wounds that are eating her alive. "Only the Fates...."

"I'm sorry." I should have brought Chloe with me. Foolish Nic. I thought I'd been protecting Addy and Chloe both by leaving her behind. My lips tremble. There's so much I want to say to her. But one thing I must ask before it's too late. "Addy, the runes. How do I use them?"

"You will know how when it is necessary." Her lips are dry and cracked. "Don't try to stop free will. And don't waste it."

A last, rattling breath leaves her. The flesh rots off her bones and falls to the floor like dry leaves. Her cheeks hollow and her skin, now the texture of burning paper, disintegrates.

"No!" The scream tears something loose from my very soul.

"Nic," Nahini is by my side, her touch gentle on my shoulder. "Nic, she's gone."

"She can't be." I shake my head, unable to believe it. Addy, the most powerful of the Fates, the Norn who cuts the thread of life, can't be dead.

My shoulders hunch. I need her. Need her help. And she's left me alone. She, who embraced what I am from the very beginning, who did everything in her power to protect me. Taught me just how fiercely I should love.

Like a mother bear in winter.

She knew this was in store for her, this horrible end. But she'd come anyway. Interfered anyway. For me and for Addison Sophia.

"Addy," I breathe and swipe at the tears that are running freely down my face. "I won't waste it. I promise."

NO TIME.

There's no time to mourn Addy. No time to rescue Aiden from Underhill's grasp. No time to wield the runes and buy more time. My plan is in tatters. The Draugar will be here soon. By unspoken agreement, we make our way to the throne room at the center of the palace. Jasmine, Freda and Taj bar the exits. I stare at the Fire Throne, numb.

The ghosts of the hunt swarm to Nahini and she whispers something to them in a language I don't recognize.

Then they all separate, moving in different directions.

Nightweaver remains, her gaze unflinching.

"Scouts. They'll let us know when the Draugar near." Nahini says.

"Can they fell them?" Soladin asks.

Nahini shakes her head. "There are far too many now. The spirits can buy us some time, but will eventually be overwhelmed."

"We can make it," Freda turns and faces me. Her golden helmet is tucked under one arm. "The cave is but an hour's ride. Have the ghosts clear a path and ride through."

"Past thousands of Draugar?" Bard cracks his three knuckled fingers.

An hour will be too long. Pharaildis won't hesitate to gut Aiden on the floor. I doubt she can kill a full god with only one fey royal heart in her grasp, but Aiden hasn't been a god since those bastards in Asgard turned on him. If Loki is freed there will be no stopping Ragnarök.

My gaze falls on the two thrones. One wreathed in shadows. The other idle. Waiting.

"If we can't get to her," Jasmine follows my line of sight.

I get to my feet. "We make her come to us."

"It could kill you." Nahini, covered with weeks' worth of filth, still looks as beautiful and ethereal as ever. "Nic, you don't have fire magic. You don't have any magic. Underhill stripped it from you."

"I've wielded it before." I stare at the chair. "It's the only way to stop her. Only a queen can set Loki free."

"You're the only one who can kill her." Freda strides forward to block my path. "The only one with the ability to end this. If you die, we are all lost."

"I can do it." A small voice speaks up.

We turn to look at the child, Brigit's last living daughter. Rowena.

She holds out her hand and a golden flame burst forth. "I was groomed for it. Father wouldn't let me."

Because even then, Rodrick had been in cahoots with Underhill? Or perhaps to do what any decent parent would do, to protect his child. "No, if it's too dangerous for me, then I'm not about to let you do it."

"It's what I was born for," she says. "What I'm meant to do."

"Nic," Freda puts a hand on my arm. "Nic, please don't. You'll die."

I suck in a deep breath. Pharaildis had numerous chances to kill me but she didn't. I remember my dream about her giving birth, hoping her babe would be an end to her loneliness. She wouldn't hesitate to kill Rowena but me….

I hand *Seelenverkäufer to Freda*. "It has to be me. I'm the only one who can lure her back here. Away from Aiden."

And have faith that my mate can free himself when I do.

Slowly, I approach the dais. The Shadow Throne sits quietly. No feeling of power comes from it. Is that because Gretchen is across the Veil? The Fire Throne hums as though it is eager for this encounter.

I reach for the fire I've only wielded once. The connection to Aiden, to Addison, must be somewhere inside me still. Carrying our daughter changed me. If I am to survive, it will be because of them.

"Any last-minute advice?" I ask Soladin and Taj.

"Don't forget who you are. Why you are doing this," Taj says. "Love is what got me through it."

The king shares a tender look with his consort.

I swallow and then nod. I can do this. I was born in shadows but my heart…my heart burns with anger, with love, with the fierce need to protect those around me.

279

"If I don't make it," I say to Harmony.

She shakes her head. "You will."

My lips turn up. "Did you have a vision?"

"No. You're too stubborn to die."

I smile, then sober. "Take care of him. And of her."

There is a silver sheen in her eyes. "Always."

Don't waste it.

Those had been Addy's last words to me. An order to do whatever it is I need to do. And right now, I must take the Fire Throne back from Underhill. To lure her to me. To end this.

"Nic," Bard shouts from his position by the window. "The dead are coming. A lot of them."

No time. No time to think or to feel anything other than hope. Aiden taught me about hope and love. Addison personifies it. I can do this.

I don't ease into it, don't reach my hand forward and trail it over the charred wood that glistens as though it has been shellacked. I pivot on the dais and sit.

And wait for the Fire Throne's judgment.

At first there is only silence. A great and terrible stillness that portends the calm before the storm.

And then I start to burn, from the inside out. All the oxygen is stolen from my lungs. The fire robs me of breath, eating away at everything that I am. The inferno rears hotter, higher until I am engulfed in a pillar of flame.

Someone shouts my name. I'm dying, I know it. No one can live through this.

Too late.

THE FACE IN THE MIRROR

Through the Man's Eyes

Pharaildis pauses with the dagger held high over her head. Her dark brows pull together.

Nic. Aiden falls to his knees. He can feel her pain, the agony she's in. His mate is dying.

The wolf rips free, seizing control faster than ever. He sees his mother cringe back, though she doesn't leave Loki's side.

"No," Underhill had been inches from carving out his heart. She staggers back. Then vanishes.

"My lady?" Rodrick's confusion is clear on his face.

The wolf doesn't waste time. Still bound in Gleipnir, he slams into the distracted fey general with all the force of a linebacker. They sprawl in the dirt. The fey's head hits the stone floor with a dull thud. Blue black blood spreads out from beneath him. His eyes stare sightlessly up at the cavern's ceiling.

If he had been in wolf form, he would have ripped the bastard's throat out.

I need to speak. Aiden tells the beast.

Hurry. The wolf recedes.

Aiden scrambles to his feet.

"Help me," he gasps to his mother. "Remove the chain."

"The wolf," she whimpers. "He'll kill us."

"I'm trying to save you, Mom. Save all of us."

Her lips tremble.

"Do it for your daughter," he snarls. "The baby you handed over to Freya because you chose to stay with his sorry ass."

Loki stares at him blankly.

A tear spills down Sigyn's cheek. "You've met Harmony."

He nods. "I have. And if you don't care about your own life or mine, care about hers. She doesn't deserve to die."

"I met your mate." Her lips twist into an expression no one would consider a smile. "She's so cold."

"No, she isn't." Nic is lava under an ice floe. "Believe me, she's everything to me. As is our daughter."

Her lips part. "Daughter?"

Though he doesn't know for a fact that the One True Queen has been born safely, he can think of no other reason for Nic to have crossed the Veil. "You're a grandmother. I haven't even met her yet. Please. For once in your life, think about us before him."

Loki remains oddly quiet.

Sigyn sets the bowl on a small ledge. Loki bellows as the venom drips onto his face. The acid burns him down to the bone. The room shakes in time to his thunderous bellow. Tears stream down Sigyn's face but her hold is true as she removes the chain from his body.

Cracks form in the ceiling overhead and stalactites fall. Sigyn lunges for the bowl and catches the stream of venom.

The snake hisses. Loki takes in a choked breath. His face is unrecognizable. The quake stops.

"I'm sorry," tears spill down his mother's cheeks. "For my part in it."

Aiden kisses her on the forehead, a benediction he isn't qualified to offer. He's sorry, too. "Thank you," he breathes and shifts to sparks.

It's a matter of moments for him to travel up out of the cave. The winds whip up, propelling him to his destination. Mountains surge up out of lakes below. Underhill is moving the terrain until the landscape looks like batter being stirred by an invisible spoon. Shifting her home field advantage. Whatever Nic's done, she has her mother's attention.

The mountain that conceals the Underground Palace appears. Aiden forces himself to travel faster. He must be faster than ever before.

He flies down into the depths of the Unseelie catacombs. There it is, the magnificent crystal palace that had been hewn on the orders of the first Unseelie queen. He doesn't pause. Doesn't count the flood of Draugar that surround it.

Aiden coalesces in the throne room to see Nic seated on the Fire Throne. Flames lick up and shadows curl around her. Her hair is ablaze. It's going to reject her. His brave mate will die trying to wield a power that isn't hers.

He lunges for her, intending to shift to sparks as soon as his skin touches hers. Her eyes open and she stares at him once. Her cracked lips mouth two words that he hears echoing inside his head.

Protect her.

The Throne explodes.

Aiden throws up a shield surrounding the small group of fey in the throne room. The pillar of flames spurts to the ceiling and shadows curl out of the corners to meet with it.

All around him their allies cough and choke.

"Nic?" This from Nahini who is nearest to him. "Where is she?"

The smoke begins to clear.

Nic is nowhere in sight.

EVERYTHING HURTS. Even my toenails. The pain is so intense that, for a moment, I don't realize what has happened.

Then it all comes back to me. Sitting on the Fire Throne. Aiden.

The explosion.

"Did you really think," a female voice says from behind me. "That you could take it from me?"

I roll onto my back. Pharaildis stands there, her purple gown unsmudged, her kohl lined eyes narrowed on the tiny tongue of flame dancing in her hand.

Above our heads the runes pulse with their eerie green light. The Draugar trundle out through the doorway. Off to collect more dead fey for her army.

I glare at Underhill. "Why bother to save me?"

"You're not my enemy," she says. "You simply side with them."

Time for some harsh truth. "I'm not your daughter, either."

She tilts her head to the side. "I don't understand you, Nicneven. Anyone else I would kill for ignoring my banishment. I offer you your life and you almost die in a fruitless effort to steal a power you can't wield."

Though it feels as if my bones will crack, I force myself to sit upright. "It's Nic. And you never have understood me."

"Why fight?" Her face is a picture of bafflement. "You had a child taken from you by another. A child you needed to help set you free. I thought you would understand."

A part of me does. "I wanted that babe for the wrong reasons. How would your life have been different if the fey hadn't taken me? You want to destroy the worlds."

"The worlds destroyed me!" she shrieks. "For love, I lost everything."

"I know. And it isn't fair. But his was the action of one man. You punished him and were punished in turn. Don't drag the rest of the living into it."

The flame disappears and her hands clench into fists. "Don't you get it? We are all wrong. Every last one of us. Twisted. Evil. The worlds need to be scourged clean."

I hold her gaze. "You're wrong. Not everyone is evil. I'm not."

"The road to hell is paved with good intentions." She waves her hand. A cabinet appears. From deep within I see the throbbing light of Brigit's heart, the power bestowed by the Fire Throne. "She was supposed to be goodness itself. Yet she traded her heart for your head."

"And I defended myself." My horrific burns are healing too slowly. I need to keep her talking.

She reaches into the cabinet and extracts the heart. "You were after this. But it's too late, Nicneven. My Draugar will capture your friends and I will take the wolf back to Loki and use him to set the Lord of Chaos free. The worlds will end."

"Not if I end you first."

Her full lips curve up in a genuine smile. "So that's your plan? You think you can kill me? You'll *become* me."

"I won't." Collecting enough strength to stand, I rise to my full height.

"You've taken innocent lives," Pharaildis says. "This prison will swallow you whole. After millennium incarcerated in this place, you will be just like me."

"It never had to be a prison though. You made it this way.

Your anger about John, about what happened to you. You are trapped in a jail of your own making."

She shakes her head. "You know nothing about it."

I move forward. Closer to her. My immortality is reviving me. "Why did you let the fey keep your child?"

She stares at me a long moment.

"Even before you had Brigit's heart, you had the power to reshape this world. Why would you allow the fey to keep your baby from you?"

I see an echo of the vulnerable girl from my dreams in her dark eyes.

"You wanted better for her, didn't you?" The same way I wanted better for Addison.

Pharaildis shakes her head. "It doesn't matter anymore."

"You treated the fey as your children for a time. Played with their magic. Giving boons and doling out punishment. You cared about them. What changed?"

"I cared for them, but they never cared for me," she seethes. "No one sought me out. I had the knowledge of centuries. Yet none came to be with me. You want to know why this is a prison? Because I am trapped with the knowledge that I don't matter to anyone. Power isn't the ability to shape the world, but to have the world recognize and celebrate your contributions."

I hold out a hand to her. "I recognize you."

She stares at it as though she's never seen anything like it.

"End this," I beg her. "I'll stay with you. I promise."

Her eyes glisten with unshed tears. "You aren't fey. You can lie."

"I can, but I'm not. I've discovered something about myself. I come from goodness. My soul was brought back by love, my body conceived in love and I've been raised surrounded by love. You never had the chance to know that. But you can have it now."

A single tear escapes. It slides down her cheek in a glistening trail.

"Please, Pharaildis." My tone is fraught with a sea of churning emotions. "I'm not your daughter. But part of her still lives in me. A portion that yearns to be with you."

"No." Her expression hardens.

I realize my mistake at once. Nicneven was one of the fey who never sought her out. I see her shut down her feelings an instant before she raises her hand. A ball of fire appears, white and blue flames. A killing blow.

"Goodbye, Nicneven."

Something clatters to her left a moment before a black blur slams into her from the side. Aiden, in wolf form. He knocks her to the ground, teeth bared.

I glance around, hoping to spy what he'd dropped. *Seelenverkäufer.* Each motion full of agony, I drag myself to it.

Pharaildis fights back like a wild thing, teeth bared, hands curled into claws of her own. The ground beneath us shifts. One blood-soaked finger traces something in the sky. A rune.

The Draugar at the far side of the cavern turn slowly to face us.

Nightweaver appears and dives inside one of the corpses. It shudders and collapses. The Valkyrie spirit emerges and then goes into the next one. Buying us time.

My hand closes around the sword hilt.

Nic, Aiden thinks at me. *I can't hold her much longer.*

Pharaildis throws him off, straight into the black water. Dead hands grab for him, ready to pull him apart.

I don't think. I lunge forward and plant my lips against hers even as I drive the blade into her stomach.

Delivering my goodnight kiss for the final time.

Her lips part. The ground beneath us stills. Black lines streak across her face. The toxin acts fast or slow depending on the dose. I give Pharaildis every drop of the poison water she once drank to kill herself and her unborn babe.

"I....I...," she sputters and her eyes fog. Her entire body shudders. A trail of blood oozes from her ear. Only moments from the end.

"I would have kept my promise," I whisper through the knot in my throat. No matter how hard it would have been, after all she had done, I would have found a way to forgive her.

Chloe is right. Forgiveness is for quitters. And I am more than ready to be done.

Her lids flutter and all the tension, all the power, leaves her.

And finds me.

Aiden dissolves into sparks, freeing himself from the corpses.

"Nic?" Aiden shifts back to human form. He's naked and sweating, covered with dirt and blood. His green eyes are wild. "What's happening?"

"Stay back." I hold up a hand as energy courses through me. This doesn't burn like fire. It's deeper, stronger. I close my eyes sensing...

Everything.

Too much. I fall to my hands and knees, retching. The land around me is dead or dying, poison is everywhere. Dizziness washes over me as all the thoughts and emotions of the fey make themselves known. Their fear and panic overwhelm me. To help or hinder? I'm losing myself in the endless sea of them.

I can feel the ground trembling beneath our feet, the land up above. I can see the fey. The Draugar, the ones in this cave and the ones that surround the palace. Can see them fall as ghosts dip into them, stealing their animation.

A hand cups my cheek. I detect his scent. Cedar, sage and wildness. Aiden whispers, "Stay with me, love."

I focus on his eyes. He's here. He's here and he's in danger. Nightweaver is slowing down, she can't take them all out. I must master the power. But not all at once. A little at a time. The same way I learned to fight. Right now, I need to shut all the noise out. In my mind's eye, I picture turning off a faucet to cut off the flow of all the panic and pain. From a torrent to a trickle and then to a drip. Until it is safely contained. The tremors cease.

"That's it." Aiden strokes my hair. "Come back to me."

And just as the last drop of sensation falls, I sense the runes. They throb like a heartbeat inside my head. Under-hill's knowledge of them has been transferred to me along with her power. Addy had said I would know how to use them when I needed to. "I think…I'm okay now."

"Nic." Aiden points to my ankle where a thin silver chain twines around my skin. "It's Gleipnir."

I look over at Pharaildis body. The chain which had perpetually bound her ankles is gone.

"You've taken her place," Aiden breathes. "You're the new Underhill. You're a prisoner."

"It was the only way." I shove hair back from my eyes. "Aiden—"

His expression morphs from concern to determination. His hand ignites and fire burns into the shape of a sword. "Duck."

I dive onto the cavern floor. He swings the sword in a powerful arc and beheads the Draugar approaching from behind. Its body smolders as it hits the ground beside me.

"Why aren't they stopping?" Aiden asks.

Because they haven't been commanded to. The dead are mindless servants and will carry out their last order until given a new one.

"Get behind me," Aiden barks. The Draugar stalk closer.

"I need something sharp," I say to Aiden.

He extends a hand which shifts to a wolf's paw. I don't hesitate as I swipe it across my arm. Then I take the blood on two fingers and trace the rune in the sky.

Rest.

As the last marking is made, the rune sparks gold. The Draugar crumple to the ground.

Aiden's sword disappears. I glance over to where Pharaildis lays among the corpses. The sight of her there, my latest victim, disturbs me more than it ever has before.

Aiden pulls me into his arms. "Do you want me to burn her?"

I can't speak so I nod.

He extends the sword again and touches it to the hem of her dress, then pulls me away.

The fire burns hot and because Aiden controls it, it burns straight up in a jet that touches none of the dead fey.

Her pyre alone.

The tears fall freely for the young woman who'd danced so beautifully, who'd once had a passion for life and who in the end, chose death. She may not have been my mother, but the two of us had been linked.

We watch until nothing remains but a pile of ash. I can't stand the sight of it lying in this dark space. There should be air and light here.

"Hold on to something," I tell him.

He asks no questions, just grips my waist in one hand and then a nearby outcropping of rock with the other.

I pull in a deep breath and nudge the faucet to a slow drip. Then I lift my hands.

A great roaring fills the catacombs. The ground beneath our feet shakes as the world reforms to my will. The peak above descends while the Underground palace is lifted higher. The solid wall of rock parts, making way for the palace to emerge.

It soars up until it sits for the first time under the night sky.

As if it had been waiting, the North Wind blows in through the open doorway. The ashes swirl up and are taken out through the other chamber.

"She's free at last," I breathe.

"You traded your freedom for hers." Aiden's gaze holds mine.

I can't read his expression. Anxiety bubbles up. Is he upset by my choice? My lips part but I don't know what to say.

"Hi." His thumb strokes along my cheekbone in a tender caress.

A smile breaks, but I need to know. "Are you bothered because I have to stay here?"

"You postponed the end of the worlds." He presses his forehead to mine. "As long as you are content to be where you are and I get to stay with you, I'm happy."

I throw my arms around him. "Missed you. You'll never know how much."

We hold each other. Just breathe one another in. It's over. It's finally over.

"How long?" he rasps. "How much time did I miss?"

"How do you know you missed any?"

"Your scent." He puts his hand on my stomach, covering my womb. "It was different when you were pregnant. So, how long has it been?"

"Too long." So many lonely nights, the constant pressure of knowing he was in danger. "It was torture."

"Our daughter?" The tone is laced with worry.

I grin up at him. "Safe in Midgard. She's sixteen."

His eyes round in horror. "Sixteen?"

"Don't worry, she hasn't killed anyone yet." I cup his whiskered cheek in my hand. "She repaired the Veil, Aiden. She's the One True Queen."

The sound of running feet and then Harmony bursts into the room. "Váli?"

I step back, knowing Harmony has longed for this moment almost as much as I have. Aiden grins. He scoops the seer up and spins her around. Freda follows close behind, Nahini at her side.

"Gods, Nic. I thought you were done for," Freda shudders.

"I was."

Nahini doesn't speak, just moves close and extends a hand. "Thank you."

"Thank you for sending Nightweaver. For a while she was all that kept me sane."

"She volunteered," Nahini admits. "I think she was tied more tightly to you than we ever knew."

I blink. "She hates my guts."

"There's a thin line between love and hate," Nahini murmurs.

I think of Pharaildis and John. "You're right. Is everyone all right?"

"The others are up in the throne room." Freda moves as if to go collect them. "The ghosts protected us until you did….whatever it is you did."

"I need to speak with them."

"In a bit," Aiden says and then pulls me tight against him. "Give everyone some time to clean up and catch their breaths."

He's right, of course. "Meet in the throne room in two hours?" I look to Aiden with my brows raised.

His hands sift through my hair. "Better make it three. We have a lot of catching up to do."

With that we dissolve in a shower of sparks.

Aiden reforms us in my old bedroom. The view out the windows is incredible and stark all at once. Stars shine brightly in the cloudless night sky, but the land itself is barren and pitted like the surface of the moon.

"Some view," I murmur.

"I like what I'm looking at."

I turn in Aiden's arms and see he is staring down at me. "I have to stay here. I can't ever go back."

"I know."

"But you can."

He shakes his head. "No."

"Aiden. Think about it for a second. Harmony, Liam and the pack, our daughter. They are all in Midgard. I'm trying to be fair to you."

He curls one finger beneath my chin, forcing me to meet his gaze. "No, Nic. I'm done being apart from you. You must stay here? Fine, I'll stay with you. Together we'll rebuild this place. Bring the fey who are left out of the dark ages. We have friends that can go back and forth. But I will not cross that Veil again without you. Understand?"

My lips tremble. "Okay."

"It's a bargain well struck." His head dips and I catch a glimpse of his wicked intent a moment before his lips brush gently over mine. Sealing our agreement with a kiss.

A kiss that heats into need.

I pull away, shocked.

"What is it?" He asks.

I lick my lips, savoring the tingle there. "I thought…part of the sentence for becoming Underhill was that I didn't have any physical urges. But I want you."

He pulls my shirt from my head and then crouches down to work the buttons of my jeans open. "Maybe your sentence is different because you chose it."

I steady myself on his broad shoulders as he drags my

pants and panties down my legs. I step out of the fabric. Nervous, because it's been so long and we'd only done it once. I lick my lips and am about to tell him when he grips my hips and buries his face between my thighs.

Nerves don't stand a chance.

An hour later, I sigh and lean against him in the bath. His hands rove over my body in steady caresses.

He tells me of Rodrick and his parents. His mother finally stepping up to help him in his time of need. I tell him about Angrboda and about Addy. I describe all my dreams of Pharaildis and her life.

"She wasn't all bad." I fold my fingers through his.

He shakes his head. "No one is. That's the whole problem."

We are quiet for a time, both of us lost in our own thoughts.

"Would you really have let her live? Knowing what she'd done?" he asks.

"Everyone deserves a second chance, Aiden. You gave that to me. I offered her the same gift." I swallow hard. "Even after everything she'd done. To the fey, to you and me. She saved me from the Fire Throne. I would have died there if she hadn't ripped me free from the explosion."

"She was going to kill you herself," Aiden points out.

"Yeah." I thought about what I'd seen in her eyes. The terror there, the fear that overrode the hope. "And then you saved the day. Like I knew you would."

"You scared the hell out of me when I saw you on the throne. If I hadn't caught your scent…" He pulls me tighter. "Sixteen years is a long time."

"What is it?" Curious at his mood swing, I tilt my head to see a muscle jumping in his jaw.

"You said Liam stayed with you. Did you and he ever…?"

The thread of possessive jealousy in his voice makes me shiver.

I can't help but tease him. "What would you do if I said yes?"

"Kill him." The answer is immediate. His hands clamp on the side of the tub so hard the cast iron bends. He releases a breath. "First, I would thank him for watching out for you and Addison. Then I would rip his head from his body."

"Even though you managed to share Nicneven with her fey nobles?"

His gaze burns into me. "You're not Nicneven. You're my Nic. Now answer the damned question."

"Nothing happened, you maniac." I shake my head against his chest, unable to suppress a smile. "Liam is honorable and decent. And I'm pretty sure he views me like a sister."

"Really?" The hands on the side of the mangled tub relax, the claws receding.

"I would have waited twice as long," I turn to face him fully. "I would wait for you forever."

His expression softens, green eyes glowing in the low light. "I don't know what I did to deserve this. To deserve you."

"You are." I lift my hips to take him inside me again. He gasps and I smile as I begin to move in a liquid rhythm. "That's more than enough."

THE ONE TRUE QUEEN

We stride to the throne room together. Aiden holds my hand in his. Nahini and the ghosts are already there. Nahini's cheekbones jut out at even sharper angles but her hair is clean.

"You need some food," I tell her.

She makes a face. "I'm too tired to find the kitchen."

I whisper something to Aiden and he nods once, then vanishes in a shower of sparks.

"Where's he going?" Freda asks as she strides into the room alongside Jasmine. Both look clean, but tired.

"We have some new thralls to break in," I say. "Former FBI, total wackos. Let's hope some of them can cook."

Nahini laughs. "Let the punishment fit the crime? They kept you now you're keeping them for a year and a day?"

"It should take us about that long to figure out what to do."

"What to do about what?" Taj asks as he and Soladin enter. By the flush of love that covers the two of them, I can tell they spent the last few hours reconnecting the same way Aiden and I did.

"About Underhill."

Aiden reappears, followed by Agent Hanson and company. Her eyes are glazed, her hair sticking up every which way and she is carrying a tray piled high with fresh bread, fruit and cheese.

"No meat?" I ask Aiden.

He raises a brow. "Since when do you eat meat?"

"On and off since I was pregnant with Addison. I blame you and your wolf for that. And Angrboda for insisting I try bacon. I am now a bacon vegetarian."

He grips me around the waist. "Woman, you have never been sexier."

"Get a room," Harmony says, but she is smiling.

There is a large charred oak banquet table at the far end of the throne room. The thralls lay the feast down on it and we wait for the others to arrive.

"So, what is this about?" Bard asks.

I take a breath and look at them all. The beings I had once believed to be my court. My friends.

"The One True Queen."

Taj's jaw drops. "You mean the prophesy?"

Harmony sits on Aiden's other side and addresses the Seelie king. "She's not a prophesy. She's real."

"Where is she?" Fern tilts her head.

"In Midgard. With Laufey and Chloe and some other friends." I take a deep breath. "I want her to rule from there."

Silence. Taj takes a deep breath. "Our people are scattered to the winds. The gods have granted us a temporary stay in Vanheim, but we need somewhere else to reunite. Midgard might be the best plan."

"Why can't they come back here?" Soladin turns to face me. "You're in charge now. Surely you will let them come home."

"The land here is toxic." I can feel it every time I turn the spigot to Underhill's power. "It won't sustain life for a long time. And I plan to release the souls that provide magic to the noble fey. They deserve peace."

"That will mean no more magic." Jasmine's eyes are wide.

I smile at her. "Not exactly. It will mean wild magic. Harder to contain or control. Everyone will have to master other skills."

"The nobles won't like that," Freda mutters.

"The nobles can fuck directly off." Harmony tosses her midnight hair. "They like the imbalance of power and the inequality it creates."

"It sounds as if your mind is made up. What do you need from us?" Soladin's tone is quiet.

I hold his dark gaze. "The fey need to come out from behind the Veil. No more hiding, no more thieving, no more poverty. They will need strong leaders to guide them."

Bard's lidless eyes fix on me. "You're talking about revealing ourselves to the humans?"

Aiden's fingers lace through mine. "Even though he was a total and complete bastard, Wardon had the right idea. An educated population of fey will mean a better world for all. We want to keep his dream alive. His son, Jedda, has already agreed to help in whatever way he can."

"This won't be an easy transition," I tell the room. "I will hold down the fort here. I won't force any to go. But I can't guarantee their survival once the souls are released from the elements."

"It's the right thing to do." Nahini had been quiet up until that point. "Not just for the fey. But the giants and trolls as well."

"Gods, can you imagine a pack of trolls roving downtown Manhattan?" Freda asks.

"No, and that's why we're going to ask the giants for help creating pocket realms."

Jasmine's eyes light up. "Like a sort of halfway house."

"Right. Teach them the rules of Midgard before exposing them to the humans."

"Like that they can't eat the humans." Harmony mutters.

"I know it's not a perfect plan. Which is why we're going to have a vote."

"A vote?" Taj blinks. "What is a vote?"

"A show of hands. Who thinks we should move forward with integration into Midgard?"

Aiden's hand is the first to rise, followed a second later by Nahini and Jasmine, Harmony and Bard.

Freda holds my gaze. "What of the Hunt?"

I shift in my seat. "That is up to your Unseelie Queen. But the Hunt is always welcome to stay with me."

She nods once and then her hand goes up as well.

"Gentlefey?" I ask Soladin and Taj. "What say you?"

The males exchange a look. "I have...reservations," Taj says.

"As do I." Soladin nods. "We want what is best for our people and ripping away the one thing they've always been able to count on, their magic, might be too much."

I lean back in my chair. He's right. It might be too much, especially for some of the ancient fey. But the younger ones.... "What if we set up a school?"

"A school?" Taj repeats with a frown.

"A place where mortals learn to read and write and do math," Jasmine explains.

"Only in this case, they will learn to harness the elemental magic." I explain. "I have used magic on the far side of the Veil. It does exist but it works differently. We can teach the fey who want to learn how to wield it. And they can teach others."

"Progress," Soladin nods. "Steady forward progress. It's something the fey haven't had in my lifetime."

"You like this idea?" Taj asks his lover.

"I do. But I will go along with it only if you want to. You are the Seelie king after all."

Taj looks around the table. "You have all helped us. Helped our people. I haven't been king long and it's easy enough for me to say I am willing to give it up. Especially if by doing so we get to live in peace. I trust you, Nicneven." He raises his hand and Soladin does the same.

I let out a breath. "Then it's agreed. The fey will cross the Veil."

Through the Man's Eyes

"STOP FIDGETING," Nic pinches him lightly on the arm. "You look great."

Aiden stares down at the outfit Nic had Jasmine retrieve for him from the farm. Dark jeans and a black tank top, black boots on his feet. He's grateful that she thought to have the girl run the errand to begin with, but he wished she had brought something more impressive. Like what he wore on his first date with Nic. "It's so casual."

"She's a casual girl. Grew up running through the trees with a pack of werewolves and healing injured rabbits and birds. Trust me." She threads her fingers through his as they wait.

A moment later, a line splits down the hall in front of them. Freda appears first wielding *Seelenverkäufer*. Alric by her side. Then Jasmine. Chloe, Liam and finally….

"Addison." The name is expelled from his very soul. She is breathtaking, as gorgeous as her immortal mother. She's tall, almost six feet with a willowy build. Long honey blonde hair flows freely down her back, perfect bow shaped lips. And her eyes....

Her eyes are his.

Pup. His wolf thinks at him, radiating satisfaction. *Strong, magnificent pup.*

Harmony comes up to stand beside him, one purple hand on his shoulder as she lends her silent support.

"Mama!" Addison runs straight to Nic first, lifting his mate off her feet and spinning her in a circle.

"Missed you," Nic squeezes her eyes shut, but not before he sees the tears of relief gathering in her eyes.

Addison sets her down and then looks directly at him.

Their gazes lock. He can feel a burning in his own eyes as he beholds this perfect, brilliant creature.

On her feet once more, Nic reaches for his hand to tug him forward. "Addison this is—"

"You're my dad?" Addison tilts her head to the side.

He starts, recognizing it as his own gesture. What other mannerisms had she inherited from him? From Nic? So much time, he lost so much time with her, with them both. Sixteen years. It hadn't registered before this moment. His throat is dry, and he can't seem to form words. He nods mutely, stranded in place even as he craves so much more.

She throws herself against him so hard that he loses his grip on Nic and almost topples to the floor.

Nic covers her mouth with both hands but he can see the delight shining in her eyes.

"Thank you for protecting her," Addison whispers in his ear.

He closes his eyes and holds his daughter close. "It's what I was born to do."

I FIND Chloe in the dungeon, staring down at the spot where Addy had died. I move to her side and put an arm around her waist.

"Did she suffer?" Chloe asks.

I don't want to share the horror of watching Addy crumble with Chloe. Part of me still feels as if it's my fault.

Chloe straightens her shoulders. "She chose this, Nic. She chose to interfere. I'm sure she knew I wouldn't get to her in time. But she came anyway. For you, for me, for Addison. For the whole freaking universe."

I nod against her shoulder and ask the question I'd been dreading. "What happens next?"

"Next?" She laughs without humor. "I need to locate other Norns and we will need to find one to elevate."

"You didn't do that when Sissy died."

"We should have. But we didn't. First out of grief and then because—" she cuts herself off abruptly.

"Because of me." I sigh. "It's okay, Chloe. Really."

"So now I have a mess. Shit, Nic. I don't even know where to begin."

I take a deep breath. "I do. You remember that girl who was in FBI custody with me?"

"Astrid?"

I nod. "She was like you."

"Like me how?"

"I saw her eyes do that swirling thing. I think that's why Hanson kept her."

Chloe goes completely still.

"Say something," I tell her.

"Shit. She was right there in front of me and I didn't even see it."

"And now she's dead."

But Chloe shakes her head. "She was shot. A mortal wound wouldn't stick."

"Wouldn't stick?"

"She would have regenerated. Only a Fate can kill another."

"Are you telling me we *buried her alive?*" And I can't go back to get her. Oh gods, oh, gods!

Chloe sinks down onto the floor and puts her head in her hands.

"We'll find her. Liam and his pack will help you. I have a lead on someone she used to know. It's slim but hopefully it will prove to be enough."

If anything, Chloe looks more upset. "All this time, she's been out there alone. Nic, you don't know. Don't know what it's like to have those abilities."

"We'll find her." I say. "We have a seer and an army of ghosts. We have werewolves. We will find her Chloe. I promise."

"No," I say for the hundredth time.

"Mama." It's not exactly a whine. Addison doesn't whine. But it's not exactly *not* a whine either.

"Nic." Aiden, my wolfish Benedict Arnold, stands by her side. "Harmony said she needs to do this."

"No." I point at the Shadow Throne, which I've been avoiding even looking at. "You haven't felt what those things can do. I have."

"It's my destiny." Addison's chin goes up. "You can't be the boss of me forever."

I hold my arms wide to encompass the whole of Underhill. "My house, my rules."

"Nic, she needs the authority to do what must be done." This comes from Taj. "The fey will only respect her if they know she is the One True Queen."

"They can take our gods damned word for it," I snarl.

Addison has changed into a long, bloodred sleeveless gown. She looks elegant and regal. She doesn't need to sit on the freaking chair of death to prove anything to anyone.

"Let me talk to her," Aiden says to the group.

Talk some sense into me he means. *Have fun wasting your breath, pal.*

"Nic," his tone is soft.

"What?" I spit and wait for the condemnation.

"I love you."

I close my eyes, unwilling to hold my mate's gaze. "I'm being unreasonable again, aren't I?"

"Maybe a little."

"She's my baby, Aiden. Our baby."

"She's taller than you are."

I shake my head. "Doesn't matter. It's my job to protect her."

"You can't protect her from living, Nic. She wants this. The fey need this. Let her do what needs to be done."

I exhale a ragged breath. "Damn it, it was easier when she was little. Eat your broccoli. Don't stick a knife in the toaster while it's plugged in. I don't know how to be the parent of a teenager."

He smooths my hair back away from my face and kisses the crown of my head. "You think I do? I have had exactly zero practice."

My lips twitch. "And you're still better at it than me."

"Just remember that when she wants to date." I can hear the snarl in his voice at the very thought and I feel a bit better.

"So how do I do this?" I ask.

"Step back. Be there to catch her. Let her spread her wings."

"Can't we start with something less deadly than the damn Shadow Throne?"

"I'll be right here with you."

"Okay." I take one more hit of his fortifying scent and then turn to face her.

She scrutinizes my expression and then breaks into a sunny smile.

My guts clench as she ascends the stairs and turns to face the gathered room. There are no words, no speeches for the crowning of a new ruler.

She sits. We all wait. One heartbeat. Two.

Lightning cracks down through the ceiling.

The throne ignites and the dais turns molten.

Addison's green eyes reflect the flames which do not touch her. Wisps of darkness curl up over her shoulders and snake around her waist.

My gaze is locked on her, my heart pounding against my ribs.

The Shadow Throne is...changing. The legs melt into the flow of lava which circles the throne like a moat. The shadows grow thicker until I can barely see her face.

"Addison," I breathe.

She rises from the darkness and walks through the lava as though walking across grass. In one hand a jet of fire flickers. She opens her other hand and a ball of ice forms.

"She's magnificent," Aiden's green eyes shine with pride.

"Long live the One True Queen," Harmony calls.

All in attendance fall to their knees. All except for me and Chloe. As a Fate, she bows to no one. And I am Underhill. She who can rearrange the worlds.

And will gladly do so for the ones she loves.

"Long live the One True Queen," I say and put a hand on Aiden's head.

EPILOGUE

"We need to get out of this bed eventually," I snuggle closer to Aiden's warmth. "We have company coming for Yule."

"Cold, love?" He snaps his fingers and a fire blazes in the hearth.

There is a knock at the chamber door and Agent Hanson, eyes still glazed in her thrall, moves forward bearing two goblets full of mulled wine. A snarl rips from Aiden's lips, but the mortal ignores us as she heads back to her kitchen duties.

"You need to relax," I told him. "You know she's locked down tight."

"Doesn't change what she did to you."

I swallow. "No, but I landed the first blow." I tell him about her husband and how his death had set her on my trail.

Aiden's thumb traces along the contour of my cheek. "Still, she was the one who married a monster. Yet she focused all her vengeance on you."

The stone floors have warmed enough that I chance stepping out of the comfort of our bed. Aiden makes a disappointed noise when I pull on a robe. He teases me about my mortal modesty, even when the two of us are alone.

I pad over to the table and pick up both cups of wine. It's been warmed and smells of cinnamon and cloves. I take a sip before bringing Aiden his cup. "Have I mentioned how glad I am that I can still taste things?"

He takes his own cup, but then sets it on the bedside table. Then he plucks my goblet from my hand and lands it next to his.

"Hey, I was enjoying that."

"I'll give you something to enjoy." He snags me around the waist and pulls me down onto his lap.

"You're insatiable." And I love that even with the two of us being together day and night, it hasn't dulled the edge of his desire for me. Or mine for him. "About Hanson and the others. She's going to have missed seventeen years in Midgard. No one will believe her stories. Isn't that punishment enough?"

"Maybe one of these centuries I'll master the art of forgiveness the way you have."

"Forgiveness is for quitters." I cup his face in my hands "And I'm officially out of the game."

Sometime later, I finally convince Aiden to leave so I can focus on getting dressed. He does so with great reluctance. I have just finished pinning my hair atop my head when I sense another presence in the room.

"I was wondering when you would show up." My gaze locks on her reflection in the mirror.

"So sure of me...Underhill." There's a smugness to her tone.

I take my time with the clip before turning to face the goddess. "I knew you'd want to gloat."

"I wanted to catch you alone. And since the wolf rarely

leaves your side, our girl talk had to wait." I detect the note of bitterness in her words.

"Can't say his name?" I raise a brow.

"He isn't my Váli any longer."

"You're right, he isn't." If the goddess needs to refer to my mate as the wolf in order to assuage her pride over his rejection, so be it. Let her have what she views as a win.

"So what's it like, knowing you'll spend the rest of your existence imprisoned here?"

I take a moment to look around the massive chamber that has become our temporary home. It's filled with stuff Chloe, Addison, Sophie and Harmony have brought from the farm or purchased as mating gifts. Blankets and books, candles, an iPod, even a laptop, though I haven't figured out how to charge it on this side. Clothing, both his and mine. A painting of the farm and another portrait of our beloved daughter flanks the fireplace. Aiden plans to build us a cabin overlooking a lake. The same one he had designed and intended to build near the farm.

Does knowing I can never leave bother me? Maybe it would, if I didn't have such a loyal pack of werewolves that hunt in the forest, if the Wild Hunt didn't swing by a few times a week to raise hell. If I had to do without regular visits from Addison and Chloe, Sophie, Garret and Tate, Fern and Laufey, Soladin and Taj. If Aiden wasn't with me, helping me figure out how to work my powers, this might be a hellish fate.

"I miss Gretchen," I say at length. With her forced to stay in Midgard and me bound to this land, we couldn't do more than wave at one another through gaps in the Veil. She's a great pen pal though, keeping me apprised of all the changes going on in Midgard and Liam's constant antics in setting up the pocket realms with the giants. That fool wolf is going to get himself killed one of these days.

If Freya is disappointed in my reaction, she doesn't show it. "I've come to warn you. There are pockets of the fey who are...less than pleased by your new edicts. They want magic to stay the same."

"Want in one hand, shit in the other. See which fills first." One of Addy's favorite truisms.

The goddess wrinkles her nose at the adage. "Don't underestimate those who are backed into a corner. It is then that an animal is most deadly. The goddess Skathi is monitoring their activities even now. Ragnarök is still coming."

"Thanks for the update." I retrieve my wine goblet and sit, crossing my legs. "By the way. I wanted to ask you about Gleipnir."

"What about it." Her tone is too casual.

I take a sip, my gaze locked on her face. "Well, it's made by dwarves, right?"

"Yes."

"And no one else can make it, correct?"

"That's correct."

I study my wine goblet. "And dwarves forge only for the gods?"

"What's your point?" Her tone is impatient.

I study my wine for a moment. "So how did Pharaildis get enough of it to ensnare Aiden?"

Her expression is carefully blank. Not a flicker of emotion.

I lean back in my chair. "I find it interesting that your own, personal dwarf helped set Aiden free from your house and then turned around and gave Underhill the means to trap him."

"He is no longer my dwarf." Freya neatly dodges the question. "He has been...dismissed."

Our gazes lock. "I don't know what you're playing at,

Freya. But I doubt the other gods would like it, especially if it means their demise."

"The gods of Asgard don't fear death."

"But you aren't a god of Asgard...are you?" Nowhere in my studies have I found any mention of Freya falling at Ragnarök.

Her lips part but before she can say anything I surge forward, sinking my nails into her flesh. "Stay away from Aiden. Stay away from Addison. If you want to end the gods, that's between you and them. But I swear that if you try to use one of my loves in your schemes again, I will move all nine worlds to end you."

Wrath and hatred flare in her cat eyes but then the door opens. She vanishes out of my grip.

"Nic?" Aiden asks. "What's taking so long? Everyone is waiting."

"Just getting my bearings." I loop my arm through his. "Ready to celebrate?"

Aiden brushes his lips over mine in a tender caress that means everything to me. "With you by my side? Always."

Author's Note

While Nic and Aiden's story is complete, there is so much left to explore in this world of fae and werewolves. Wanna meet Liam's mate? Her journey begins in Savior's Spell. Read Chapter One on my website now!

IT'S NOT MY WORDS THAT COUNT.
IT'S YOURS!

Please consider leaving an honest review for this book. Reviews help readers like you find books they enjoy, or warn them off from ones they won't. Reader reviews help the authors you love sell books and help them put money toward the next title. Even a sentence or two can mean the difference between a series that continues and one that flops. I found one of my favorite series from a two star review. So if you want more, tell the world.

Thank you for reading!
Gwen Rivers

ABOUT THE AUTHOR

Gwen Rivers is the changeling of a *USA Today* bestselling author Jennifer L. Hart. When not writing urban and rural fantasy with kickass heroines, you can find her poring over Norse mythology, dicing with the Fates, cavorting with werewolves or hunting for fairy wine in the deep, dark woods.

Want exclusive behind the scenes access to what she is working on next? Become a Patron today!